Desolation Row
An Austin Starr Mystery

Kay Kendall

ISBN 978-0-9859942-1-1

Visit Kay online:

kaykendallauthor.com

STAIRWAY≡PRESS

Cover Design by Guy Corp www.grafixCORP.com

www.stairwaypress.com
1500A East College Way #554
Mount Vernon, WA 98273

In memory of David Thompson

His vast knowledge and passion for mysteries

were infectious and helped me get my start.

CHAPTER ONE

1968

Austin hurried down Harbord Street in the deepening twilight. She'd tried the usual meeting place at the University of Toronto, but some bearded hippie said the anti-war group had moved, gone to the United Church on Bathurst. Which she was having trouble finding. She was tired of rushing, her feet hurt, and her skirt was too tight. Carrying the container of muffins was awkward and slowed her down. Why did she bother to bake anything anyway? David's anti-war colleagues would just gobble up her food and keep on arguing.

Hiking several more blocks, Austin reached Bathurst and turned north, searching for the flashing lights that marked Honest Ed's. The popular cut-rate department store was near the church, and she hoped her weary legs wouldn't collapse during those long, final blocks.

She stopped and slumped against a lamp post, catching her breath. Why didn't she throw the blueberry muffins away and be done with them? That would be foolish and wasteful though, given how little money the transplanted Americans had. The draft resisters didn't often thank her, but they'd be grateful for free food.

"Boo."

Her heartbeat tripled while her gaze pierced the darkness. After an eternity, a small figure slithered out of the shadows. A devil's red face, topped with horns, loomed before her.

Her jaw dropped open and she stifled a scream. What the hell?

"Trick or treat."

Damn it. Halloween had completely slipped her mind.

"My goodness, you're very scary." Austin tried to slow her

thudding heart by taking deep breaths, then leaned closer to view the devil better. He stared back, swinging a pillowcase no doubt filled with treats.

"I've got goodies. Do you want some?"

The devil child nodded solemnly, then grabbed the offering and skipped away shrieking. His cries were probably joyful, but to Austin they sounded sinister, like a ghoul howling into the urban wilderness.

She turned in a circle and examined her surroundings, noted for the first time the jack-o-lanterns decorating the stores. In her frantic rush to make the meeting on time, she'd ignored the signs of Halloween. A wave of homesickness washed over her. Back home in Cuero, Texas, Daddy would be dressed like an abnormally tall ghost and doling out candy with a lavish hand.

She set out once more, tramping past tacky storefronts that hadn't seen a paintbrush in years. While she'd never dream of walking alone at night in a similar American neighborhood, she assumed it was okay in Toronto. Everyone did it. Everyone said the crime rate was low here. But while she'd felt safe just moments before, if worn-out and cranky, now she was rattled, even a little scared. Phantom lizards hopped around in her midsection.

When she finally reached the United Church, it opened its brick arms to her, representing a safe haven. Puffing, she raced through the side door, only to slam into a deathly silence. She'd expected the usual cacophony of arguing voices to greet her, to lead her to the meeting, but the old building felt like a mausoleum, not a meeting place or house of worship. The frustration of failure crashed against her fatigued body.

Summoning her last few ounces of energy, she dashed down the dim hallway.

"Ye better watch out," an ethereal voice called. "I mopped the floor, and it's still wet."

Austin jerked to a stop and lost hold of the box she was carrying. It hit the floor, and the muffins burst out. She watched her baking—a labor of love shoehorned into a too-full day—rolling across the wet floor. She howled, sounding just like that devil child.

A stooped old man emerged from the shadows and shuffled to her side as she fought back tears. He leaned on a mop, using it like a crutch, and then reached down to help her.

"It's okay, lassie." He wheezed between words. "Your treats are only a wee bit dented. Look—some are still wrapped up pretty." His hands trembled, but he managed to tuck a few wayward muffins back in the box. He tried to scoop up another, but had to stop, both hands gripping his mop, as he struggled to catch his breath.

"Thanks for your help, but I'll get the rest." She crouched down to finish cleaning up while the old man stood by and watched. Straightening, she said, "Do you have any idea where the anti-war meeting is? I'm late."

"Those lads ran off somewheres. Maybe try the university, eh?" The janitor tried to lift up his mop, but his hands were so unsteady that he dropped it. The mop clattered on the linoleum, making Austin jump.

What was wrong with him? Austin inhaled a long breath—what was wrong with *her?* She felt guilty that he'd exerted himself to help her. He looked as old as her grandfather, and Gran was eighty. Now drenched in remorse and stymied, she simply wanted to flee.

"I can't carry this stuff another step. Think I'll just leave everything in the kitchen for y'all to enjoy tomorrow." She shifted several steps away down the hall.

"But I must go," he called after her, "and canna help you." A violent coughing spasm interrupted him.

"That's okay," she stopped to yell over her shoulder. "I've been here before and know my way around." Then remembering her manners, she swung around to thank the old man, but he'd already faded back into the dark, a slick move appropriate for Halloween.

She began to jog in the direction her memory dictated,

listening to her footsteps echo in the empty hall. When she turned a corner to see a sign pointing to the kitchen, she grinned with relief.

"Something's finally going right," she murmured.

Austin pushed the door open and entered a room as dark as puddled ink. Promising herself never to bake for the group again, she inched through the murk, feeling along the wall for a light switch. Her ears seemed to catch the sound of scampering feet, and she quivered; mice gave her the creeps. After several cautious steps, one foot slipped. She almost fell, but instinctively grabbed the counter and righted herself.

With greater care, she edged ahead.

Her left foot hit something solid. She pitched forward, not managing to catch herself a second time. But the object she'd tripped over had some give to it and cushioned her fall.

"Damn, that was a close one." She spoke aloud in the darkness, needing to fill the silence. Lying on the floor, she thought about just staying put. That had to be better than anything else she'd tried that day. Yet the smell of dust and something oddly metallic made her change her mind. She sneezed and reached for her purse, needing a tissue, but instead her fingers met a sticky, moist goo.

Her heart slammed against her breastbone, and she gasped.

The dark was no longer her biggest worry.

She lunged to her feet and felt her way back along the wall. Her quivering fingers found the switch and flipped it. Florescent lights crackled and illuminated the room.

Austin's eyes slowly adjusted to the sudden flood of light.

Before her sprawled a man in a pool—no, a lake—of blood, and her blueberry muffins covered the most beautiful suede jacket she'd ever seen. She knew not to touch anything and squelched an urge to brush crumbs off the body. The blanket of baked goods made the man's condition appear comical.

It was anything but.

She recognized him. No one who'd seen Reginald Simpson in action would ever forget him. But she mustn't think ill of the dead.

Her legs were unresponsive planks. Frozen in place, Austin could only stand and gape at the corpse. Or what she guessed was a corpse.

Reg lay on his back. Blood covered one side of his head, catsup-colored and slick, shimmering in the light. The blood was wet.

So his was a recent death, if in fact he was dead. She needed to check but hesitated, trying to recall her CIA mentor's advice for daunting moments like this.

"When you need to forge ahead but don't really want to," Mr. Jones used to say, "then just breathe deep and focus. Empty your head of expectations so you can absorb all the data that surrounds you."

One gulp of breath was not enough. She took three more. Emptied her mind of fear and crept back toward Reg. Leaned down close, turned her face away to breathe deeply again, placed her fingers on the skin beneath his beard, and felt the truth. This was an inert thing, not a man.

Reg was gone.

Warm bile rose in Austin's throat. She needed to vomit but swallowed and gagged instead. Eyes closed, she willed the wave of nausea to pass. She'd never seen a dead person before, other than an aunt who had passed away peacefully of old age. But that frail body, lying in a satin-lined coffin in a pristine funeral home, belonged in a reality much different from this grotesque one with its figure laid out on a worn tiled floor.

Austin began shaking and grabbed the kitchen counter to steady herself, then jerked back, afraid to leave more fingerprints. After a few moments, her racing heart slowed and her curiosity overcame her initial fright. Here was an event plucked from one of her favorite mystery novels. It was morbidly compelling.

Using the hem of her blouse, Austin rubbed the place where she'd clutched the counter. Okay now, she told herself, get it together. What should she do first?

5

She'd often wished she could step into an Agatha Christie novel or work alongside Nancy Drew. Once Austin startled a friend when, upon entering a room, she abruptly declared, "That brass candlestick would make a good murder weapon." However, surveying this scene, Austin didn't see a single candlestick—or any other obvious implement good for killing.

She stepped back from the body and moved around the kitchen slowly. She peeked into an open container for trash, but it held nothing. Either the trash had been cleared away before the murder or the killer had taken it with him.

The closed cupboard doors called to her. "Open me," they clamored. And so she did, again covering her fingertips with her blouse. This operation took a long time—using her blouse was awkward and added complexity to the process. And the kitchen was enormous and held many cupboards. Twenty-two. She counted them. Twice. The tedious process calmed her teeming brain.

Her gaze swept the room, searching for clues. For anything out of place. Anything unusual. Satisfied that there was nothing suspicious, she decided it was time to call the cops.

Sure, but what cops—the city police or the state police? Ontario was a province. Damn it, how could she get in touch with them? What were they even called? She and David had talked to officials when they'd crossed the border into Canada, but she didn't know if they were border police—did Canada have those?

Maybe she could call the Mounties. After all, Sergeant Preston always got his man. But no, the pamphlet designed for assisting Americans emigrating to Canada to avoid the draft warned that some members of the Royal Canadian Mounted Police sought excuses to export draft-aged boys back home. Officially, they weren't supposed to harass them. Unofficially, they did.

She felt a fool for dithering while a body, adorned in her baking, lay on the floor of a church kitchen. But she truly didn't know who to call.

She gawked at Reg's body and felt more out of her element

than usual. Maybe she should call the operator and let her choose the right cops to contact. Okay, check. Her first step would be to locate a phone. The church office was a likely spot, but that door was probably locked. Also, if she left to find a phone, what about Reg? It didn't seem decent to leave him alone like this, now that she'd found him.

She gulped. "You're not going anywhere, are you?" she asked the body. It didn't respond. She'd half expected Reg to answer; that would've been a fitting climax to this evil day.

"Oh, no." Austin slapped her forehead. What if she went for help and then someone came in and saw Reg? She'd be a suspect!

She wasn't a citizen, and Canada would be happy to deport an alleged murderer.

She looked again at Reg.

Deportation sounded rather appealing. At least that would make her family happy, although her mother would mostly be mortified. Good heavens, she was mortified enough already, her only child having fled to the Great White North with a draft-resisting husband.

Austin shook off her circling thoughts. This was not the time to be obsessing about her mother. She clamped her hands together; they were twitching like they'd suddenly acquired a case of St. Vitus Dance.

"Slow down and take just one thing at a time." Austin spoke aloud the words her father often used to counsel her, back in the good old days, back when her worries didn't include politics, flight from her own country, and a corpse staring up at her from the floor.

She studied the body again, saw how the fringes of Reg's western-style suede jacket were absorbing more blood. The crime scene was changing already. How long had she been stuck here, hesitant about what to do? Probably hours.

And what if the killer were still lurking somewhere in the church? No, she refused to consider that possibility. She shook her head, hard, forcing those fears from her mind.

Checking her watch, she was flustered to see she'd been in the kitchen only a few minutes. Her mind had been rocketing around at the speed of light, spinning totally out of control, until passing time had felt like an eternity. She shook her head hard, again, in an effort to stop dawdling and finish her mission—finding a phone.

Austin decided to abandon Reg and the once-precious muffins and leave the kitchen. She peeked into the hall and looked for the janitor. He was nowhere in sight.

She rolled her eyes. "Just my luck."

Then, realizing she'd need a dime for a payphone, Austin turned back to the kitchen. Careful not to touch the body, she grabbed her purse. It had fallen clear, away from the blood, and looked unscathed. She wished she felt the same. Her breath came in short gasps as she rushed back into the hall and began trying every door along the hallway.

Each was locked.

She ran to the exit, made her way out to the street, and looked up and down the sidewalk. Where did Canadians put their phones? Austin stepped off the curb without checking the traffic, and instantly a car horn blasted on her left.

The first horn she'd heard in oh-so-civil Canada.

She waved a placating hand and made it to the opposite curb. She walked up Bathurst toward Honest Ed's, keeping an eye out for a payphone. A woman walked ahead of her, loaded down with packages, and Austin hurried up to her to ask where she could find a phone.

The woman's eyes widened, and she stepped away.

Austin glanced down, saw decorations of blueberry bits, purple spots, and blood stains on her jacket. Such evidence could place her at the crime scene. This frightened her, and tears trickled down her cheeks.

For the first time since she'd found Reg, she wondered about David. Where was he? If he were here, he'd know what to do.

Nothing ever rattled him.

David thought Reg was a showboat—all flash and no substance. Maybe that was why she hadn't thought of getting help from David right away. Although he never passed judgment on his fellow draft resisters, she sensed that David loathed Reg. David wouldn't be overcome with grief over Reg's murder.

She bit her lip, contrite. Her assumption was harsh and unfair. David was a moral and highly ethical man. But she herself didn't have to be a do-gooder. She could walk away from the old church and the gruesome contents of its dark kitchen.

Her apartment beckoned, a sanctuary far removed from Reg's bloodied body. Her new home had never seemed so welcoming before.

No, that was a copout, a cheater's way out. Austin would stand her ground. After all, she had an ancestor who'd defended the Alamo. How dare she even contemplate for one second fleeing from the scene of a crime? Besides, what was it Mr. Jones had said so often during her CIA training?

"Don't imagine you can outrun foreign authorities. They're devious, even if they don't let on that they suspect you."

The mental image of Mr. Jones, now lodged more or less permanently in her brain, reminded her that those damned muffins back at the church might as well have worn a sign: Austin Starr was here.

She imagined the old janitor arriving at work the next day, finding the corpse littered with baked goods, remembering their hallway encounter, and turning her in to the cops. Then a policeman would find her on campus, pull her out of class, and march her down to some police station. The police would charge her with the murder of Reginald Simpson, the show-off firebrand who divided his listeners into warring camps—those who thought he was a jerk and others who swore he possessed the oratory skills of Lincoln, had Lincoln been a vain and profane revolutionary.

Austin didn't like that scenario one bit. She pulled the

scattered pieces of her mind back together.

Totally refocused now on finding a phone, Austin was barely aware of the hordes of children and parents out trick-or-treating. She plunged past them down the street, but in her haste, and with her sensibilities dimmed by tunnel vision, she reeled into an unseen guardrail at the corner of Harbord and Croft. She fell for the second time that night.

Lying on the cold cement made her shiver. Her teeth chattered as Austin inspected her skinned knees and bruised hand. She'd live. Too dazed to stand, she raised herself a few inches and rested on the curb.

She picked up her purse, detected smudges of blood on it, and rubbed them off. Then she stood on wobbly legs and surveyed her surroundings. Two doors down, she spied a British-style pub.

Glory be, in front of it stood a beautiful payphone.

The thrill of success jolted through her. Dodging a surge of drinkers exiting the pub, Austin approached the phone. A telephone directory chained to it simplified her task. When she found a listing for the Toronto police under the category of city government, she felt another moment of triumph.

Austin took a dime from her purse, stuck the coin into the telephone, and placed the call.

"I want to report a dead body in a church on Bathurst."

CHAPTER TWO

Austin decided it was better to wait outside the church for the police rather than return to the interior with its gruesome kitchen, a perfect setting for film noir. Halloween would never again be just a time of fun and candy.

She stood on the sidewalk and eyed the seven steps leading to the massive wooden door, the main entrance to the United Church. The pitch was steep and even though there weren't many steps, still they intimidated her.

Once upon a time back in grade school, Austin had fallen backwards down the stairs of a slippery slide. Since then, stairs had unsettled her. The church's side door, the one she'd used earlier and the one without stairs, was now locked.

There was no handrail to hang on to, so she chose a step only two up from the sidewalk. She brushed sodden leaves away, sat down, and was instantly chilled. Shivering again, she pulled her jacket tight. Toronto was frosty in October, and Austin's thin Texas blood rebelled. Heat and humidity she could take in stride, but freezing temperatures and blizzards were unknowns. A brutal Canadian winter lay ahead, and she dreaded it.

She glanced at her watch. Eight o'clock. No sounds of police sirens yet. Only ordinary traffic noises and occasional childish peals of laughter reached her ears.

How long would it take for the cops to show up? She glowered into the darkness, her eyes seeking any sign of the authorities or danger.

Off to her right, she detected a red mailbox, and the sight

brought her up short. She flashed back to the first one she'd seen. The British royal coat of arms painted on its red background had pierced the bubble she'd inhabited, the one built on *Everyone's* advice that moving to Canada would produce no culture shock whatsoever. She'd banked on that advice, coming to Toronto under that illusion, only to find that Canada was full of differences. The rampant lion and unicorn shouted that Everyone had been wrong. Now, it would appear, even dead wrong.

Where were the stars and stripes? The American eagle?

All Canadian mailboxes now shrieked at her, symbols of her naiveté.

How trusting, how stupid she'd been to believe that Canada would feel just like the States. Why hadn't she raised a fuss before moving north? Being compliant hadn't saved her from harm. After all, here she was on Halloween night, convinced she was about to get mired in a murder case, while little kids scurried around holding their loot bags close to their scrawny little chests for safekeeping.

Oh, why couldn't David just plop down beside her, like magic? But she had no way to contact him and beg him to come help her. *Where was he? And where had all the anti-war activists gone?*

She should've known this day would be difficult—it had such a rough beginning. When the alarm clock had failed to go off, she and David were rushed getting ready for class. Then the bacon burned and the scrambled eggs went dry. She singed her thumb taking biscuits from the oven, but at least they were perfect. She'd mixed the dough the night before, a trick of her grandmother's. A wife for only seven months, Austin was still eager to do her new job properly. And still learning the ropes.

In the distance a siren blared and snapped her back into the present. The noise came closer and closer until a police car pulled up to the curb in front of her and two stern-faced men in uniform emerged. They were young, probably in their early twenties, same as she was.

The red-haired one came toward her, cap in hand. "Hello,

miss. I'm Constable Peters. Are you the person who phoned about the dead body?"

"My name is Austin Starr. I called, yes."

"Pleased to meet you, miss," Constable Peters said.

"*Missus*. It's Mrs. Starr."

"Our apologies, Mrs. Starr." The second officer stepped forward. "I'm Constable Higgins. We need you to take us to the body."

Austin rose from the step as a second squad car pulled up behind the first. The flashing lights from both created a psychedelic effect. Her head throbbed and her vision blurred, but before she could steady herself, a third car pulled up. Not a police car, thank goodness, so it added nothing to the light show. It was an ordinary dark sedan, and out of it climbed an ordinary, pleasant-looking man in a windbreaker and sport coat.

Who was he?

"Hello, sergeant." Constable Higgins spoke to the man exiting the second police car. "You made it fast."

The man in the windbreaker approached the three policemen with an outstretched hand. "Officers, how can I help? I'm Reverend Baxter, and this is my church."

Austin watched the men introduce themselves until finally they remembered her. Reverend Baxter came forward and put his arm around her in a consoling manner.

"You must have had quite a shock. I'm so sorry you've been drawn into this," he said. "Officers, how long does she have to stay here? She's shaking."

The sergeant said, "She can't leave until someone from the homicide squad comes. He'll want to question her. Meantime, let's go inside and see what the situation looks like." He pointed to Constable Higgins. "Wait out here for the detective sergeant."

Leaving him outside, the others followed Reverend Baxter into his church, down the hall, and right up to the kitchen door, where Austin stopped abruptly. "I don't have to go back in, do I?"

"You can stay here in the hall until our superior officer arrives. Then he'll decide how to proceed." The sergeant pushed the door open.

Austin turned her face away. She knew what was in there. She didn't need to see it again. The image of Reg's corpse was forever burned into her memory.

Austin slid down the wall and landed with a thump on the cold tile. She stretched her tired legs in front of her and watched the tweed-clad back of the minister recede down the hallway. He'd draped his windbreaker around her and gone to get chairs so they wouldn't have to stand or sit on the floor.

Too late now. She'd spent half the night on the cold Canadian ground; why stop now?

Waiting for the minister to return. Waiting for the homicide detective to show up.

Most of all, she was waiting to run home to David. He must be very worried about her by now.

Would this horrible night never end?

Up and down the long hall were many doors, eleven in all. She had tried each one earlier when searching for a phone to call the police. She looked across to the other side of the hall, at the entrance to the kitchen. Counted nine tiles from where she sat to that door. She was looking for something else to count when noises came from down the hall.

Raising her head, she eyed two male figures slowly advancing toward her. Her vision seemed clouded by exhaustion, but as they drew nearer, she was able to discern that each wore a brown tweed jacket and tan slacks. Her mind was so befuddled that she couldn't tell which man was Reverend Baxter and which a newcomer.

Wasn't the minister supposed to be bringing chairs? Maybe he'd forgotten. He probably had no more experience with a murder inquiry than she did. God would forgive him for not keeping his promise, and so would she.

Suddenly both men stood before her, and the air filled with talk.

Talk. Talk. Talk. She couldn't keep it all straight.

Only two things dented her consciousness. One of these men was a detective sergeant from the homicide division. And she had to return to the bloody kitchen.

Someone pulled her to her feet. Austin took a few steps, then stopped. Her mind balked at the thought of walking back in to see Reg laid out on the floor. But she had to do it. She was a good girl. She always did the right thing.

Well, almost always. She *was* in Canada, wasn't she?

Now one man in a tweed jacket took her left arm and the other took her right. Together they maneuvered her through the kitchen door and into that evil room.

"He's right where I left him. Now may I leave?" Her voice sounded thin and reedy, not low and confident as it usually did.

"Afraid not," one of the cops said. She had no idea which. Did it even matter? She was so tired, so very tired. How could she help them? She knew she wouldn't make sense.

"Would you like a glass of water, Mrs. Starr?"

"Yes, please, but not from that tap." She pointed at the kitchen faucet.

One of the young constables went into the hall and returned with a paper cup filled with water. She sipped from it. "Thank you. I feel better now."

One of the tweed gentlemen stepped forward. "Is this room the way you left it?" he asked.

She nodded.

"What did you do when you were in here?"

Austin hesitated, trying to remember. "It was dark. I came in when the lights were off. I stumbled. I didn't know where the light switch was. Then I fell when my foot hit...my foot hit..." She gestured at the corpse, but her eyes remained locked on the kitchen door.

"I was tired of carrying the muffins. You see them now." Again she waved at the dead body without looking at it. "I dropped them when I fell. I felt something sticky on the floor and got scared. Got up, fiddled for the light switch. When I could see, when there was light, there was Reg. I knew who he was. I'd met him before. He was dead when I fell on him."

"How do you know?"

She shuddered and drew in a sharp breath. "I suspected, but I made sure."

"How?"

"I felt under his chin, under his beard. There was no pulse." She was on automatic pilot now. She could answer anything.

"Why did you come to the church tonight?"

"Came for a meeting of the anti-war group, but no one was here."

"What did you touch?"

"Nothing. No, that's not right. The light switch. The countertop. The doorknob. After I saw what had happened in here, I tried not to touch anything else. Knew I shouldn't. I read lots of mysteries you see. That's how I knew." She started to giggle but stopped herself. If she continued, she might never stop. "Will you take my fingerprints? Will I have to go to a police station? My husband will be worried about me. He doesn't know where I am. I'm late."

"No, the equipment will be here soon. Where is your husband?"

"I don't know." Her tone was almost a whimper.

"Your accent suggests you're not from Canada. Are you a Canadian citizen?"

Oh dear, now this was tricky terrain. "I've got landed immigrant status." She added a touch of pride to her voice. Surely the Canadian policemen would like that, wouldn't they?

"Where are you from originally?"

"Texas."

"Why are you here?"

"We're graduate students at the University of Toronto. My husband and I have teaching fellowships there. He studies mathematics, and my area is Russian history."

She took a peek at her questioner in time to watch his eyebrows shoot up so high that his glasses slid down his nose.

"Russian? Are you a fellow traveler, a supporter of Communism?"

"Of course not." Austin felt hot indignation flash through her. *Of all the nerve.* "The Russian past is exotic and foreign, and I adore history, but American history seems dull by comparison. I like all the English kings and queens too. It was Queen Elizabeth's coronation that got me interested in history. All that pageantry is beautiful." She stopped to breathe.

"You're babbling, Mrs. Starr." The voice was kind.

She turned to face him and saw that her questioner's expression was surprisingly pleasant. "Do you like history too?" The minute she asked, she felt stupid.

"As a matter of fact, I do."

"I'm sorry I'm babbling. I'm a mess."

"We understand. You've had a shock."

Austin shut her eyes tight, tossed her head back, and wiggled it back and forth until her neck crunched. "There, that's better. Do you think you can find the killer?" Her words startled her. "Oh my gosh, I'm sorry. Of course you can."

The man grinned at her. "Of course we will." The man in tweed turned to one of the younger men. "Take her back into the hall. Let me know when the fellow comes to take her fingerprints; I'll need to talk to her again."

"Yes, sir, Detective Sergeant McKinnon," the younger man said.

When he led Austin from the room, she looked back to see McKinnon following her with his eyes. She was surprised to sense only concern in his gaze.

She hoped she hadn't blown everything by gushing about Russia. That was so unlike her. How bizarre. What would their future dealings be like?

She didn't doubt she'd be seeing the detective sergeant again.

CHAPTER THREE

"Where've you been? It's after midnight." David threw down the book he'd been reading and ran to the door.

Austin flung herself into his arms and burrowed her nose in his sweater. The familiar scent of him was reassuring. She didn't speak for several moments, then muttered, "I was at the church, just like I promised."

"All this time?" He grasped her shoulders, shifted her farther away, and assessed her expression. "What's wrong? Are you all right?"

"All this time, yes, I was at the church. Right where you were supposed to be."

"Oh, babe, I'm sorry. Word came of a huge rally at Queen's Park, and we all dashed over there." He coaxed her to the couch, they sat, and he grabbed her hands. "You're cold. Do you want some tea?"

"No."

He cocked his head and regarded her closely, question marks seeming to leap from his eyes. "I figured you'd find us, and it's a pity you didn't. It was really cool, a happy demo for a change. Johnson's finally called off the bombing in the north." He paused. "But we can talk about that later. Why on earth did you stay at the church so long? Didn't you know I'd worry?"

A hint of exasperation crept into his voice.

Her perception amazed Austin. Sensing his feelings was usually like trying to read tea leaves without being taught how. But after stumbling over a corpse, coming home to find him upset was too much. She burst into tears.

"Honey, honey, what's wrong?" David sounded distraught, and he clearly didn't know what to do.

Through her sobs, she managed only a few words. "You have no idea, just no idea. It was all so horrible."

He drew back, and his eyes widened when he noticed the blood and blueberry stains on her clothes. "Are you okay?" He threw his arms around her and spoke into her hair. "Did someone attack you? Tell me."

Austin's reply was shaky. "No, nothing like that. No, no."

David's sigh of relief puffed against her cheek. "Everyone says Toronto's safer than America, but—"

"Yeah, right. *Everyone* says." Austin's laugh bordered on hysteria. "Reg Simpson is dead, and I found his body."

"Wha-what?"

"You heard me. Reg was murdered in the church. I phoned the police. They came to the church and grilled me. The whole thing was a big, god-awful nightmare, and now I'm exhausted." She cuddled deeper into his arms and kept on crying.

David held and rocked her for a long time, not saying a word until she settled. Then, leaning forward, he wiped tears from her face and gazed into her eyes. "Who questioned you?"

"At first I couldn't decide who to call and couldn't find a phone and—the Metro Toronto Police."

"Nobody from the RCMP showed up?" David sat up straight, and his fingers began to twirl a lock of his long hair.

"The Mounties weren't there. But why would that matter?"

"Thank God, only the local cops. Good thing they talked to you, not one of the guys."

"You'll *all* have to talk to the police pretty soon anyway."

"That's bad, really bad." David took his glasses off, polished them on his denim work shirt, and put them back on. He twirled his hair again.

Despite her agitation, Austin noted this new gesture. What did it mean? She watched the obsessive twisting and wondered why he didn't cut his hair. The hippie look didn't suit him.

"You're not exactly heartbroken that someone killed Reg, and maybe that's not remarkable. But you don't seem very upset over my ordeal either." Austin tried to keep from sounding angry. She wasn't sure if she succeeded.

"Honey, how can you say that?" David's hands moved from his hair to her shoulders, and he hugged her to him. "I got frantic, didn't know where you were. Why didn't you call?"

She explained about her problem finding a phone. "And after that I was with the police, and then it got too late to call. Didn't want to wake you up."

"I wasn't asleep." He took a deep breath and lowered his voice. "It's just that you've never been late like this before. Promise me the next time you fall over a murder victim, you'll call me."

Austin giggled and kept on giggling, unable to stop. Soon David joined in, and then they were both laughing so hard they gasped for breath.

Once they regained their composure, he said, "Okay, let's take it from the top. Tell me everything that happened tonight. And tell me if I'm right about this: part of you thought the whole episode was fascinating."

Her face grew hot, but she said, "You're right. You know how I love murder mysteries and spy stories. I couldn't help being intrigued by the circumstances of Reg's death. I've always wondered what it would be like to be caught up in a real mystery. What makes it hard, though, is not being on home ground. I don't know the jurisdictions, the laws, even the names of the officers' ranks. It's all different from back home. *Unsettling.* I would've felt more competent if this happened in Texas."

She crossed to the window, pulled aside the sheet they were using in place of drapes, and pondered the darkness. Without looking at David, she said, "I really don't want to agonize over everything that happened, not right now anyway, so here it is in a nutshell. Two young cops and a sergeant showed up, and someone rounded up the church's minister and brought him in. Next, a senior man came, Detective Sergeant Bill McKinnon.

"They questioned me, over and over, about the same things. They naturally tried to trip me up, and so I only repeated what I knew for sure, but I was scared." Austin stopped to dig out a tissue from her purse. She blew her nose and wiped tears from her face.

"The minister was comforting though, said what a decent person I was, calling the police and not running away." She snorted. "After that, I was ashamed I'd even thought about slinking off into the night and letting someone else find the body."

She paused, eyes on the ceiling, considering her next words. "Still, you're right, David. The whole evening was mesmerizing, like being caught up in an episode of *I Spy*."

"Aren't you mixing up spies and cops?" He was restacking the books piled beside him on the couch.

Austin froze. She didn't want to talk about spies. She'd never admitted to David that she'd done several weeks of training with the CIA. He wouldn't have approved. Besides, Mr. Jones warned her not to confide in anyone, and then she'd married and rushed off to Canada, putting a stop to her fling with international intrigue.

Now she chose her words carefully and adopted a spritely tone. "You never know—maybe Reg's murder did have something to do with spies."

Her face lit up. "David, just think. Maybe federal agents hopped over the border to take out Reg because he was being so effective against the war."

"That joker? Effective?" David yelled. He never yelled.

"Hey, come on. Have some respect for the dead." Austin rubbed her eyes and tried to erase what she'd seen. "It was so grisly. Blood seeping out of him, spilling on the floor. I tracked through some of it when the lights were off, couldn't help it. And his beautiful suede jacket got saturated with it."

"That ridiculous thing? Looked like he was dressed up for Halloween."

David's harsh manner grated on Austin. "Then you did see him?"

"Sure. He was at the meeting, ranting against LBJ. Reg said stopping the bombing of North Vietnam was just a ploy to help Humphrey beat Nixon in next week's election. Reg boasted like he always does. Said he knew lots of politicians, that they're all no good, just like the military brass."

David slammed a book on his knee. "I'm sick of all his hints, that he knows so many big shots. He's just like the rest of us—he knows what he reads in the newspapers. He gave a decent speech tonight, though. I didn't agree with his analysis, but he did get the guys fired up. Hard to do now, you know. Most of them are pretty gloomy, living so far from home and on so little money."

"So Reg's speech turned out to be his swan song, and he won't annoy you ever again. Maybe he'll become a martyr for the cause. Songs will be written about him, like for Joe Hill."

David sniffed. "Now *that* would be a shame. Reg was no hero. You don't know what kinds of things he's been up to lately."

Austin's head snapped up. "What do you mean?"

David didn't answer. He sat still, avoiding her gaze. Finally, he asked, "When do you think the cops'll talk to me?"

"Soon, maybe even tomorrow. Already gave them your name and how to contact you."

"Gee, thanks a lot."

Austin made a face. "You know I had no choice. But I hope DS McKinnon will be the one who calls. He's really nice."

"I'm sure." David's voice was laced with sarcasm. "This is going to be complicated, you know." He was twirling his hair again.

The only time Austin had ever seen him fidget was when he told his parents about moving to Canada. Now she realized how much tension he must be holding in. She carefully said, "Why would things be tricky? After all, we're here legally. You haven't even been drafted yet, and we're following all the rules."

David stopped twirling and glared at her. "Still, I'm worried."

"Why? We've got nothing to hide."

"Yeah, sure, but you never know."

Austin had a sudden thought. "By the way, David, where'd you go after the rally? You can account for all your time, can't you?"

He turned away and contemplated a poster of a peace sign. "Umm, sort of."

"What's that mean, for pity's sake?" Austin felt her blood pressure soar. Now she'd have to add David's interview with the police to her ever-increasing list of worries. If only someone would come up with a pill to take anxiety away. Booze and pot never helped her—neither one worked right. They either made her mood darken or her mind speed into paranoia.

"After I left Queen's Park, I went back to campus," he said. "I studied for a while and came back here about eleven o'clock. Doubt if anyone saw me after the rally." David jumped up and knocked over a coffee cup. He stooped to mop up the spill with a sock from a pair that he'd left on the floor.

Watching her husband's endearingly sloppy habit made Austin smile, made her want to wrap up the evening on a tender note. "Shall I make some herbal tea before we go to bed? I'm dead exhausted, but my mind keeps racing anyway. Maybe chamomile will slow me down and help me sleep."

David ignored her olive branch and stalked from the room, leaving Austin alone in disbelief and silence. What was wrong with him? *He* didn't trip over a dead man and then have to deal with the cops.

Why was he so upset? She sensed he was nervous about tangling with the authorities and being a draft resister, although if asked, he would no doubt deny it. Okay, so she understood that, but still.

She scooped up the wet socks and empty cup on her way to the kitchen. She dropped the cup in the sink and took the socks to the clothes hamper in the hall. The cowboy shirt on top of the laundry heap caught her eye. She'd given David that shirt on the anniversary of their first kiss. Each time he pulled it on, he winked at her and talked about one of their early dates.

What had happened to that sensitive, romantic guy? Political exile was changing him more than she'd expected it would. More than she'd planned for. It was probably changing her too, but she couldn't see the changes in herself as clearly.

When they'd begun dating in their junior year, David's alabaster skin and Kennedy-esque hair had transfixed her. She eventually decided that his looks made him a ringer for Warren Beatty, but it was his intelligence and seriousness that won her over.

However, her sorority sisters found David "too pompous for words," and she cried secretly after she overheard one say how pretentious he was, intently solemn as he smoked his pipe. But Austin adored the image the pipe projected. It suited his math and philosophy double major. His intellectual intensity challenged her, and she felt safe with him.

By their senior year, the war in Vietnam began gnawing at students' nerves, unsettling their projections for life after college. For those who made the "Ballad of the Green Berets" a hit song, however, their game plan was to fulfill their ROTC commitments and go off to Asia to "kick some gook butt." Austin's sorority sisters got busy and organized their weddings, having snagged their grooms before the men escaped to fight in the dank, dark jungles of 'Nam.

Austin had seldom thought about Vietnam unless she caught Walter Cronkite's coverage on the news. But the war escalated until she couldn't escape it. Vietnam flew off the television screen and into everyone's lives.

When President Johnson needed more manpower to fight the war, the draft rules grew tighter. Graduate students, once allowed to defer military service, were no longer able to do so. If David had graduated only one year earlier, he could have gone to graduate school and remained there under the earlier rules, avoiding the draft forever.

Austin couldn't imagine why any military board would want to draft David. He was thin and pale and scholarly—a real bookworm—not like Daddy, a big, beefy graduate of Texas A&M, who became a major in World War II.

She picked up David's shirt from the heap of laundry, held it to her cheek, and nuzzled it, remembering all their former plans for the future.

Back in the spring of 1967 when they'd graduated from college, they'd believed their futures were cast in stone. Columbia University awarded her a graduate fellowship in Soviet studies, and David won a math fellowship from Princeton.

Since then she'd learned an old Yiddish saying, one that perfectly suited that period in her life. When man makes plans, God laughs.

During the summer, waiting for her graduate career to begin, Austin had lolled around her home in Cuero, killing time. She was either at the swimming pool with her friend Earleen or hunkered down beside the air conditioner devouring mysteries—three times for John le Carré's novel, *The Spy Who Came in from the Cold.*

But time had hung heavy in the sweltering Texas air. Austin envisioned it inching forward, crawling along on bloodied knees. Each month of the calendar took an eon to turn.

Now she put down David's shirt and went into the kitchen where their calendar for 1968—festooned with Canadian maple leaves—hung on the wall. It was past midnight, so she ripped off the sheet for October and tried to focus on November.

Still, she couldn't help returning to the past. Flashed back to June 1967 when Israel won their defensively strategic Six-Day War, seizing the Sinai Peninsula and the Gaza Strip. To July, when federal troops were sent to quell deadly race riots in Newark and Detroit. Casualty counts, both at home and abroad, had dominated the news. The onslaught was relentless.

In August, LBJ ordered half a million new troops for Vietnam. Then David began calling daily from his home in Dallas. "What if I get drafted? I don't know what doing my duty means in this war. It's so confusing."

"Don't worry." Her tone and her heart had been so blithe. "Grad school'll take your mind off your draft worries." She'd been flippant, so sure that everything would work out the way she wished. Now she cringed at the memory.

When she'd finally arrived at Columbia, she'd brought everything she cherished—including her unrealistic hopes and expectations. Her fellowship money flowed in like an old-fashioned Texas gusher, and Austin could afford bus rides to see David at Princeton every weekend. She loved him and didn't want to lose touch. Wanted to marry him, in fact.

She deployed the heavy feminine artillery traditionally used in campaigns to win husbands and by Christmas, she and David were engaged. When cities across America were in flames in April 1968 after the assassination of Martin Luther King, Jr., they wed, and by the time Bobby Kennedy was assassinated in June, they were living in Toronto.

Even so, Austin was astonished to find herself in Canada, although she'd been an active—if not entirely happy—participant in the decision. She had made good, in the end, on an unthinking promise.

Two months before their wedding, David had said, "My mind's made up. This war is immoral, and I can't fight. If I'm drafted, I'll either go to prison or Canada."

"Don't be ridiculous," Austin had snapped. "Nobody's going to draft you and if you are drafted, you can't go to prison. If that happens, well, I'll go with you to Canada or something."

David sent for Canadian graduate school catalogs. She took that in stride; he was merely being prudent. Later he said, "We need to pursue Canadian schools now." And although his draft board had as yet shown no interest in calling him up, the two of them applied to three grad schools in Canada.

And they got lucky. One university accepted both of them and offered each a fellowship. "Lucky-schmucky," Austin had confided to her girlfriend Earleen.

"That settles it," David said. "We'll transfer to Toronto and continue our studies up there. Our two fellowships will give us enough money to live on."

Whoa!

Okay, Austin old girl, she'd told herself, *you've gone along with this little charade long enough. Time to clue him in. There's no way you're moving all the way up there.*

"Guess what, honey, I've changed my mind." That's what she should have told David, but it didn't go down that way. No, in her family, once you made a promise, you never went back on your word. Besides, she honestly didn't think she could be happy if David languished in prison.

And now, standing alone in their Canadian apartment, Austin turned away from the calendar full of maple leaves and returned to the old cowboy shirt. It smelled like David, a decent and honorable man who was going through a rough patch. Even though he pretended to enjoy being in Canada, she knew he was homesick too. The murder investigation shouldn't actually involve her much. She should probably just hunker down and focus on making a good life here.

She undressed in the hall, added her clothes to the pile of laundry, slipped on David's shirt instead of her nightgown, and tiptoed into the bedroom. As she crept into bed beside her husband and curled around his unyielding back, Austin felt as desolate as if her last friend had begun an expedition to the North Pole. Visions of Reg in his bloodied suede jacket were embedded in her mind and try as she might, she couldn't drive them away.

She couldn't help but worry what wretched events lay ahead.

CHAPTER FOUR

Two pigs pushed their snouts into a trough and rooted around in the bright red slop until they found their targets. They snorted in glee and gobbled the muffins that bopped up and down in the sludge. A shout grabbed the pigs' attention. They lifted their heads. Rivulets of blood ran from their mouths.

Austin woke up with a start, her heart pounding.

The shout repeated. She frowned; that couldn't have been part of the dream.

"Wake up, sleepyhead," David called. "Better get up or you'll miss your class." A door closed, and quiet returned.

David's warning transformed Austin. She flipped over and snatched up her watch from the bedside table. Her Russian history class would start soon.

She sprang into action. After dressing quickly, she rushed into the kitchen so fast that she crashed into David, who stood in front of the fridge, drinking orange juice from the container.

"Dang it." Austin massaged her aching shin. "Can't move an inch in here without hitting something. Cabin cruisers on Lake Houston have bigger galleys."

"Sorry, sweetheart. Have you got time for eggs? *I* made some for a change." He proudly held up eggs scrambled in their old iron skillet.

Although her time was tight, she didn't want to disappoint him. "Then I'll have some, thanks."

He prepared her plate and poured juice. "You sleep okay after that ordeal last night?"

"Pretty much. But you know what they say: the murder seems like a bad dream. Today I just want to concentrate on my studies. I'd rather think about a revolution fifty years in the past than what happened last night."

David served her and then turned on the radio.

Austin groaned inwardly. Listening to news was the worst part of their morning routine.

David squeezed past her and sat at the table. "I can't get enough news about the election up here." His voice reeked with disgust. "Even the CBC doesn't give details."

Tired of his morning rants against the Canadian Broadcasting Corporation, Austin changed the subject. "Professor Klimenko expects Nixon will beat Humphrey and—"

David choked on his coffee. "What's he know about presidential politics? He's an expert on communism." He eyed the new coffee stain on his shirt and scowled. "Humphrey's got to win and get us out of Vietnam." He picked up his fork, put it down again. "We shouldn't mess in a civil war. It's not like World War Two, with Nazis spreading evil everywhere in Europe and the Japanese raping and pillaging and subjugating their Asian neighbors. I would've fought in that war, like our dads, but not in Vietnam— no way."

The atmosphere in the kitchen shifted, like tectonic plates grinding past each other along fault lines.

"Please don't upset yourself so early in the morning." She reached out and took his hand. "If Humphrey does win, will we have a shot at going home to Texas?" She shifted in her chair, waiting, hoping for a favorable response.

David studied her face. At length he said, "We'll probably never live in the States again. You know that. We've talked about it often enough." In a lighter tone, he added, "Besides, the cold up here will make us snuggle, and you sure can't say that about back home." He stared at their intertwined fingers. "This is hard on you,

I know, but give it a chance, okay?"

"You're right. Sorry I brought it up." Austin looked down at her plate but discovered she wasn't hungry.

David scooted his chair back and stood. "By the way, I wanted to make grits but couldn't find any. Where'd you put them?"

Her head fell into her hands. "We're out, and grits aren't exactly a staple of Canadian cuisine. Next time Mother calls, I'll ask her to send some."

"Don't say they're for me. She'll add poison."

Her head snapped up, and she laughed. "Hey, come on. She's not happy her only child moved to a foreign country. Still, she believes in the whole whither-thou-goest bit."

He arched an eyebrow. "If you say so." He took three steps to the other side of the kitchen, then gazed out the window while rinsing his cup. "If I don't hurry, I'll be late for class." Stripping off his shirt now spotted with coffee, he left the room.

Austin eyed the eggs congealing on her plate, and her stomach flipped. Did the cold eggs bother her, or was it the prospect of living in Canada for the rest of her life? It was so much the antithesis of Texas. She cleared the table and scraped her uneaten breakfast into the trash. She'd grab a doughnut on campus.

David returned in a clean shirt. He pulled a sweater over his head and put on a jacket. Seeing him swaddled in layers of clothes was an eye-opener. Before the inevitable arrival of snow, they'd need to buy heavy coats. Their Texas clothes weren't going to cut it.

David hugged Austin and nibbled on her ear. Her knees went weak, and her heartbeat quickened. His physical effect on her was always immediate.

"And one more thing," he said. "Another draft resister's coming to stay next week, with his wife and kid. I told the organizing committee it was fine."

Austin gaped at David. "The last dodger left only three days ago and—"

"Don't say *dodger*. It's *resister*." He shook his head. "Don't make us sound like cowards or criminals."

Austin squeezed his arm. "I admire how you stand up for your principles, but honestly, David, some of these people who land on our doorstep are utterly hopeless."

"So the movement needs all kinds." He shrugged. "Let's talk later. I have to hurry."

Austin leaned her head against his chest. "All right. I have to run too."

He kissed her again and left the apartment, shutting the door quietly behind him.

Emotions swirling in turmoil, Austin hurried into the living room to watch David from the window. Would he remember their ritual or was he too caught up in anti-war fervor? He got to the sidewalk and, just as she was losing hope, turned and waved. She broke into a smile and waved back.

But her giddiness turned to nervousness. Any day now she was sure he'd forget.

They'd lived in Toronto since June. As the months passed, she worried about the mounting stresses on their relationship. The only time she didn't fret was when they were in bed together.

Her mother had warned against moving to Canada. Since Austin routinely ignored her on everything except matters of style, remembering her words now only made Austin feel worse. She picked up her wedding picture, traced the intricate pattern of its frame, then restored it to the brick-and-board bookcase. The elaborate frame looked silly among the no-frills, graduate student décor, but her mother had insisted only sterling would do. Taken last April in Texas, the photo showed two happy people in a simpler time—a tall, glowing bride and her groom, taller still. His full beard and long hair accentuated the serious look on his handsome face.

She'd first seen David rushing in late to government class in her junior year at college, and she fell in love with him on the second day when he arrived early enough to take the seat beside her. David proved to be the sweetest, smartest boy she'd ever met. His occasional prickliness reminded her of Mr. Rochester's manner with Jane Eyre. David's own mix of sweet and sour, something like a Chinese dish, intrigued her.

Excited voices from the radio interrupted her thoughts. The CBC announcer was describing a controversy over the schedule of Quebec's new premier, Jean-Jacques Bertrand. The non-American pronunciation—*shed-yule*—plus the unfamiliar French name set Austin adrift in a sea of unease. She longed to hear some good old Texas twang.

She switched off the radio and listened instead to the lonely silence.

She ran all the way to Sidney Smith Hall and slipped into her seat, breathing hard, just as Dr. Klimenko entered the classroom. Despite all her rushing, Austin felt she never got anywhere in anything, let alone ahead.

She watched her professor prepare to give his lecture. He looked the way she pictured Jo March's professor in *Little Women*, a big bear of a shaggy man, with clothes awry, beard uncombed, and a face alight with goodwill. Only, Dr. Klimenko always wore a black leather glove on his right hand. The glove seemed to handicap him—taking out notes from his briefcase was a long process.

Growing bored, Austin turned to her fellow grad students. Without exception, they sat quietly in their seats, waiting patiently for Dr. Klimenko to begin. If this had been one of her college classes in Texas, everyone would be talking to someone else, busy being friendly. Here in Toronto, however, everyone was dutiful—patient and silent. She wanted someone to chat with, to confide in about her dreadful evening with the dead body. But she hadn't made any friends yet, so she too sat, but maybe not too patiently, awaiting the professor's talk.

"Today we will discuss how dangerously ill-prepared Tsarist

Russia was at the beginning of World War One," Dr. Klimenko began.

And Austin's mind began to drift.

What could have caused someone to kill Reg? Rather than taking lecture notes, she began listing possible motives for murder. She hadn't known Reg long, but within seconds, she thought of three possibilities.

First, Reginald Simpson IV came from a wealthy family. Although he portrayed himself as only a poor student, he had money and lots of it. She'd witnessed as he handed out baggies of pot and treated a crowd to beer, and his dramatic suede jacket was worth more than her whole wardrobe. The jacket's cost could underwrite a year's rent for another draft resister. Therefore, she reasoned, Reg might've been a target for a robbery that had gone terribly wrong.

Second, Reg pushed his anti-war views—freely, loudly, and often. While he had a way with words, his staunch belief in his own charisma was an inspiration to some and a turnoff to others. Austin assumed her husband wasn't the only guy who despised him. Someone who possessed a less temperate nature than David could've gotten into a political argument and lost his cool after Reg had zoomed up to his usual full-blown level of condescension.

And third was that favorite old standby, sexual jealousy. Reg was known to prey on other guys' women, something that Austin herself knew all too well. She'd had a run-in with him at a party a few weeks earlier.

David had been debating with other draft resisters the consequences of the assassinations that had rocked America earlier that year: would the murders of Dr. King and Bobby Kennedy hurt or help the anti-war cause?

After ten minutes, Austin had wearied of the argument. She wandered into the kitchen, where she found a sink full of ice and stubby brown bottles of Canadian beer. She was opening a Molson when a hand stroked her hair. And ran down her back.

That hand belonged to Reg Simpson.

"Ever since I laid eyes on you the first time, I've wanted to get you alone." Reg pushed back her protective armor of hair and whispered in her ear, "You're good enough to eat, even better than those pretzels, and they're far out." He gestured at a snack bowl, licked his lips, and stuck his tongue in her ear.

"What're you doing?" Austin yelped. "You know I'm a married woman." She pulled away and drew up to her full height, all five feet eleven inches.

"Shit, makes no difference." He wiped his mouth on his sleeve and shuffled closer. "Tell you what. I scored some LSD, so let's go out to the porch and try it. Whaddya say?"

"I say it's too chilly out there and, as I said, I'm married." She held up her left hand and waved her ring in front of his glassy eyes. "Besides, you don't interest me."

"You're sure stuck-up, like your stupid prick of a husband. But I know what you need, and I'm just the man to give it to you. Baby, you've never been fucked till you've been fucked by me." He grabbed Austin and pulled her to him.

"If you're so eager, go fuck yourself."

"Oh, baby, you're gonna be wild in bed and—"

Austin wrenched free and bolted out of the kitchen. In the dining room, she checked to see if anyone had noticed her tussling with Reg. Seeing David still deep in discussion, she ran into the bathroom and locked the door.

No one had ever treated her like that before. Her friends said that good-girl vibes emanated from her and those, combined with her height, usually protected her from casual sexual advances. So she didn't know how to handle them. With admittedly little to judge from, she still wondered how anyone could see Reg's come-on as enticing. She splashed water on her face, sat on the closed toilet lid, and took deep breaths.

She'd stunned herself, uttering the F-word for the first time. Her Texas friends didn't swear, but the Toronto anti-war crowd flung four-letter words to the air all the time, where they hung thick like mosquitoes after a Gulf Coast downpour. She smiled, thinking no one should mess with a Texas girl. Austin stayed in the bathroom until an irritated soul pounded on the door and yelled to get in.

Ever since that party, she'd given Reg a wide berth. Deciding not to add to David's growing dislike of him, she'd held her peace about the encounter. She assumed her husband knew nothing about the episode, but wasn't sure. Someone could have told him, but David never brought it up. Perhaps Reg's murderer was some bad-tempered man who discovered Reg sniffing around his own girl and wasn't content to let his girl handle Reg.

Austin put down her pen and looked out the window, past Dr. Klimenko, at the maple trees glowing in the autumn light. She sighed. Several students sitting near her spun around to glare, and her professor stopped lecturing.

"Mrs. Starr," he said, interrupting the history lesson, "why the sighs? Did your family suffer traumas during the war or the revolution that followed? Do you have family experiences to share with us?"

Austin felt heat rise to her cheeks. "Forgive me, Dr. Klimenko. My family isn't Russian, and we lost no one in either World War. I was, however, actually thinking about how wars can alter the paths of so many lives, even those who never go off to fight. Sorry I interrupted. It won't happen again."

He nodded and resumed his lecture. Austin picked up her pen to signal her concentration and tried to ignore the buzzing in her head that told her to flee. The classroom clock showed that class was almost over, and she planned a rapid escape.

Looking for some distraction, Austin fixated on the black leather glove that Dr. Klimenko wore on his right hand. Of course Dr. Strangelove came to mind. How had she missed that before? In the movie, Peter Sellers used a black glove and a German accent to illustrate his sinister character. Dr. Klimenko had his own distinctive Slavic accent, but the gloved hand was a mystery. The Strangelove movie had made her laugh at the ease with which men got caught up in the stupidity of war. Yet the more history she studied, the more she realized how close to reality the satire was.

Dr. Klimenko didn't strike her as sinister, but he must have fought in the last Great War. He was the right age to have been wounded in World War II, and the Russian front had been notably brutal. Who knew what atrocities he witnessed—or committed— in order to escape with his mangled hand as a memento?

"Class is dismissed," Dr. Klimenko said, once again interrupting her thoughts. "Next time we will discuss how Lenin's return from exile changed the course of world history."

Austin stood and gathered her books.

"And, Mrs. Starr, please stay a moment. There's something we must discuss."

CHAPTER FIVE

Austin delayed joining her professor until the other students left the classroom. She tapped her foot, waiting her turn, and was reminded of David twirling his hair last night. She needed to relax.

But if she had to work so hard at it, how relaxed could she be?

At last her turn came. Dr. Klimenko stood at the lectern, rubbing his gloved hand.

"I had an unusual visitation in my office this morning before class, most unusual," he said. "Since I left the Soviet Union more than two decades ago, I've missed the, umm, *pleasures* of being interviewed by the police. Now, thanks to you, Mrs. Starr, that's no longer true." He paused, looked down, and fingered his lecture notes.

His sarcasm didn't escape her. Did he want her to say something? She waited for him to continue, assuming it was safer to remain silent until she heard what he had to say.

"I don't like dealing with authorities, madam," he said finally. "My past has taught me to avoid officials at all costs. True, Detective Sergeant McKinnon was a pleasant man, but I would gladly have foregone the experience of meeting him. Shall I tell you what he wanted?"

"Please."

"I imagine you already know."

"I don't. Do tell me." Was Dr. Klimenko toying with her? If so, she didn't appreciate his method.

"When McKinnon learned you were my graduate student, he

came to ask how he could see you on campus. Alas, it was my duty to answer, and so you can expect to meet him when you exit this building. I thought it only fair to alert you."

"Thank you, sir. I appreciate the warning."

He cleared his throat. "May I be so bold as to inquire what happened to make the police interested in you, Mrs. Starr? To be blunt, you don't seem yourself today. Should I worry about your welfare? Your safety? You've only recently arrived in Canada, *da?*"

Austin struggled to respond. This was her first command performance to describe briefly and succinctly the events of the previous evening. So she stumbled through the story, knowing she'd have other chances to hone it to perfection. She bet the police would talk to her again, and all the guys in David's group would want to hear her story too.

While he listened, Dr. Klimenko kept twisting his gloved hand into the other one. When she finished, he leaned against the lectern. "I feel compelled to advise you," he said, "how to handle authorities who question you about dangerous subjects. Unfortunately, I am skilled in this area due to frequent practice. Although that's all blessedly in the past, the lessons are burned into me." He looked pointedly at the glove he wore.

"If you've nothing to hide," he said, "then you must be straightforward and honest. Yet, don't offer more information than necessary. Extraneous details can get you into trouble. Canada isn't the Soviet Union, needless to say, so you needn't worry about the horrors that I encountered. Nevertheless, please heed my advice. At a minimum you'll avoid mental anguish and legal fees." His lips twisted into a lopsided grin. "Your fellowship is not large enough to cover such costly expenses."

Every word burrowed into her brain. She said, "I'll remember, and thank you for your concern, professor."

"Furthermore, if you need someone to confide in or if your situation becomes difficult, please seek me out. My door will always be open to you."

Dr. Klimenko's good hand reached for his briefcase. Austin took this as a signal that their conversation had ended. She was wrong.

"And now, despite your problems," he said, "you must read Edmund Wilson's brilliant book, *To the Finland Station*. Wilson charts the philosophical underpinnings of radical thought from the French Revolution in 1789 to the Bolshevik Revolution in 1918. I dare say those same revolutionary passions, found now in the modern culture of protest, are alive and well among your friends." He put his gloved hand over his heart and bowed. "I bid you good day, Mrs. Starr."

Had her professor actually linked her to Lenin? She certainly was no revolutionary, and neither was David. Befuddled by Dr. Klimenko's mix of messages and changing moods, intrigued by the hint of appalling misfortunes that had befallen him, Austin left the classroom.

She searched for signs of a lurking policeman, but saw no one. She did spot a nearby ladies room—she couldn't bring herself to say *washroom*, as Canadians did. Before facing more questions from the police, she ducked inside to collect her thoughts. She pulled a brush out of her purse and used it to smooth her rebellious hair. This usually calmed her, but today the ritual took longer to work. She observed an inordinate number of hairs stuck in the brush. *That's just great*, she thought. *I'll be bald by the time this investigation is finished.*

"You're a nut job," she scolded herself, talking to her reflection in the bathroom mirror. "You've got more important concerns than hair loss. You're only twenty-two. Your hair won't fall out anytime soon, no matter what your mother says."

When her mother had encountered fluffs of hair around her daughter's dressing table, she had warned, "If you always backcomb your hair, Austin Amelia, you won't have any hair left when you're forty." If her mother said that once a week, she'd said it ten times. As usual, Austin had ignored her advice. Right now, however, she would gladly flee back to the safe but tense bosom of her family, willing to endure her mother's constant criticism—if she could only escape the clutches of the Metropolitan Toronto Police.

She sighed—recognizing she was doing it—and chided herself for being nervous about talking to the nice policeman again. She was a good girl, had done the right thing. Therefore, she should have nothing to fear.

At last she was ready to face DS McKinnon, and she expected him to be lying in wait outside Sidney Smith Hall.

The policeman did not disappoint.

"Mrs. Starr, come over here, if you please." McKinnon stepped forward and confronted Austin as she descended the steps outside the lecture hall. "Dr. Klimenko said I would find you here after his class ended. If there's time before your next one, I'd like to talk to you."

When Austin saw McKinnon, her body felt electrified. She swore her freshly brushed hair began tingling at its roots. In truth, she now felt more upset than when she'd stumbled onto Reg's corpse. The dead man could no longer threaten or hurt her, but this one could rain all kinds of havoc down upon her head, torturing her with constant demands to repeat her experiences in that blasted church kitchen. Why was she so nervous? She could kick herself for feeling so insecure in Canada. She'd never react this way back home in Texas.

"I can spare ten minutes," she said through clenched teeth.

"That's fine. Let's talk over there." He motioned to a bench beside a tree.

Austin sat as far from McKinnon as possible. She placed her purse and books on the ground between them, imagining they formed a Maginot Line that would protect her. Yet she feared her defenses were just as weak as that famed system.

A sense of doom nibbled at her nerves.

DS McKinnon carried a large leather notebook. He placed it

on his knees and calmly removed a pair of glasses from the pocket of his Harris Tweed jacket. The jacket made Austin yearn for home—her father had one too. Incongruous in steamy Texas, heavy wool suited nippy Ontario.

He riffled through his notebook, withdrew one sheet of paper, and began reading from it. " 'Get two hundred dollars for DS. Meet at church, eight thirty tonight.' " He held out the paper, a stern expression on his face.

Austin looked at the words. *DS? Her David?* She pursed her lips in disgust. "Why show me this?"

"I copied these words from a scrap of paper found in the pocket of Reg Simpson's jacket, the one he was wearing when he was murdered. They mean anything to you?" His glasses slid down his nose, and he pushed them back up.

"I've no idea. I told you, I didn't really know Reg."

The policeman looked steadily at Austin, searching her face— for a clue, perhaps—before he spoke again. "Also in his pocket we found a chunk of hashish wrapped in tinfoil, a pipe, and a switchblade."

"Don't know anything about those either." Austin started to comment on what the items suggested about Reg's character, but stopped when she remembered Dr. Klimenko's warning. She'd better keep her mouth shut. Extra words could hurt her. And she certainly wasn't going to comment on the oddity of her husband's initials appearing in the dead man's note. Initials meant nothing.

"Are you sure you know nothing about all this?" he asked again.

"All news to me."

"All right then, here's my theory. *DS* stands for David Starr, and Reginald Simpson planned to see him last night after the meeting. Reg planned to take two hundred dollars with him to the church, but the money disappeared by the time we got to the scene."

He cocked his head. "Any idea where the money went?"

"No." Austin's shoulders tensed, crept up to her ears.

"Any idea if Reg usually carried a switchblade?"

"No. No. This is all preposterous."

Austin felt she was losing her cool. She couldn't feign nonchalance anymore. "What on earth do you expect me to say? Naturally I don't agree with your so-called theory." She took a deep breath and tried to regain her composure. "My husband's the most balanced, cautious, thoughtful person you'll ever meet."

"I look forward to judging that for myself, but your husband seems to have disappeared."

"That's ridiculous. Three hours ago he was in our apartment, and now he'll be here on campus somewhere."

"I don't share your confidence, Mrs. Starr. Still, if you run across him, please tell your husband that I'll be at your apartment this evening. Shall we say around seven o'clock?" The wayward glasses had slipped down McKinnon's nose again, and again he adjusted them.

"David always comes home for supper before he goes back to campus in the evenings. I'm sure tonight will be no exception," Austin said. "I'll give him your message. I gave you the address last night, right?"

"You did. Now before I leave, have you anything to add? Anything at all?"

"Not really, although I have a question." She glanced down at her lap, then up to meet his eyes. "You don't really suspect my husband of the murder, based on the spurious connection of his initials on that note?"

Unexpectedly, McKinnon broke into a grin. Austin sensed he was struggling not to laugh.

"Oh, you graduate students. You do fling around uncommon words, don't you?" he said. "I used to do that too, back in my day. You might have used the word *specious*, don't you think? That synonym would've had the same effect."

McKinnon's sense of humor pleased Austin. He appeared to

be—dare she think it?—almost human. She said, "I know the meaning of *spurious*, but wasn't too sure about *specious*."

"They're both excellent words, particularly given all the lies I hear, but I don't usually have an opportunity to bandy them about." Again McKinnon grinned at her. "I hope you find your husband and that we have a satisfactory conversation this evening. Unless you've given me a spurious address." McKinnon winked and bobbed his head. "Until then, adieu."

Disarmed by his humor, Austin visualized her imaginary Maginot Line crumbling.

So, if he were really a good guy, then DS McKinnon should wear the red coat of the Mounties, like TV's Sergeant Preston of the Yukon. Then she imagined McKinnon yelling to his sled dogs, "On, King. Mush, you huskies." Among Austin's heroes, Sergeant Preston ranked alongside the Lone Ranger as a man who courageously fought villains and won.

She smiled, and her heart grew lighter. It was only as he strolled along the sidewalk, whistling, that she realized McKinnon had dodged her question.

How could he possibly think her David was one of the bad guys?

CHAPTER SIX

Austin chewed on a ragged cuticle as she watched McKinnon walk away. His sport coat hung on his lanky frame, and his long steps made short work of getting to Willcocks Street. When he turned a corner and disappeared, her heart grew heavy again.

Homesickness for her father flooded her. She knew it was simply the familiarity of the tweed coat stirring up thoughts of home, but she felt the tug strongly. Daddy and McKinnon were about the same age, and they bantered in similar ways. How she missed that kind of talk. Mother monopolized their phone calls, and the words from Daddy were few.

She didn't know what to make of McKinnon. He was so friendly at the end of their talk that she almost expected him to stop and wave before he crossed the street. On the other hand, he appeared to believe her husband was guilty of Reg's murder.

Left alone on the bench, Austin sank into a funk, mindlessly watching students bustle past in the brisk autumn air. She envied them, betting none were caught up in a murder inquiry. She kicked the bench and cursed her luck.

Ever since she'd found the body and reported it, Austin had expected to be pulled into the investigation. But David? What an astounding development. The homicide detective called it a theory that Reg planned to meet David last night—he never said he was wedded to the idea. Plus, theory or not, that didn't mean David knew about Reg's plans. Still, she had an uneasy feeling.

Austin glanced down to see fluff from her sweater mounded

on her lap. She'd been plucking at the soft mohair. An ancient memory surfaced—Mother's promise to buy a new blanket if she quit picking at her old one. Every morning when Mother woke her for kindergarten, piles of blanket fuzz surrounded Austin's bed. Austin had longed for a sibling to share her mother's perfectionism, but her older sister had died at age four.

This was old ground for Austin, and going over it yet again did no good. She needed to do something useful, dissipate the nervous energy building inside her.

What if she did some digging on her own into Reg's death? She'd get closer to Reg's friends than the police ever could. Maybe she'd find evidence or a witness to prove David was not the murderer. She could even track down the real killer! Her pulse quickened, and adrenalin brought a lust for the hunt. Where should she begin?

She knew she could do it. When she'd dallied last year with joining the CIA, she'd picked up enough knowledge to discover how much she liked sleuthing. Her grad school career had precluded any further evaluations on the CIA's side and had necessarily squelched further inquiry into the agency from her side, but she'd had a blast with the scenarios and testing situations.

Her CIA test scores had been stellar. Her contact, the enigmatic Mr. Jones, advised that a job offer was forthcoming. Despite his deadpan demeanor, he couldn't hide his disappointment when Austin chose school over the Central Intelligence Agency.

"If graduate research ends up boring you, and I expect it will," he'd said, "then call me. We'll always need bright young people like you, especially ones who speak Russian. You'd better hang on to my card."

She'd been a Nancy Drew has-been before she'd ever gotten a chance at being a real Nancy Drew. Now Reg's murder offered her a second chance.

Austin had kept "Mr. Jones's" business card. Although she often pulled it out, she never called. Not given her current situation in Canada. But now she mused about asking him for advice.

She could just imagine that phone call.

With eyes shut tight, she put herself in a mindset labeled "Jones" and advised herself to search out the people who knew Reg Simpson best and question them. She hadn't enough data to work with yet, and oh how she loved data. Looking at patterns that revealed a deeper truth made her brain sing. On a good day, her history studies were like that too.

Her head fell to her chest, and she opened her eyes. While she let her mind relax, she focused on the paving stones surrounding the bench she sat on. She began counting them.

When the count reached two hundred, she sat up straighter, and her thoughts sharpened. Two names burst into her head. A draft resister named Pete had been Reg's chief acolyte. However, he wasn't a student at the University of Toronto, and she didn't know where to find him—Toronto was a huge city. But Dulcie, Reg's girlfriend of record, was a U of T student. She gave Austin a place to start.

Her books and purse lay on the ground, scattered underneath the bench where DS McKinnon accidentally kicked them as he walked away. She smiled when she realized she was using the shorthand from British mysteries, thinking of McKinnon as DS. She understood the usage now—thinking and saying *detective sergeant* all the time was a pain.

She collected her belongings and brushed off the mohair that still clung to her macramé purse. Then she headed toward University College where Reg's girlfriend sometimes hung out at the Junior Common Room. Austin had seen Dulcie there often but assumed she'd be holed up somewhere else now, in mourning. But maybe her friends could advise Austin how to find her.

Austin sought excuses to visit the Junior Common Room. It boasted ornate wood paneling and plaques listing members of the Literary and Athletic Society back more than a century. Reminders of antiquity always soothed her soul, and the Romanesque revival architecture of University College let her pretend she was in medieval Europe.

She took the long way through the inner courtyard to the JCR and daydreamed of wandering through a cloister in twelfth-century France, surely a safe haven.

Ultimately this choice of route was inspired, leading her straight to Dulcie. Austin rounded a corner and spied the short, curvy girl lounging against a courtyard column and smoking.

Austin's approach startled Dulcie, who hastily stubbed out her cigarette and ran up to Austin.

"Isn't it awful about poor Reggie?" Dulcie wailed in greeting, and then her eyes filled with tears. "I saw him hours before he was murdered. How can he be gone, snap, just like that?" She sniffled. "Killed in a church too. What a bummer. Everyone's talking about it."

"What're they saying? I slept in, barely got to class on time, and haven't talked to anybody yet." Austin knew she had to seize the initiative if she was going to learn anything new.

"For one thing"—Dulcie adjusted her tie-dye blouse that showed more of her ample cleavage than was decent—"I hear you found him. If that's true, then you must know more than I do."

"I found the bo—that is, I found Reg, but I don't know much."

"How was he killed?" Dulcie asked, still fiddling with her top. Even her outer jacket didn't cover her chest.

Austin glanced down at her shoes and shuffled her feet. She looked back up at Dulcie. "A really hard whack to the head, I guess. Blood was everywhere. I never knew a head wound could bleed so much."

Dulcie made a face. "Yuck. Poor, poor Reg. You must've been so upset."

Yuck? This girl was all heart. Austin said, "Upset? Obviously I was upset. I'd never seen a dead body before, except at a funeral."

"And that's not the same thing at all, you poor thing." Dulcie leaned against Austin, and her bosom pushed into Austin's arm.

Being so close, Austin was able to smell the marijuana mingling with the cigarette smoke on Dulcie's clothes. No wonder she was so mellow. "Any idea why someone would want to kill Reg?"

Asking the question, she felt like a real detective.

Dulcie shook her head. "Nope, nada, zilch. Hey, but wait just a sec. I do know he was bummed about something the last time we were together. But even though he was angry, the sex was good."

Dulcie's smirk made Austin blush.

"When was that?"

"Let's see…must've been Tuesday night because he stood me up on Wednesday, and Thursday night he was killed." Dulcie ticked the days off on her fingers. She seemed spacey. "I walked by his house late yesterday afternoon, and that's when I saw him and Pete going off to their meeting. Reg called out to me, said he'd see me later at Grad's. But I went there and waited and waited, and he never showed. Then I learned why."

"What upset him on Tuesday?" Austin fought to keep impatience from creeping into her voice. She had to keep in mind this girl had suffered a blow, even if she didn't act as if she had.

Dulcie pulled her jacket up around her neck and shivered. "Look, if we're going to talk, let's go to the JCR. I'm headed there for lunch anyway. I had to split, had to leave my pad and get out among people. I was going batty all alone, remembering all the good times Reggie and I had." She leaned in close to Austin again. "I consulted the *I Ching* first, to make sure it was all right for me to go out."

"Sure, lunch, if you want. I skipped breakfast." Austin also skipped her normal blistering comments about the *I Ching* and tried for a casual tone. Her encounter with Dulcie, the not-so-grieving girlfriend, might bear fruit after all. If Reg had played around on her, she could even turn out to be a suspect.

* * *

In the Junior Common Room, Donovan was performing, courtesy of piped-in U of T radio. While he sang about being mellow yellow, an amateur tried to play a Bach fugue on the corner piano. The din made Austin's head spin.

Dulcie and Austin settled as far from Bach as possible, in chairs beneath the plaques engraved with the names of students from the past. While Austin ate yogurt and a doughnut, Dulcie munched a roast beef sandwich.

"I'm trying to go macrobiotic, but it's not working. I can't give up beef, but Reggie says it doesn't matter." Dulcie looked contrite. "Shit, I keep forgetting he's gone. I know he made some people crazy, but not enough to kill him. It doesn't make sense."

"You were going to tell me why he was upset on Tuesday."

"Yeah, I know, but you don't want to hear it."

"Why?"

"Because it's about your husband, that's why. Reggie told me that David was trying to oust him from the group. He wouldn't talk details, though. He only said David's a creep and jealous of him. Reggie said he'd never done anything to David, so he couldn't figure out why he was so hostile. But once people crossed Reggie, it was game over. Reggie hated them forever."

"I know David didn't like Reg," Austin said, "and I figured the feeling was mutual. However, I never heard my husband say anything about wanting to drive him out of the group. Are you sure you don't know what that was all about?"

"I told you everything Reggie told me," Dulcie said, "but it's his anger that sticks in my mind. He banged things around and swore, acting like a real shithead. I'd never seen him so mad."

"Had he bad-mouthed David before?"

"Sure, in an offhand way, like calling him a know-it-all and a fool, stuff like that. Nothing major."

"Who else did Reg dislike in the group?" Austin hoped she

50

didn't sound as desperate as she felt.

"He only singled out your husband. But listen here; I know what you should do. You should talk to Pete. He knew Reg best." Dulcie wrinkled her nose. "It's kinda mean to say, but Reg always made fun of Pete. Said he wasn't too bright. Pete sure was devoted to Reggie, though."

"How long were they friends? I don't know when either one came to Canada, do you?"

"They both hit town last winter, more or less at the same time, and they landed in the same boarding house. Must've been early February. I remember Reggie gave me candy for Valentine's Day, and I thought, wow, outta sight. We've been together ever since." Dulcie slapped the table. "Oh shit, there I go again. I keep forgetting he's gone." She pushed her sandwich away, took a cigarette out of her purse, and lit it. Blowing smoke rings seemed to relax her.

Austin watched. Was this a performance or a display of real emotion? If it was real, it was a pretty pathetic display. But people grieved in different ways, and she had no experience with watching reactions to murder.

While Dulcie continued to smoke and Austin reflected, the music changed. Gordon Lightfoot began singing, warning his lover she would lose everything because of him. When he hit the chorus, Dulcie began to cry.

Austin leaned down and pretended to search for something in her purse. She rummaged diligently for several minutes and waited for Dulcie's tears to stop. Austin had witnessed close girlfriends cry, but never a mere acquaintance. It wasn't hip to let someone see your tears.

Dulcie wasn't embarrassed, however, and she wasn't finished talking.

"You know, Reggie could be nice sometimes, when he wanted to. I know he hit on other girls, but he always came back to me. He said I understood him. And I did. He had lots of sadness in him, you know. When he was stoned, he'd say his folks didn't love him."

Dulcie stubbed out her cigarette and lit another before she continued.

"We were in here one day eating lunch when U of T Radio played an old Al Jolson song. It depressed Reggie. He said his dad loved Jolson and so he tried to like him too, to create a bond. But his dad laughed at him, said he was too young to understand how important Jolson was to the 'great American songbook.' After Reggie told me this, he cried. He actually cried. So you see what I mean? That wasn't the picture the rest of you guys had, now was it?"

Dulcie held her cigarette in front of her face and studied it. "Reggie said his dad was always too busy for him."

"What about his mother? Did he mention her?" Austin wanted every detail.

"He said she wasn't any better. His mother was always going off to Europe to buy art."

"Good grief, they were that rich?"

"As rich as God. That's why it's so weird, Reggie staying in that old boarding house."

Austin swiftly filed this fact away in a new mental folder she'd just opened and marked *anomalies*. "Do you know where Reg lived in the States?"

"Somewhere in the east, around New York maybe. Sorry, I'm hopeless at geography. You should talk to Pete. He'll be able to tell you more than I can."

Austin felt a quick pang of remorse. "I'm sorry if talking about Reg made you feel bad. This whole thing has me on edge too. And I have a feeling the police could get really tough on, well, on all of us who knew Reg."

Dulcie patted Austin's hand. "Listen, I'm glad we had this chance to rap. And things'll be okay pretty soon, you'll see. Darkness before the dawn, and all that crap. Don't people always say that?"

"I guess so. Where I'm from, though, people always say that God doesn't shut a door without opening a window, but that never made me feel any better. Who wants to climb out a window?"

Dulcie burst out laughing and patted Austin's hand again. "Hey, cheer up. Things could always be worse." Her expression brightened. "Look, it's real groovy here in the so-called banana belt of Ontario. I grew up in Saskatchewan, where it gets super cold, so when pals gripe about Toronto winters, I thank my lucky stars I'm here, not somewhere worse. You should try it. Works wonders for your mood."

Austin hesitated. *Banana belt? Yikes.* "Well, if you say so."

Dulcie stuck her cigarettes in her purse. "Now I better get myself straight before my next class starts." Her face changed, and her expression softened, eyes alight with sympathy. "Let's stay in touch, okay?" She gave Austin a parting hug and sashayed out of the room, waving at friends as she passed.

Austin wondered what to make of the girl from Saskatchewan, a place that sounded like the back of beyond, which, if it were truly colder than Toronto, she never wanted to visit. Austin had warmed to Dulcie, despite her initial reactions. Sure, Dulcie was kind of ditzy, but she conveyed real understanding of her murdered boyfriend's tortured psyche. Her advice to interview Reg's only other friend was helpful too.

If only Austin hadn't forgotten to ask where to find Pete.

CHAPTER SEVEN

Austin left the JCR propelled by a fit of nerves, flew down the short flight of stairs to the ground level, and exploded outside. When she backtracked through the courtyard of University College, this time the pseudo-medieval atmosphere held no magic.

Questions about Reg's past buzzed in her head, and she slowed down, moving as if in a trance. Finding herself in front of the main library, she couldn't remember walking there. The stacks beckoned her, whispering about research she needed to finish for her paper on Lenin, yet she sensed that trying to study would be hopeless. The only thing now worth her time was discovering Reg's killer.

Austin changed course and headed for her apartment.

The minute she opened the door, she knew David was inside. Her nose sniffed the evidence—the aroma of the endless pot of coffee he kept brewing. "Yoo-hoo," she called. "Honey, I'm home."

David sat in his favorite chair, smoking his favorite meerschaum pipe and pouring over his favorite journal, *Annals of Mathematics*. He was in his element, and the sight should've pleased Austin. However, seeing the Princeton University journal made her fume. When Princeton's math department had offered David a full graduate fellowship, his life's dream was close to being fulfilled. He'd always yearned to study where Einstein had worked. Yet once the evils of the Vietnam War obsessed David, he gave up his dream of following in the great physicist's footsteps and headed north to Canada.

David glanced up at Austin. "You're home early." He carefully placed a bookmark between pages in the journal.

She flounced over to him, knocked the journal out of his hands, and planted a big smooch on his lips. "Thanks for making sure I got up on time."

"Hey, I was reading that. You lost my place." He began tickling her in the ribs.

"Stop. Stop. I can't breathe," Austin said, pushing against his hands.

"Listen, babe, you had a tough time last night." He picked up a newspaper that lay on the floor, turned to the movie section. "The Varsity's still showing *Rosemary's Baby,* so why don't we go tonight? Since it's Friday, we don't need to rush off to class tomorrow, and we could do with some fun. We've been under lots of stress lately, even before the murder."

She sat at his feet and leaned her chin on his knees, wondering if she would classify *Rosemary's Baby* as fun. She took a big breath. "That's sweet of you, but something's come up. Detective Sergeant McKinnon is coming over tonight after supper."

"Here? Tonight?" David laid down the paper and focused on Austin.

"McKinnon ran me down on campus, but all he wanted to talk about was you. He believes you and Reg planned to get together after last night's meeting."

David inhaled sharply. "That's preposterous."

"I know, honey, I know. That was the very word I used to McKinnon, but it seems the police found a note in Reg's pocket that had your initials on it. They decided that *DS* stood for your name."

"But that could've meant all sorts of things. Maybe he was going to see, umm, a detective sergeant. And that possibility just came off the top of my head. There are endless others."

Austin swallowed a chuckle, thinking it unseemly at such a serious time. "Maybe so, and the detective knows that too. McKinnon said it was only a theory, and by the end of our talk he loosened up a lot. Maybe he's just coming over to check you off his list." Austin rubbed her hand along David's leg. "If only someone had seen you on campus last night, you'd be set."

"Told you before." David slid her hand aside and stood. "No one else was around." He began to pace. "This doesn't sound good, not good at all."

"True, but it's way too early to assume the worst." Austin hesitated and considered how to phrase her idea so he wouldn't object. "David, I've been thinking. Why don't I go around and talk to other people who knew Reg and see what I can find out? I already saw one of his girlfriends, Dulcie. I'm betting I can uncover some clue that will point to the killer."

He stopped pacing. "That's a lousy idea. Don't do that."

"But I'll get more information out of his friends than the police can and—"

"Promise you won't do that." The words flew from his mouth, and Austin flinched. "You could get us in more trouble than we're already in." David's lips formed a grim line across his tight jaw.

"Okay, I won't do anything." Austin only complied because he was adamant—and then she wondered why he was. When her nerves subsided a little, however, she reconsidered her answer. David hadn't convinced her to change her mind about sleuthing. And what he didn't know wouldn't hurt him.

The living room in their apartment had limited seating. When Detective Sergeant McKinnon arrived, he sat on their dilapidated couch and David took the armchair. Not wanting to sit next to the policeman again, Austin plunked down on a large cushion on the floor. She was sorry to see David already twisting his hair, while she was so nervous she was chewing on her cuticles.

McKinnon was calm, almost stoic. He had experience and authority on his side and was probably a veteran of World War II; he seemed the right age. One way or the other, to him carnage and mayhem would be nothing new. Without preliminaries, he jumped into the subject of death.

"My team investigates ten to twelve murders each year and even though we don't have as many murders as an American city of similar size, nevertheless we are the elite homicide squad in Canada."

He stopped, looked at Austin, and cocked his head. "You all right there on the floor? You look uncomfortable. Why don't you sit up here on the chesterfield? I promise not to bite."

Austin couldn't help herself. She blushed.

McKinnon blinked, appeared to realize he'd made an error, and quickly resumed his discussion of murder investigations. "When we handle a homicide, we look for one of three primary motives. Revenge. Greed. Lust. And sometimes there are other motivators, like politics. In the case of Reginald Simpson's death, we assume that politics may have played a part."

David's face brightened. "I had none of those motives to kill Reg, or to kill anyone, for that matter."

Too late, Austin realized that she had failed to pass on Dr. Klimenko's warning to David. He was already volunteering too much information.

"I disagree with you, David," said McKinnon. "You have two—perhaps three—of the motives that I listed. The political angle, certainly. Revenge figures in too. And perhaps greed."

"But with respect, sir, I can't agree. Reg and I held similar political views," David said.

"All right, you and Reg were on the same left end of the political spectrum," McKinnon said, "but that's not to say that you agreed on everything. I have information, in fact, that you differed on quite a few topics. People say your fights during anti-war meetings were vicious."

David had paled. He sat frozen, his hands pressed between his knees. At least he'd quit fidgeting.

After a few moments he responded, drawing his words out with care. "It's true that I disliked Reg and we argued a lot. That does not mean, however, that I wanted him dead."

The policeman held up two fingers, indicating the second possible motive. "Then there is revenge."

"That's absurd," David said. "Why would I want revenge on Reg?"

"Because he tried to seduce your wife."

McKinnon studied David. David stared at Austin. Austin dropped her eyes.

No one spoke for a long time.

McKinnon cleared his throat. "Am I correct to assume then, David, that you knew nothing about this?"

"Nothing, nothing." David's face had gone from pale to scarlet. He turned to Austin. "Why didn't you tell me?"

Before she could respond, the detective spoke again.

"Several people witnessed an incident between Reg and your wife at a party and told us about it. You young people would say that he was hitting on her. Is that right? Did I use the term correctly?" McKinnon swung toward Austin, then back to David. When neither spoke, he continued.

"We have it on fairly reliable authority, however, that Reg did not succeed. Austin didn't respond to his amorous intentions. Nevertheless, David, since you were at the same party and standing nearby, it's possible you saw his attempt at seduction and were angered by it. Perhaps this caused you to seek revenge against Reg."

David stood, walked unsteadily over to a bookshelf, and began adjusting a pile of journals that were tilting slightly. He kept his back to them and spoke straight ahead. "Since I didn't know about any of this, I think I can be excused of that motive entirely, don't you?"

McKinnon said, "Perhaps you weren't fueled by revenge after all, but we shall see."

David whirled around and chopped the air with a math journal. "Just because someone comes on to my wife at a damned party doesn't mean I'll try to kill him. I'm not that kind of person.

I've never initiated a fight in my life."

"Frankly, I don't think you're the combative type either—at least not physically combative." McKinnon began to smile, evidently thought better of it, covered his mouth with his hand, and coughed. "But let me finish my list before I give my opinion.

"Your third motive could be greed. You and your wife apparently have little money while Reg had a lot. The note found on his body could mean that he was bringing two hundred dollars to give you at the appointed time, eight thirty last night, after your earlier meeting concluded."

David shook his head. "I didn't have an appointment, and I don't have extra money now. You can search me and this whole fu—this whole frigging place." His arms spread to indicate the minuscule apartment.

"Thank you, but that won't be necessary," McKinnon said. "I came here tonight because I needed to talk to you myself. Despite the suppositions I've just detailed, I don't believe you're a killer and are what you seem—earnest and smart, but also naïve and misguided. At the present time you are not a suspect in the death of Reginald Simpson."

Brimming over with relief and joy, Austin pushed up from the floor and hurried to David. She hugged him, but he stayed rigid.

The telephone rang. Austin moved to answer it.

"Just let it go," David said. "We don't need any interruptions."

"No, please answer," McKinnon said. "I gave your phone number to my colleagues and told them to call here if anything urgent came up."

David left the room only to come back a moment later with the receiver stretching a long cord. "The call's for you, sir."

"Thanks. This shouldn't take long." McKinnon grasped the receiver and strode out of the room.

Austin hurled herself into David's arms, and they huddled together. He started to speak, but she shushed him. "Let's try to eavesdrop," she whispered. Try as she might, however, all she could hear from the kitchen was an occasional murmur.

She shouldn't count her chickens before they hatched, as her grandmother always cautioned, but she couldn't help herself. On the strength of DS McKinnon's promise that David wasn't a suspect, her hopes rose. Maybe she wouldn't need to dig up clues or disobey her husband. They'd go out to the movies after all. It would be a celebration.

McKinnon returned.

He appeared to have aged in his brief absence, dragging himself to the couch and dropping down with a soft groan. He closed his eyes and rubbed his temples before he spoke in a tone replete with exhaustion. "You need to sit down. The case has new developments."

David and Austin obeyed. Austin's heart was pounding, and her arms felt so wired that she expected them to rise above her head of their own accord.

"I was not aware of this," McKinnon began, "but it turns out that Reginald Simpson's father is a United States senator, one unfortunately not shy about throwing his weight around. He went straight to the top, calling the prime minister's office. Mr. Trudeau has assured Senator Simpson that we will find his son's killer and that it will be done quickly."

Austin swiveled toward David, but he ignored her, tipping his head down and staring at his feet. She looked to McKinnon, whose expression did not bode well. Their fates seemed to hinge on his next words.

"And there is more bad news," he said, not meeting Austin's eyes. "I've just spoken with the police commissioner. David, a witness has come forward who places you leaving the church around seven—"

"No way," David shouted. "At seven I was at the demonstration."

McKinnon pressed his lips together and stared at David for a moment before continuing. "Nevertheless, the decision has been made to arrest you, on reasonable and probable grounds for the murder of Reg Simpson." He paused to rub his temples again. "I'm sorry. There's nothing I can do."

Austin's brave new world, only just beginning to take shape, shattered.

CHAPTER EIGHT

Austin lay curled up on the living room couch. On her second night without David, she still avoided the bedroom and couldn't sleep alone on the futon. Every creak of the old building unnerved her. Every shadow that flickered across the wall made her fear an intruder, when it was only trees swaying in the wind outside her window. Worn out from dealing with the legalities of David's arrest, Austin only wanted to sleep. But sleep wouldn't come.

Scenes from the catastrophe kept spooling through her mind.

She had followed in David's wake—to a small jail on Claremont, from there to 22 Court, then to the Old City Hall, and finally to the notorious Don Jail off Gerrard. Told she couldn't visit him for several days, she'd broken down and cried. McKinnon lent her his handkerchief.

David had been led away in handcuffs, not even allowed to kiss her goodbye.

She'd grabbed a passing jail attendant. "Where's he going?"

The man cackled. "To a famous place—the cell next to the gallows. I was here when the last prisoners were hanged, just three years back, eh. I got so many stories of this old place, older than Canada it is, one hundred years and a bit. Want to hear 'em?"

Austin turned and fled toward the exit. She guessed the Dickensian place would play a starring role in her nightmares.

Most of the authorities who processed David through the system had been straightforward and civil. A lawyer from Legal Aid took David's case. If he were arraigned, however, she'd been advised to hire a private lawyer. David and Austin hoped that wouldn't happen, but nevertheless they couldn't help fearing the worst.

Sometime during the fraught weekend, Austin had called the Starrs, collect, at their home in Dallas. The dire turn of events had them ranting against the Canadian authorities. Obviously their son had been targeted because of his anti-war stance.

When David's parents offered to fly up, she minimized David's predicament. "I'm sure he'll be released soon," she'd lied. Tending to them was more than she could handle, even under normal circumstances.

Lying on the couch now, Austin felt waves of woe lapping at her legs and worried about going to sleep, afraid that by morning those waves would cover her nose and smother her. Before the murder she'd been drenched in homesickness, but now she was drowning in gloom. Her distress had never before reached these depths. In Texas, whenever she got down, she'd used her friends to help siphon off the heavy waters. But that was long ago, in the now-hallowed time *Before Canada*.

Austin stared at the wallpaper above the couch. Its floral design appeared to predate her birth. Never a fan of flowery patterns, she recalled the last words of Oscar Wilde as he lay on his deathbed in a ratty hotel in Paris: "Either that wallpaper has to go or I do."

But *she* wasn't going anywhere. She would help David fight to clear his name, and they would succeed. She just needed someone to talk to.

In Toronto there was no one. And Austin never phoned friends in Texas since long distance rates were exorbitant. David had warned their budget wouldn't allow those calls, but now that their circumstances were calamitous, she was sure he'd want her to talk to someone. Isolated and alone, she considered reaching out to friends thousands of miles away.

She yearned to talk to Earleen, but *her* new husband was

serving in Vietnam, doing what he saw as his duty. So how could Austin intrude when she was so certain their problems came from David protesting that same war? David was a ready-made target.

Although their friendship dated from first grade, she assumed that Earleen wouldn't want to hear from her. Not for this reason.

Pushing her worries aside, Austin marshaled enough energy to get off the couch. Her footsteps echoed as she circled the lonely living room looking for her Russian history textbook. The paper on Lenin was due the following week.

She plopped onto the floor and rummaged through the low-lying bookshelves. Her dog-eared copy of Lenin's famous *Chto Delyat?* fell off a shelf and into her lap.

Hmm, good question, she mused. *Chto delyat;* what's to be done? Russian revolutionaries had argued for decades what should be done to pull Russia out of its backwardness and improve conditions for the Russian people. That question had consumed them. And here she was, puzzling over what was to be done about her own problems. They loomed as large to her as had Lenin's question for him and his radical colleagues. What needed to be done to find Reg Simpson's killer and free David?

She didn't have decades to find the answer.

What would Lenin say? She giggled at the absurd question. If her studies taught her one thing, it was this: Lenin had not been afraid of action. She should be decisive too—do *something*. Almost anything. She jumped up from the floor and ran into the kitchen, snatched up the phone, and dialed Earleen's number in Texas.

"Hi, it's me," she squealed when Earleen answered.

Austin and Earleen played catch-up at first. They took turns ranting and raving about their lives.

Austin said, "Can you believe what's happened to David?"

"What'd you expect when you left your home and country?" Earleen shot back.

"Not this. Who could guess David would be jailed for murder?" Austin was carefully tiptoeing around the subject of the war.

"True enough, but now your job is to pull up your spirits and take care of yourself," Earleen said. "You think the police will keep looking for other suspects or..."

"They think David's their man, and I've got to prove they're wrong. No one else will try from the looks of things."

"Good for you. I can just see you now, bustling around Toronto asking people tons of questions. You're the most curious person I know." Earleen paused and took a depth breath. "And remember what your mother says about you."

Austin could only groan.

"She's right. You're exactly like a dog with a bone."

"Go right ahead and call me Lassie."

Earleen barked and then laughed. "Gosh, it's great to talk again. Been way too long since we had one of our heart-to-hearts. So what're you going to do next?"

"*Chto delyat?*" Austin said.

"What?"

"Just a Russian saying. I won't get into it now since this call's getting costly."

"It ain't cheap, but it's certainly worth it. But before you hang up, tell me your next step." Earleen's voice was strict. "I'm afraid if you don't have a plan, your world will shrink to the size of the sofa you're sleeping on."

It was Austin's turn to laugh. "Reg's girlfriend said I should talk to someone named Pete. Pete was the last person to talk to Reg before he died."

"As good a place to begin as any," Earleen said.

"Maybe Pete can tell me what Reg had on his mind before he was killed."

"You're thinking Reg's state of mind will hint at a reason for his murder?"

"Something like that. I've got to start somewhere." She checked the clock. "It's only eight thirty here, so if I hurry, I can get

65

to Grad's before it closes. Lots of the draft resisters hang out there, and maybe someone can tell me how to find Pete. Better to meet him in a public place, not his rented room."

"You be careful, Austin. Don't get into trouble yourself. One person in jail's more than enough for one family."

"I promise to be careful," Austin said. "Thanks for your help."

"Holding you to that. Adios, *kemosabe*."

When Austin heard her old friend's familiar sign-off, she no longer felt so alone.

Austin needed a jacket for her walk to Grad's, but that meant going into the bedroom, a danger to a psyche bruised by David's absence. She pushed aside thoughts of him and entered what should have been their refuge. The bedroom was a mess, with clothes spilling out of open drawers and scattered around the floor. Looking for evidence of a crime, the police had concentrated on this room and left chaos in their wake.

Austin managed to find a jacket and was reaching for a pair of shoes when a piece of paper caught her eye. It lay in a jumble in the bottom of the closet, and she recognized her husband's back-slanted handwriting. She picked up the scrap.

She read, "TD Bk, Cdn T, LCBO, and Tl 2 RS."

She recognized immediately what it was. David made to-do lists and shared them with Austin to help organize their time. She'd learned to decipher his homegrown shorthand and knew that once he did everything on a list, he ripped it up and threw it away; therefore this list was recent and indicated tasks he'd intended to do before his arrest.

Decoding the first two items was easy—Toronto Dominion Bank and Canadian Tire. They banked at the first, and David loved shopping at the second, although wandering through aisles of hardware and auto products bored Austin to tears. Everyone in Ontario knew the third item, Liquor Control Board of Ontario, the only place to buy alcohol in the province. And Tl 2 RS might mean that he needed to talk to RS.

But how could this be? David shunned Reg Simpson and only spoke to him when he couldn't avoid it.

What caused him to break his pattern? Fear quivered through Austin, and her arms felt tight again. What would she do if she uncovered something that implicated David? She'd been so certain that David and Reg weren't planning to meet the night of the murder.

Standing with her back to the closet, Austin eyed the clothes and other personal items unearthed and strewn around by the police. The list probably fell out of David's pocket, small enough to escape prying eyes.

The voice of Austin's mother—permanently lodged in a corner of her mind—was in full cry, like a pack of hounds following a terrorized deer, barking that sloppy housekeeping had allowed the paper to fall behind a warren of dust bunnies. Brushing aside her mother's voice, Austin stuffed the paper—along with her curiosity about whether David had planned to meet with Reg—into the pocket of her skirt, threw on the jacket, and headed out of the apartment.

She would find Pete. She needed to do something and wanted to decide for herself *chto delyat*—what was to be done. Studying how Lenin's choices fouled up Russia might earn her good grades but wouldn't help her present situation. She would try to avoid making bad choices while investigating the murder. At least she'd be doing something.

Movement was good. Paralysis was bad.

Austin dashed over to Grad's on College Street and arrived half an hour before closing. Smoke stung her lungs. Many customers puffed on cigarettes, and the smell of marijuana hid out in corners. People plowed through mounds of French fries—too many attacks of the munchies to count. Pete and three other draft resisters chatted in a booth along the back wall.

A giant display rack of pies stood on the counter, and she chose a stool that let her cower in its shadow. Sneaking a peek through the racks, she assessed Pete and his motley group. Anyone from her father's generation would take one look and declare, "Filthy hippies."

Pete was smaller than the others. His skin was pitted, his facial features slightly irregular—a little off kilter. His teeth were so crooked and dark, Austin concluded he'd never sat in a dentist's chair. A leather headband encircled his oily hair, and his beard was matted. What a charmer.

Who knew how they'd greet her after David's arrest? If they assumed that David had killed Reg, a killer's wife might be guilty by association. Austin wished she knew more about Pete. She'd never spoken to him and regretted not getting details from Dulcie.

The group Pete sat with was too far away for her to eavesdrop on. Besides, the joint was noisy. Many of the guys were yelling from table to table, arguing about the debacle four nights earlier when the Montreal Canadiens swept the Toronto Maple Leafs.

"Zero to five. Shit, man, I coulda played goalie better myself."

"Yeah, the Leafs stunk up the Gardens. The way they played, you'd never know they took the Stanley Cup last year."

"Wish they'd dump Imlach."

"Right on. He's a crappy GM."

To become truly at home in Canada, Austin knew she had to learn all about hockey, Canada's national game—more like obsession, really—but now was not the time. Her big decision was how to approach Pete. She sat at the counter, keeping an eye on him, and mulled over whether to accost him with his friends or not.

Before she had time to decide on her tactics, however, Pete stood, threw some money on the table, and slouched toward the door. Austin waited while he stepped out onto College Street before she followed. Once outside, she tried to catch up, but he was walking too fast.

"Wait up, Pete," she called. "I need to talk to you."

He spun around and, when he recognized her, scowled. "What do you want?"

"I need to ask you about Reg."

"Shit." He spat on the sidewalk. "You've got some nerve. He was my best friend."

"Please, Pete, I know my husband is innocent. He didn't kill Reg."

"Oh yeah? That's what killers always say." Pete turned and marched away. Over his shoulder, he called, "I think the Mounties have their man."

Austin hurried after him. Cars whizzing past drowned out their voices. She shouted, "The RCMP doesn't have jurisdiction. It's the Toronto police."

He kept walking, again snarling over his shoulder, "I don't care who nailed your fucking husband, as long as they got him in jail. He can rot there for all I care."

Austin was unnerved but pressed on. "But David's innocent."

Pete stopped. "Not my problem. Let the heat figure things out."

"That's rich." Austin felt her blood pressure rise. "Guys like you aren't usually so quick to trust cops."

Pete blinked and scratched his beard. "Yeah, that's right," he mumbled.

Austin saw that she had confused him and took heart. "Cops are cops, no matter what side of the forty-ninth parallel they work on. They can make mistakes in Canada just like they do in the States."

Austin remembered what Dulcie said about Pete's brainpower—or lack thereof, according to Reg. If Pete wasn't too bright, surely she could argue him into submission. She might as well give it a shot. She pulled down the hem of her jacket, straightened its collar, and imagined Pete in the middle of her crosshairs.

She took a big gulp of air. "What if you were the one the

police falsely accused of murder? Wouldn't you want your friends to help prove your innocence?"

"Uh, guess so." Pete looked at the ground and scuffed his boot.

"So it follows that you should help me. Does my husband seem capable of killing someone? You've known him for months. What do you think?"

"Hey, I never thought of it like that." He smirked. "Your old man looks like he's never done anything in his life but read books." Pete waved a hand. "Uh, sorry. No offense."

"Nope, none taken." Austin was glad she got through to him, but she hadn't finished her argument yet. "So what would make David change so much that he'd murder someone? He came to Canada to avoid being forced to kill people in Vietnam. Why would he become a cold-blooded killer when he got here?"

"When you put it that way, guess you've got a point. Still, Reg was my friend, and it ain't right to help you, of all people."

"So you're mourning Reg, but you're letting his killer get away?"

"Not if it's David." He snickered, but when Austin glared at him, Pete added, "Nah, I was joking. You know that, don't you?"

She refused to be provoked. Wouldn't give him the satisfaction. "It won't hurt the memory of your dead pal if you talk to me and in a way, you'll honor his memory. You'll make sure the Toronto police don't make mistakes. We both know cops can get things wrong."

"All right, all right." He threw up his hands. "So what do you want to know?"

Austin managed to suppress a joyful whoop, but her excitement was short-lived. The thought of David behind bars, terrified and alone, gave her increased urgency.

"You probably don't want to be seen with me inside Grad's, so let's walk around the block while we talk."

"Right on." He stared at the passing cars. "Everybody's down about Reg's murder, and most of the guys think you're married to a killer."

"That's what I figured." Austin tried a different tack. "You know, Pete, you're very brave to talk to me." A little flattery might soften him up.

"Thanks." Pete mumbled so low that Austin could hardly hear him. "So let's walk."

They started off toward Spadina Avenue. Although Pete was a good five inches shorter than she was, Austin had to hurry to keep up with him. She gasped, "Can we slow down? I can't get my questions out when I'm rushing."

Pete snorted. "Thought you'd be some kind of superwoman, you being a smart-ass grad student and all. Guess I'll go slower since you can't keep up."

Austin stifled a sharp response. Better to hide her growing animosity in order to get on his good side, assuming he had one. "Thanks. Now, how much do you know about Reg—his background, where he came from? Did you know his dad's a U.S. senator?"

Pete whistled. "Shit, man. You mean the rumor's true? Some guy told me that today, but I didn't know if I should believe him. Damn, old Reg sure had a hotshot family. Go figure."

Pete stopped in the middle of the sidewalk and fiddled with the zipper on his jacket. Austin had the impression that he was upset but trying to hide his emotions over the death of his friend.

When he finally spoke, his voice was low and sad. "Reg never talked about his life before Toronto. I told him all about mine, but he never mentioned his. If I asked him, he'd say he wanted to move on, forget the past, become a real revolutionary—travel light, you know? After a while, I quit asking."

Pete's pain registered with Austin, and she decided to make use of it. "So Reg didn't really trust you after all, did he, if he didn't share much with you?"

"Shit, I didn't say that. Reg told me all kinds of things." Pete's voice rose. "Just not about his past. Who cares about the old days anyway?"

Bingo. Now she had him.

"You really believe he told you things no one else knew?"

Pete tilted his head, thinking about her question. "Reg was always talking about our anti-war group. He had such big plans, thought we'd influence American politics, even from way up here in Canada."

"Could any of that translate into someone wanting to kill him?"

"Sure." Pete snickered. "Reg hated your husband. He thought David's politics sucked. You of all people know how they argued. David wasn't Reg's favorite person. But that's not what you want to hear, is it?"

"I have to know everything if I'm going to dig up the truth." Austin grimaced and put her hands on her hips. "Go ahead. Tell me about their political battles. I saw heated exchanges, sure, but nothing that would turn deadly. Half the time, I tuned out. All their rhetoric was a little much for me."

"Yeah, know what you mean," Pete agreed. "Got kinda steep sometimes." He paused to scratch his beard and chew on a fingernail.

Austin fought to keep from tapping her foot. And from yelling for him to hurry.

"Reg hated the military and wanted to destroy the system that propped up American life, but your guy David only seems to care that Vietnam is the wrong war to fight. Reg said there'd *never* been a good war. He knew this cuz his dad was supposed to have done something big in World War Two. Everybody thought his dad was so great, but Reg knew he was a fraud."

Hearing his own words as a revelation, Pete perked up and laughed. "Hey, he told me about his family after all. How about that?" He puffed out his chest like a turkey before Thanksgiving.

"You know something specific about Reg's father not being a hero?" Austin asked.

Pete started to speak several times and stopped each time. He finally shook his head. "Here's all I remember. Reg's dad won a medal in one of the big battles. Don't remember, but think it was in the Pacific. Anyway, Reg said the whole thing was complete shit, and his old man was no hero. Not ever. Reg was fierce when he talked about it."

Austin thought it possible that Reg had information proving his father had never earned his medal, but couldn't figure how that would help David. "Don't you remember anything else, Pete? Think hard."

Pete jabbed a finger at Austin. "Told you everything I can remember. Now get off my ass."

Austin stumbled back, jolted by his outburst. Pete got right in her face, so close that she smelled his body odor.

"Shouldn't be talking to you anyhow," he snarled. "Now bug off and leave me alone."

Pete pivoted away from Austin and hurried down College Street, but then unexpectedly whirled around and ran back. She braced for another eruption.

In a soft voice, Pete asked, "Your old man is in jail, right?"

"You know that." A tremor ran down her spine.

"You shouldn't be alone at night around here. I can walk you home—maybe you've got more muffins, huh? They're really good." Pete inched closer to Austin.

"No thanks, I don't live far from here and—"

Pete was undeterred. "Whereabouts do you live?"

"Not far." She pulled her jacket tight around her neck and folded her arms across her chest. "Look, I'm tired and want to go to bed."

Too late, Austin sensed her mistake.

Pete smirked and winked at her. "Bed, right. I'm tired too."

He took her arm, but she jerked away. She couldn't keep up with his mood swings. Did he hate her or was he attracted to her? She couldn't tell. Maybe he was just having trouble handling his feelings about the death of his friend.

"You really piss me off," Pete said, hissing at her. "Here I was being nice. Reg always said you was an ice queen."

Austin used all her willpower to resist punching him. Sensing there was still something he wasn't telling, she reined herself in. "Come on, Pete. I need your help. Please, it's not fair that David's in jail. He didn't kill Reg!"

"Life ain't fair, bitch. You're old enough to know that by now." Pete turned around and stomped away.

CHAPTER NINE

The telephone was ringing when Austin entered the apartment. She rushed to answer, hoping for good news about David.

"Austin Amelia, it's time for you to pack up and come right home." Mother spoke without preliminaries.

Austin's teeth clenched, and her stomach tightened in knots.

Mother pressed on, not waiting for a response. "Your father and I agree that's the best thing to do. We'll wire the money for a plane ticket tomorrow. How soon can you be ready to leave?"

The moment she heard the words "Austin Amelia," Austin had prepared for the thousandth battle with Mother in their ongoing war. Her middle name irritated Austin since it was Mother's first name, making it harder for Austin to ignore her connection with the woman who'd tried to control her since time immemorial. Or at least for as long as she could remember.

How wrong Austin had been, thinking she'd won independence by marrying David. Mother merely changed the nature of the war and moved to another battle, one called "how a young matron should behave." The distance between Cuero, Texas, and Toronto, Ontario, was seventeen hundred miles, but unfortunately, the mail and the telephone could bridge that gap.

She focused on the provocations pouring from her phone.

"Your father's very concerned about this turn of events."

"Naturally Daddy's upset, and who wouldn't be? Don't you think I am?" Austin's anger was reaching gale force. "This is no picnic for me either, you know."

"My point is that you don't want to upset your father, do you?" Mother's tone was civil, but nevertheless she'd upped the stakes of the current battle by deploying her not so secret *Daddy* weapon. It was obvious to everyone—especially to her mother—that Austin adored her father, a fact that infuriated Mother. And it was always Mother—never Mama or Mommy. But Daddy got the loving endearment.

"Where's Daddy? Put him on and I'll tell him why I can't leave Toronto."

"He's not here. He's sitting on another well and won't be back for days. But I know what he'd say if he were here."

Austin's family ran an oil production company, and her father and uncle were often out in the field while new wells were drilled. How she'd envied their freedom.

"Mother, you're the one who always told me that a woman's place was beside her hus—"

"Not if he's in jail." Her mother's voice went up an octave, and the word *squawk* leapt to Austin's mind.

"All the more reason to support David," Austin said. "He's been wrongly accused."

"And what makes you so *sure*, Austin Amelia?"

"Mother!"

Austin banged down the receiver, then looked in awe at the phone. That was a first. She doubted anyone had ever hung up on Amelia Lander before. She allowed herself a smile. She was feeling better already. If only she'd remembered to ask Mother to send boxes of grits before she hung up on her.

She ran to the refrigerator and opened the freezer compartment. She unwrapped a package of brownies, used a butcher knife to separate them, and began gnawing on one. She immediately relaxed. Thank God for baked goods and chocolate.

The freezer in her parents' garage held leftovers from their daily desserts. The freezer was padlocked, ostensibly so no one could sneak into the garage and steal her mother's prized baking.

Austin knew the real reason had been to keep *her* from doing the sneaking. The goodies were meant for Daddy, who loomed large at six feet five inches, but Austin always wanted to eat as many cookies as he did.

"Little ladies do not eat like that," Mother would say, the words often intermingled with the warning, "No boy will want to marry you if you're fat."

Alone in her rental kitchen in Toronto, grinding through frozen brownies, Austin recalled hunting for the freezer key she'd known was secreted in the garage. She eventually found it but until she had, she'd obsessed over the mystery.

Right now she felt the same. Obsessive.

Someone had murdered the senator's son, and that someone wasn't David. Austin had no choice but to track down the killer. All she had to do was find the missing key.

Screech, screech. Screech, screech.

The low sound kept repeating, waking Austin. Someone was trying to be very quiet and not succeeding. Befuddled by slumber, she was slow to realize that an intruder was breaking into her apartment.

How could she protect herself? Austin sat up to look for a weapon. Nothing likely was handy. The most deadly gadgets were in the kitchen, a long way from where she was.

Then she realized her error—the noise was made by the branches of a maple tree scraping against the living room window. She'd avoided the bedroom again, still unable to use the futon she shared with David.

She flopped back, disgusted with herself, but hit her head on an armrest of the old couch. Rubbing the sore spot, she stared out the window, surveying the results of a storm that had blown in overnight. Bits of debris were plastered against the glass, illuminated by a weak sun filtering through shifting clouds. It was Monday morning, day three of David's incarceration.

It was still early. Without a husband anxious for his eggs and bacon, she could sleep for another hour. Unfortunately, her brain failed to cooperate. It snapped back to the groove it left when she'd nodded off the night before.

What if David had in fact killed Reg? Austin damned her mother for planting the pernicious idea. Yet a little voice in her head quibbled that perhaps she'd feared this all along. Mother had merely summoned the dread into the light of day.

The CIA's mordant Mr. Jones once advised her that one of the thorniest jobs in sleuthing was deciding when to follow instincts and when to guard against them. Emotions could help form useful hunches, but more often they led operatives astray. She'd never told David about her brief fling with the agency and had tried to put it out of her mind. But now with the murder…well, what she'd learned kept surfacing. David would scalp her if he ever found out about the campus representative who recruited in her Russian language class. But she'd signed papers promising to tell no one, so surely that absolved her from guilt, didn't it?

She flopped onto her side, and years of dust embedded in the upholstery assaulted her nose. She sneezed five times. *Allergic* would've been a better middle name than Amelia. With no one else around, she was tempted to wipe her nose on her nightgown but concluded that was too gross. Besides, she hadn't fallen that far yet. She found the Kleenex box under the couch, but dust bunnies attacked from there, causing another chorus of sneezes.

The wind was blowing harder outside, strong enough to rattle the windows but not hard enough to blow every what-if out of her mind. She'd go nuts if she didn't analyze, with someone other than herself, the information she'd gotten from Dulcie and Pete. Her phone conversation with Earleen was a good start, but it had whetted her appetite for more. Using friends as sounding boards helped her clarify her views. In Toronto, no one but David could provide that service, but she couldn't visit him in jail for several more days.

Over in the corner beside David's desk, his briefcase looked lonely. She lost herself in memories of David lugging it around, of him pulling out his notes and papers, absentmindedly rubbing the leather. She sat up abruptly. Its black leather jogged her memory of Dr. Klimenko and his offer to talk. *Whenever*, he'd said. What the hell; whenever was now.

He wouldn't be in his office at seven, but she'd get there at nine and hope to see him before class. A smile lit her face and courage filled her heart.

Austin began her day, convinced that help was at hand.

CHAPTER TEN

Austin dressed carefully to meet Dr. Klimenko. He'd seen her in class every week for two months, but she still wanted to walk into his office looking her best. Her mother had drummed the importance of personal appearance into her head, and she couldn't shake the lesson, just as she couldn't kiss David goodbye through an open car window because her grandmother repeatedly warned that kissing through an open window guaranteed bad luck.

After digging her favorite brown dress from the closet, she put it on and added an amber necklace bought in the Soviet Union during her summer term abroad. The Russian amber might produce such warm feelings in Klimenko's Russian soul that he'd let her talk as long as she needed. She shook her head. That was as silly as thinking bad luck could come from a kiss through an open window, but she was going to wear the necklace anyway and hope for the best.

Austin sat at her dressing table to put on her war paint, as David called it. He preferred the natural look, but she wasn't giving up make-up, even for him. Her eyes were her best feature, and she had to play them up because, as her mother often remarked, her daughter had no face without the use of cosmetics.

Austin was skilled at applying make-up, but this morning she couldn't control the mascara brush. Black went everywhere but on her lashes. After three failed attempts, Austin gave up, placed her shaky hands in her lap, and decided that mascara wasn't going to help free David anyway.

She steeled her will and set off to find Dr. Klimenko.

After the short hike to campus, Austin arrived at her professor's office at nine o'clock sharp, only to find someone else already waiting. Sitting cross-legged on the floor beside the closed door was a girl Austin's age, reading an academic journal. Austin tried to read the title upside down, but then, to her mortification, the stranger looked up and caught her.

The girl's nose was thin and straight, the kind Austin most admired and coveted. She wore her soft brown hair in a long flip and smiled at Austin with lips so perfect, she could be the identical twin of Jean Shrimpton, the only model to rival Twiggy's international fame. The stranger's beauty was so overpowering that Austin felt blood rush to her face. Blushing only made Austin more embarrassed.

"I'm...I'm so sorry. Didn't mean to be rude. I wanted to see if that's the same journal I'm using for class."

The stunner smiled again, tossed her shiny hair out of her eyes, and gestured at the floor beside her. "Why don't you sit down? Another student just went in, and it may be a while before the professor's free."

She closed the journal and showed Austin the cover. "This is the new issue of *Canadian Slavonic Papers*. Are you using it?" Before Austin could answer, the girl added, "My name is Larissa." She gave a huge smile, showing perfect teeth. "Larissa Klimenko. What's yours?"

"Then you're related to——?"

"My father." Larissa pointed her exquisite chin toward the closed door. "You're one of his students, yes?"

"Yes." Thank heaven it was an easy question since Austin's mind was otherwise engaged, working overtime to process how this gorgeous creature was related to the not-so-handsome professor. Their only similarity was dark brown eyes. Otherwise, they were beauty and the beast.

"I'm Austin Starr."

"I know who you are," Larissa said. "Your husband was arrested for murder, and my father is very worried about you."

Hearing true concern for the first time in days, Austin broke. The tears she'd held in since leaving David at the jail flowed freely down her cheeks.

When Dr. Klimenko opened his door thirty minutes later, Larissa knew everything Austin had endured since arriving in Toronto—her fear David would never leave jail, her passion to prove his innocence, and her homesickness.

"Papa!" Larissa bounded up from the floor to greet her father after he ushered his visitor out the door. "Here's Austin Starr, and she *must* talk to you. She's in so much trouble and feels so bad. I know you can help her. You simply must." Larissa hugged her father, who caressed her head with his gloved hand.

Beauty and the beast indeed, Austin thought, admiring the beauty's enthusiasm and thoughtfulness.

"Please come in, Mrs. Starr," Dr. Klimenko said. "I hoped you'd come, and here you are. Now, how can I help? The burden you carry must seem enormous because you're very young and also American."

"What's being American have to do with anything, Papa?" Larissa asked.

"Americans aren't used to hardships, as a rule," he said. "At least not those of Mrs. Starr's social class. I must hear how things stand so I can give better advice. Will you be staying, Larissa?"

"I have an appointment. Besides, I already know everything Austin will tell you, and we're going to meet for dinner tonight. I've promised to keep an eye on her. And I like girl talk more than you do anyway." She cackled—a strange sound to issue from such a pretty mouth—and her father reached out again to tousle her hair.

"Go along, *krasivaia maia.* I promise to help your new friend."

Krasivaia maia. So, the father recognized his daughter's beauty.

Dr. Klimenko ushered Austin into his office, and at once she felt comfortable. The room was lined with books on three sides, and no doubt the fourth wall would have held books had it not been a window. Books had always been Austin's friends. They were so much easier to deal with than people. Perhaps Dr. Klimenko felt the same.

Austin recounted everything she'd told his daughter, and as soon as she finished, he was ready with suggestions. Austin visualized herself as a sponge prepared to soak up every word.

"Despite learning more about the victim," he said, "you still don't have another suspect for the murder. What's worse, the powers that be, both here and in the United States, have decided your husband is the killer. They now have a vested interest in showing that they are correct by prosecuting him for the killing. Moreover, they'll wish to do it quickly. In short, they've little or no incentive to search for another suspect."

Dr. Klimenko rose and prowled around his office. "You're right to make your own investigations. If David has a lawyer, will he assist in this regard?"

Austin made a face. "Only somebody from Legal Aid, and I could tell he defines his duties narrowly. He has no interest in trying to catch the killer. I'm on my own."

"You're not battling alone anymore. I told you already about my experience confronting rough authorities. Never mind that those with whom I dueled were far beyond rough." He paused to adjust his glove, eying it with a look of grim determination.

"Rejoice that you're in Canada, a civilized democracy," he continued. "If you discover—no, *when* you discover—the killer, the authorities will assuredly want to prosecute him rather than your husband. Canadians have a definite sense of fair play, no doubt inherited from the British."

"What should I do now, sir?" Luckily for her, he didn't know her true feelings about Canada. She'd suspected her nitpicking was petty, but his words nailed her misgiving.

The professor returned to pacing, stopped to stare out the

window, and finally turned to face her again. "You must do two things immediately. First, speak to Detective Sergeant McKinnon. Get as much information as you can about the case against your husband. Second, go back to the church on Bathurst Street."

Austin shuddered. "Do I *have* to go back there?"

"You must return to the scene of the crime." Grinning at his own witticism, he settled in at his desk. "Interview the minister. He was kind to you and after all, that's what ministers are supposedly good for." He shook his shaggy head. "In truth, however, I haven't known many who were."

"How can Reverend Baxter help me?"

"When the police questioned him about the murder, he probably picked up information that can help in your own inquiry. You can *never* have too much information." His gaze bored into Austin like a drill. "I cannot stress this enough."

"Don't worry. That's my natural inclination. I love data—the more, the better."

A smile lit Klimenko's face, and he became almost handsome. "And here's one more rule of thumb. When you try to get people to tell you something, it's better to talk in person. Use the telephone only when a face-to-face meeting is impossible."

"Thank you, Dr. Klimenko. I'll remember that. I'm overwhelmed by the kindness you and Larissa have shown me."

"It's our duty and our pleasure. Many people helped me during my troubles, and I would not be alive today or in the safety of Canada if others had not provided assistance. The few who were sympathetic to my plight offset the cruelty of the many who wanted to kill me. I pass their tradition of kindness on as tribute."

He leaned across his desk. "And don't forget that you're a graduate student at a great university. You're obligated to fulfill your potential as well as live up to the trust placed in you when granted a graduate fellowship. You must keep up with your classes. Besides, learning about something other than murder will clear your mind. Studying something vicious but fascinating, like Russian and Soviet history, is perfect."

He stood. "Are we clear on all this?"

"Yes, sir." Austin squelched a desire to salute, straightened her shoulders, and marched out of Klimenko's office, mentally prepared for battle.

CHAPTER ELEVEN

Even if the professor in her next class had announced the destruction of Washington, D.C., by a nuclear weapon, Austin might not have noticed. Her mind was too busy deciding how to proceed with Dr. Klimenko's extracurricular interviews.

Austin sat through her class on Soviet political history contemplating which was scarier—talking to a policeman charged with the task of proving her husband a murderer or returning to the church with its grisly memories. DS McKinnon and Reverend Baxter had both shown her compassion, but McKinnon's authority worried her more than the reality of the crime scene. She opted to begin by visiting the church after her last class ended that day.

She and David had purchased a Volkswagen Beetle for their Texas-to-Ontario expedition. In Toronto, however, they seldom drove because David had declared a three-mile rule. For moving around the city, if the distance to travel was less than three miles, they should either walk or take public transportation. He wouldn't know if she broke his rule today, but Austin decided that walking to the church would be good for her. Sometimes her easy obedience to David's rules surprised her.

She left campus, went west along Harbord, and turned north at Bathurst. Only when she saw Honest Ed's gaudy façade did she recognize her route as the one she took the night of the murder, when life changed from calm and boring to tense and unmanageable.

Still, she slogged onward. Courageous people were those who

kept going regardless of the fear. Okay then, as the hippies were all saying these days, she'd just keep on truckin'.

The United Church stood in all its Victorian glory at the corner of Lennox and Bathurst. Austin tugged down her skirt, always riding up on her hips, and trooped into the building. She found the office and waited while the church secretary finished a phone call.

"May I help you?" the woman asked as she hung up the receiver. Springy gray curls covered her head, making her look like an aging Shirley Temple. Her smile was warm, and Austin relaxed a little.

"I need to see Reverend Baxter please, if he's not busy. I'm the one who found the body."

The woman peered intently at Austin over the top of her spectacles. "Then you're Austin Starr. Wait a moment while I see if he's available." She disappeared into an adjacent office and soon reappeared with the minister. He ushered Austin into his office and closed the door partway.

He indicated a chair. Austin sat down in front of his desk and surveyed the room. The place was a mess. Piles of paper lay everywhere, and Reverend Baxter himself looked rumpled. He wore a Shetland wool sweater underneath a tan corduroy jacket. Aside from the heavy clothes, however, he reminded her of the Methodist minister back home in Cuero. His welcome seemed genuine, and she recalled his kindness to her the night of the murder.

"I'm sorry your husband was arrested for Reginald Simpson's murder," he said.

"David's in jail, and that's why I'm here." Austin sat up straighter and stuck out her chin. "He's innocent, so I'm looking for information the police might have overlooked. Can you help? Have you learned anything new since the night of the murder?"

Reverend Baxter pressed his hands together. He made a church steeple with his index fingers, the way she had as a child. He held this amusing pose, silent for a moment, and then cleared his throat several times before he spoke.

"As you can imagine, the police swarmed all over and questioned everyone in our church family. In fact, today's the first time we've been rid of them." He sighed and regarded his cluttered desk. "My impression is that the forensics people didn't learn a lot, but I did pick up one interesting fact."

Reverend Baxter looked hard at Austin, as if ensuring she was paying attention. She scooted forward in her chair. Her whole body felt ready to engulf his next words.

"I overheard a policeman say that massive force slammed Reginald Simpson's head on the floor; there was no weapon. Brute strength killed him. Only a healthy male could do that."

Austin bobbed her head. "I assumed the killer was a man, but thank you for confirming it. Did you learn anything else? No detail is too small."

"I understand, and I'm sorry for the situation you're in. Only yesterday I talked to the dead boy's father, Senator Simpson. He came to the church to see where his son died. Obviously he's grieving, although I gather they were estranged."

"I didn't know that Reg's father was in town." Austin struggled to downplay her shock. "Do you know how long he'll be in Toronto and where he's staying?"

"The senator won't be here long, only a few days. He's taken a suite at the Royal York Hotel. He gave me the room number, and I've got it here somewhere." Reverend Baxter began searching his jumbled desktop. When papers fell on the floor, he stopped. "Never mind. Just give me your phone number and address; I'll contact you again if I remember anything or hear something new."

She wrote down the information for him, guessing he'd have trouble keeping track of it.

"Are you affiliated with a church, Mrs. Starr?"

"I'm a Methodist, but I haven't seen one Methodist church since I came to Toronto. It's very strange."

Reverend Baxter smiled. "Then you'll be interested in this bit of history. More than forty years ago, the Methodists, Congregationalists, and Presbyterians joined to become the United Church of Canada. I hope you'll consider making this your church home here in Toronto."

Austin made an indistinct but polite murmur. She wasn't as concerned about the state of her immortal soul as she was about David's name and getting him out of jail quickly.

"You'll also be interested to hear," he persisted, "that the United Church is supportive of young Americans who move to Canada because of resistance to the war in Vietnam. Assistance goes well beyond providing meeting space. Our secretary of evangelism and social service even offers emergency aid to draft resisters."

Austin blinked. "I had no idea." Her shoulders relaxed, and she sank deeper into her chair.

"Let me know what I can do to help. And I wish you luck in exonerating your husband." Reverend Baxter came around to her side of the desk and took her hands in his." I'll be praying for both of you."

Austin thanked him and said goodbye. When she walked past the secretary's desk, the woman looked up.

"My name is Agnes Duncan," she said. "If you need anything else, please call me. I answer the reverend's phone, and I'm around much more than he is."

The woman's Scottish accent was evident, and Austin wondered how she'd overlooked it before. "I'll keep that in mind. I gave Reverend Baxter my phone number. I'm looking for clues, specifically any detail pointing to a killer who's not my husband."

"You dear wee thing, how can you find something the policemen can't?" Mrs. Duncan's voice was comforting and concerned. "This must be hard on you, so young and so far from home. Do you want to just sit and talk to a willing ear?"

Tears prickled in Austin's eyes. "I'm trying to keep my chin up," she admitted, "but still, I'm pretty upset, too anxious to sit and chat, although I appreciate your offer." She liked this woman, the only person who ever called her a *wee* anything. Obviously, Mrs. Duncan had lost her mind. The word *wee* didn't fit Austin, who towered over most women and even some men.

"Anyway, before you go," Mrs. Duncan said, "would you like a shortbread biscuit? I bake them ahead of time for Christmas and put them away so they can mellow." She reached under her desk and brought out a tin box. "The reverend loves these, so I let him cheat." She chortled when she said the word *cheat*. "He gets to taste them before Christmas, special-like."

The sight of the shortbread changed Austin's mind. She decided to sit and talk and took one of the shortbread cookies— unable to think of it as a biscuit, no matter what Mrs. Duncan said. She bit into the cookie. When the buttery flakes melted onto her tongue, her taste buds sang a song of joy, and Mrs. Duncan rose into Austin's personal pantheon of cooks.

"These are heavenly." Austin tried not to grab another cookie. "Someday I hope you'll share the recipe, unless it's a family secret." She licked her lips. "I really love to bake. Muffins are my specialty."

"I'd be glad to share."

"Excuse me," Austin said, "I don't mean to change the subject, but is your old janitor around? I need to talk to him too."

"He's not here today. In fact he's only been at work once since Thursday night. He came in yesterday for our Sunday services, but his wife called this morning to say he'd gone to see his doctor." Mrs. Duncan chewed on her shortbread before saying, "She says the murder upset him terribly."

"When he does return," Austin said, "please tell him I'd like to talk to him."

"Of course, dear."

"And by the way, what's his name?"

"It's Ferguson. Gordon Ferguson."

Austin couldn't help it, she just had to ask. "Is everyone in Toronto Scottish?"

Mrs. Duncan laughed. "No, dear, only the smartest of us are Scots. My family moved here from Scotland more than a century ago, and Mr. Ferguson came with his family after the First World War. After his father was killed in the trenches, his mother moved her sons here to live with relatives. You're right, of course. Many Scots emigrated to Canada. Just check out the names in the phone book to see how many of us there really are."

Austin had a sudden memory of her latest encounter with a Toronto phone book, and her stomach lurched. She wished she'd quit being so darned jumpy.

"Wouldn't you like another shortbread?" Mrs. Duncan lifted the lid off the cookie tin and offered the cookies to Austin. "Eating something sugary and fattening always cheers me up."

Despite her queasy stomach, Austin accepted a second cookie. Fuel for the quest, she rationalized.

After a few minutes of pleasant conversation, feeling well fortified with real Scottish shortbread and the milk of human kindness, Austin left the church. She tramped to a bus stop, found a route map, and looked for a way to get across town to the police station.

DS McKinnon didn't realize it yet, but he was scheduled to become her next informant.

CHAPTER TWELVE

Austin got off the bus across from the Manufacturers Life Insurance Company on Bloor. She crossed the street to get a closer look and marveled at its pristine grounds. The grass was like a putting green—so smooth that she fancied tiny minions used manicure scissors to ensure that each blade was cut just so.

She stood at the imposing wrought-iron fence that surrounded the perfect lawn and grasped a bar in each hand. Thunderstruck, she realized this was David's daily pose, though she assumed the view from his cell was anything but pristine and beautiful. She'd be glad when she could visit him. Only two more days to wait, but she felt she had to live through an entire ice age.

Austin went back across Bloor and walked south down Jarvis to police headquarters. With the modern city blaring around her, she felt far from Cuero, where the population, all seven thousand of them, gloried in their connections to the Chisholm Trail. Cuero celebrated its cowboy heritage in ways big and conspicuous. In contrast, she saw no evidence of Toronto's fur-trading beginnings.

Cuero's police station was located inside the city hall, a cozy arrangement compared to the multi-storied headquarters of the Metropolitan Toronto Police looming ahead. She'd often visited Daddy at city hall during his tenure as mayor, but those visits made her smile. Now that she felt outside the law, she had no reason to smile.

The enormity of Toronto pressed against her. She sensed every one of its million-plus citizens watching her. Good lord, she was no stranger to big cities. Her parents had taken her to see relatives in Houston and Dallas, where they shopped at Neiman Marcus, ate at elegant restaurants, and toured museums. Yet she'd never spent one Canadian dollar at Holt Renfrew in Toronto or dined at any of the city's fancy restaurants. In Texas, she had belonged. In Ontario, she was an outsider.

Austin reached the police headquarters and, clutching the handrail, mounted the steps to the entrance. In the lobby, men her father's age were coming and going with purposeful treads. Overcome by the air of professionalism, she felt suddenly lightheaded.

Why had she thought she'd get useful information out of DS McKinnon? She was the wife of a suspected murderer. And she'd never felt so alone. She shivered and huddled into her jacket. Maybe the friendly detective sergeant would be unavailable, and she'd put off talking to him for another day.

Austin spied an information booth and inquired about the homicide squad and the location of McKinnon's office. The guard directed her, adding, "You're lucky, young lady. He's rarely here at HQ; he's usually out chasing criminals." He followed his words with a big wink.

Not feeling worthy of a wink or a "young lady" and certainly not feeling lucky, Austin trudged to the elevator. Should she rejoice or curse that he was in?

When she reached his room, Austin tapped timidly on the half-open door.

DS McKinnon beamed when he saw her. "Come in, Mrs. Starr." He laid aside his reading glasses, sprang to his feet, and put on his tweed jacket. "I was just thinking about your husband."

"Oh my God, has something happened to David?"

"Nothing like that. Sit down, sit down, and I'll bring you up to date. You know he's been remanded into custody and—"

"I know," she interrupted, "but what does that mean? *Remand?*"

"He is sent to prison subsequent to a preliminary hearing

before a judge."

"And are you still looking for other suspects?" Austin asked, her eyes narrowing.

"I wouldn't say that exactly. We're continuing to pursue the case and still interviewing people who knew Reginald Simpson. We're also looking into your husband's background."

"So you're saying that you—that is, the police—are satisfied that David killed Reg. Is that right?"

"We wouldn't rule out that someone else committed the homicide, but we aren't actively pursuing other suspects at this time."

Her head fell to her chest, and she grasped the arms of her chair.

"Are you all right?" The tenor of his voice underlined his concern.

"I'm fine." Rethinking her answer, she pursed her lips. "Not great, but fine. Do you have time for more questions?"

"Fire away."

She folded her hands together and pressed them into her lap. He must be indulging her since, as a co-called young lady, she didn't have to be taken seriously. As she composed herself, Austin scrutinized the office. In contrast to Reverend Baxter's office, this was a monument to order, with only a few files stacked neatly on the desk and binders standing in straight rows on bookshelves.

Ducking her head again, not looking him in the eye, she asked, "When you were at our apartment Friday evening, before you received your phone call, you said you didn't believe David was the killer. What changed?"

She raised her head to scowl at him.

"I'd hoped it would be obvious to you." He took off his reading glasses, rubbed the bridge of his nose, and leaned back in his chair. "This is delicate. I can't reveal the internal workings of the police department, let alone the prime minister's office." He lowered his gaze and spoke to his desktop. "If you catch my drift."

Austin frowned. "Ah, I get it. I'm not stupid."

"Never said that you were—quite the opposite, really."

McKinnon's expression was kind, and Austin felt he either found her amusing or was at least getting a kick out of their talks. Something about him reminded her of Daddy, but she couldn't put her finger on what it was. If everyone in Toronto insisted on being kind to her, she'd have to rethink her criticisms of Canada.

"Have you talked to Reg's friends yet?" Would he at least answer this question?

"Well…" McKinnon drew out the syllable. "The friends we could find, yes, we talked to them."

"Did you learn anything useful? Anyone have ideas who could've killed Reg?"

McKinnon murmured something indistinct.

"Excuse me?"

He didn't look up. "I said no one had any theories. A few thought David was incapable of murder, but no one was what I would call forthcoming."

"Do you know what my biggest fear is?" she asked abruptly.

"What?" He met her gaze and held it.

"If someone hands you evidence showing another person killed Reg Simpson, I worry that you—umm, the authorities, that is— would still pursue the case against my husband."

"I can put your mind at rest; we would never do that."

Austin cocked her head. "Never?"

"Never." McKinnon's voice was firm, and his eyes held steady.

Austin was having trouble breathing; all the questions she'd wanted to ask had fled her mind. She could take this conversation no further, so she jumped up. "I hope you're right because I plan to find the killer myself." She sucked in a deep breath. "Probably I shouldn't say this, but I believe I can find clues that you can't. Besides, you've essentially quit looking and—"

"Don't do anything silly, young lady." McKinnon pushed back his chair and stood. "If you're right and someone else committed the murder, you're putting yourself in danger."

Now she understood why he reminded her of Daddy.

"What choice do I have?"

"You could wait and trust the judicial system." He almost barked his rapid response.

"And lose months or years of our lives in the process? No, sir. I may be young, but the prospect of wasting time appalls me." She scooped up her purse and stepped toward the door. "I appreciate your taking the time to talk to me."

"You're certainly determined. If I had a daughter, I'd want her to be just like you."

"Funny thing, sir. I was thinking how much you and my father have in common."

McKinnon moved from behind his desk and clasped her hand.

Austin became too choked up to speak, so she nodded her goodbye. She decided that McKinnon would be straight with her, even in the face of pressures exerted by senior officers and politicians.

Would events prove her hunch to be correct? With all her heart, she hoped so.

CHAPTER THIRTEEN

Trudging home from police headquarters, Austin concluded she'd never endured such a stressful day. She longed to recline in a hot bath and read a good book. Yet it was almost six o'clock, time to meet her new friend for dinner.

Larissa had suggested George's Spaghetti House on Harbord. Since her apartment was nearby, Austin could stop there first to refresh her make-up and fix her hair. She didn't want to look bedraggled when she met Larissa. Attaining the Russian girl's level of beauty was impossible, but at least Austin could be neat and tidy, one of Mother's cardinal rules.

Austin's feet churned faster as she hurried the final blocks. She rushed through her building's front door but stopped abruptly at the mailboxes. Maybe, just maybe, she'd get some good news for a change. Flipping through the mail, she found bills, advertising flyers, and one envelope apparently delivered by hand.

Nothing from Texas.

She studied the odd envelope.

No address, no return, no stamp. Only her name typed on the outside. The anonymity of the envelope told Austin that this was no ordinary letter. She shuddered and her stomach fluttered.

On her way to the stairway, pausing in the dim light of a wall sconce, Austin ripped open the envelope and pulled out a single sheet of paper. Centered and typed in capital letters was a short message: MIND YOUR OWN BUSINESS. OR ELSE.

Austin staggered over to the stairs and sank onto the bottom step. She didn't know whether to laugh at the cliché or immediately get the hell out of Dodge.

Could Mother be right after all? Should she fly home to Texas and do it soon?

The anonymous note writer obviously meant to scare her, but was this a prank or a real threat? Austin's mind clicked into overdrive.

If the threat was a prank, anyone could have left the note. Maybe some draft resister, furious at David, wrote it. But people wanting to scare her away from digging into the crime were limited in number, except for all of Reg's friends. No, strike that. Other than Pete and Dulcie, Reg had no friends in Toronto. Unless Austin completely misread her, Dulcie would never send a threat like this. Pete would accost her in person rather than sneak around. He'd shown he could go toe-to-toe with her and defend the honor of his dead friend.

Now that Senator Simpson was in town, he was a possibility, as farfetched as that seemed. The threat hardly seemed worthy of a powerful politician, although that could be the point—to throw her off or disguise the sender's identity. And how would he know where she lived? Wow, she must be getting paranoid.

The longer she clasped the note, the more her knuckles whitened. The bottom line—someone wanted her to stop nosing around the murder. That didn't necessarily mean the killer sent the warning. The note was a mixed blessing—frightening but energizing at the same time.

Whatever the writer hoped to achieve hadn't worked. Instead, Austin was thrilled that the killer might've threatened her. The note was proof that David was falsely accused. She got up from her perch on the steps and mounted the stairs to her apartment with rising confidence.

When she reached the third floor landing, Austin heard her telephone ringing. She fumbled with her keys, unlocked the door, and rushed inside.

The caller identified himself as Ian Campbell. "I'm with the *Toronto Star*," he said. "I want to ask about your husband's arrest."

Austin didn't respond and bit back the only comment she wanted to make: the thrills just keep on coming.

"Hello? Hello? Are you there?"

"I'm here." Austin struggled to be civil. "You caught me at a bad time. I'm not sure I want to talk to you anyway."

"Don't worry. I won't hassle you."

"It's not that. It's—"

"Prime Minister Pierre Trudeau calls Canada 'a refuge from militarism.' My readers deserve to know what's happening to the Vietnam War resisters we've welcomed to our country." He waited a beat for her to respond and then said, "Now then, to get the record straight, tell me, is your husband a deserter or a draft dodger?"

Austin's arm muscles tightened. "You heard me. I'm not talking to you. Just leave me alone, please."

"Fine, but you'll hear from me again tomorrow. I'm going to tell your story, with or without your help. Your husband's side will come out better if you participate."

"Goodbye, Mr. Campbell." Austin slammed down the receiver. She looked at the phone with sympathy. One more bad call and surely the unlucky contraption would crack. She fell onto a kitchen chair and kicked off her shoes.

What would hit her next? All this stress was causing her to act in uncharacteristic ways. Here she was hanging up on people, which wasn't like her. She stretched out her legs, flexed her feet, and contemplated an uncertain future. Her toes ached from all the unaccustomed pounding she'd done, running around downtown Toronto. They seemed to demand she make at least one change.

No more hoofing; enough with David's three-mile rule. Besides, he wasn't around to enforce it anyway. Tonight she'd drive the Beetle. Plenty of clues were hiding in this cold city, and she was geared up to uncover them.

CHAPTER FOURTEEN

"Have you seen today's newspapers?" Larissa asked.

Austin shook her head. "Nopth, I didn'th." Garlic bread filled her mouth.

"Right." Larissa smiled. "I knew you wouldn't have time to read them, so here they are—the *Globe and Mail,* the *Star,* and the *Sun.* All carry stories about the murder and David's arrest."

Larissa passed the clippings to Austin across the restaurant table. The *Toronto Star* slipped through Austin's fingers and slid into a puddle of spaghetti sauce. Red liquid quickly saturated the paper. Austin wiped off the sauce with her napkin and tried to read the first paragraph. "This clipping looks drenched in blood."

"Oh, don't be so morbid," said Larissa, pausing with a fork halfway to her mouth.

"I'm not being morbid, just symbolic or ironic or something like that. Haven't you heard black humor keeps you from wanting to slit your wrists?"

"What's gotten into you?"

Austin yanked the anonymous note from her purse. "Look what landed in my mailbox."

Larissa read the note, and her eyes widened. "We've got to tell my father about this. Have you told anyone else?"

"Only you."

"Then let's get out of here and go see Papa. I'll get the check."

They rushed out of the restaurant, ran to Austin's Beetle, and drove straight to Larissa's home. Austin's stomach was in knots. If only she hadn't consumed her weight in garlic bread. She hoped she wouldn't walk in the door of the Klimenkos' house and throw up in the foyer.

The home was a late Victorian pile of brick located in Rosedale, the toniest part of town. Maple Avenue, clearly named for the trees lining it, would amount to Canadian kitsch if it weren't so splendid. Fall was fading into winter, and mounds of leaves covered the yard and sidewalk. Recent strong winds roaring down from the Arctic Circle—much too close for Austin's comfort—had pushed more leaves up to the front porch. There they all rested, exhausted.

Larissa hopped out of the car, but Austin remained behind the wheel. If she lived in a quiet enclave like this—or better yet, in a home like this—then she might learn to tolerate Toronto. Architecture—what her art history prof had taught her to call "the built environment"—really turned her on.

"Come on." Larissa stood at the driver's side of the car. "Are you afraid to talk to my father?"

"Enjoying the view."

"Well, stop it. Scoot inside and get safe. The killer could be here, lying in wait."

"Good grief, your imagination's wilder than mine."

"You never know. The creep could've followed us from the restaurant."

"All right, all right. I'm coming."

Larissa ran up the steps. Austin followed slowly, feeling squashed like an armadillo on the side of a Texas highway. Only her outer shell held her together.

But when she stepped inside the house, she entered another world and felt momentarily transformed. An icon of St. George slaying a dragon greeted her from a corner, its silver halo shining in the light cast by an ornate chandelier. An oriental carpet welcomed her tired feet. Oil paintings depicting Imperial Russia's high society calmed her spirit.

"Papa recreated his grandparents' home in Moscow," Larissa said. "Do you like it?"

"If I lived here, I'd never leave," Austin whispered.

Larissa unleashed a brilliant smile. "Mama inherited this place but"—her smile withered—"only lived here a year before she passed away." An expression of deep sorrow flitted across her beautiful face.

Austin scarcely had time to adjust to this passing storm of emotions before Dr. Klimenko emerged from a back room.

She registered his disheveled hair, crumbs lodged in his beard, and his shirt parting ways with the waistband of his pants. He hurried to pull on the glove he used to hide his damaged hand. Austin wanted to see what it looked like, how badly it was mangled, but couldn't stare without being rude. How amazing he'd married a Canadian heiress. How had that happened? She'd bide her time and delve into his mysteries later.

Earleen called her nosy; Austin preferred to think of herself as politely inquisitive.

"You're home early, Larissa," Dr. Klimenko said. Then he noticed Austin. "Why, Mrs. Starr, what a surprise to see you too."

"We've got a problem, Papa." Larissa flapped her arms and began talking as fast as an auctioneer. "Let's go to the kitchen. I'll put on the kettle and make tea while we tell you what's happened to Austin now. You're not going to believe it." She pushed her father down the hall.

In short order Larissa made tea, the girls related the latest installment of Austin's perils, and the professor mused aloud over what was to be done.

Again, *chto delyat?*

Despite the problems facing her, Austin relaxed more than she'd been able to in days. Nestled between her two new friends in their snug home, sipping tea with cherry jam Russian-style, Austin got a reprieve from her nightmare. The bad dream that was now her life would begin again soon, but she allowed herself some pleasure before diving back into her new world of homicide and havoc.

Dr. Klimenko's face was grave. "Here are my suggestions for how you should proceed. First, Mrs. Starr, you need to stay with us. You're not safe in your apartment right now."

Larissa clapped her hands. "Papa, what a grand idea. There's a pretty guest room next to mine, Austin. You're going to love it."

"Be that as it may," her father went on, "we'll keep an eye on you until the police can figure out if you're in danger. Speaking of them, tomorrow morning you should make an appointment with Detective Sergeant McKinnon. You must show him the note. From his point of view, it may be flimsy evidence, but if he's as perceptive as you say, he'll believe you. Someone else, however, may question whether you wrote the note yourself."

"I'm optimistic that McKinnon will trust me about the note."

"I just met you, but I already know you'd never fake evidence." Larissa's tone was firm.

"Of course," the professor said, "but someone who's not as discerning as you, dear heart, might disagree."

"Why don't I call McKinnon and tell him everything on the phone?" Austin asked. "I saw him this afternoon and don't want to pester him. Won't he get upset if I bother him again? He likes me, I think, and I want to keep him on my side."

Klimenko lifted one brow, his gaze boring into her. "Remember what I said about talking in person? You need to *show* him the note—which, by the way, he'll keep for evidence."

"Hadn't thought about that," Austin said. "Okay, I'll see him tomorrow but make an appointment first, as you suggest."

"Furthermore," he said, "McKinnon will watch your face while you describe finding the threat in your mailbox. Remember, he'll watch you, and you should watch him."

"Gosh, there's so much to all this. How do you know these things, Papa, how to deal with the police?" Larissa's face glowed with admiration.

"Life in the Soviet Union produced experiences you'll never have. I believe the expression is that I learned about life the hard way." He turned to Austin again, but before he could continue, Larissa interrupted.

"When will you tell me about *your* adventures, Papa? I'm twenty years old and still waiting."

"Indeed, my adventures." He coughed, stirred his tea, and took a sip. "I would call them catastrophes." Sadness darkened his voice. "Another time, I promise."

"But you're always promising *another time*."

"Larochka, I meant *soon*. Right now we must concentrate on helping your new friend." He tilted his shaggy head toward Austin. "I don't mean to frighten you, but you must remain aware of your surroundings at all times. You've been threatened, and someone may be following you."

"That's what I said too." Larissa was obviously pleased with herself.

Klimenko regarded his daughter sternly. "If Austin is being followed, it's not a game. If there's a killer running amuck, then this fellow will be enraged if he sees her return to police headquarters." He turned toward Austin. "In short, Mrs. Starr, be aware and be cautious. You are not a character in a novel. You could get hurt."

"I'll be careful, sir." Austin clutched the arms of her chair. "It seemed like a joke when Larissa said the killer might be watching me." Her eyes felt as if they were bugging out of her head. Was this how it felt to be truly alert? She scowled and tipped her face to the ceiling. "Professor, why don't I talk to Senator Simpson too? What do you think?" Austin glanced at Klimenko and then at Larissa. Both their faces registered apprehension.

Larissa found her voice first. "Why on earth would you try that? He won't talk to you."

"Wait," Klimenko said. "She may have a point. There are details about this murder we know nothing about. We're missing many different angles, in fact." He began rubbing his gloved hand.

The motion seemed to signal the professor's deepest concentration. Austin waited for him to say more, but finally grew impatient. "I can pop up at his hotel tomorrow and catch him by surprise."

He shrugged. "Wouldn't hurt to try, although you'll probably only talk to one of his underlings. Nevertheless, you might learn something from an aide even if you can't speak to the senator."

"An entourage?" Larissa asked. "Are senators such a big deal in America?"

Larissa's enthusiasm was admirable, but sometimes it was exhausting. "A very big deal," Austin said. "McKinnon said Simpson's the senior senator from New Jersey, so he's no lightweight. I plan to ask a friend back home to find out more about him."

Klimenko said, "The *Globe and Mail* noted this morning that Senator Simpson isn't up for re-election for another two years. That means he is not on the ballot tomorrow."

"Oh my God." Austin's hand flew to her mouth. "The election! Thank heaven I already sent my absentee ballot. If I missed the chance to vote against Nixon, I'd never forgive myself."

"What's wrong with Nixon?" Larissa asked.

"If I answer, I'll get so worked up, you'll think I'm deranged."

Dr. Klimenko smiled at Larissa and then Austin. "This sounds like a discussion for another day. In the meantime, you two should go upstairs and get situated for the night."

Larissa hopped up and kissed her father on the cheek. She grabbed Austin's hand and tried to haul her out of the kitchen, but Austin resisted.

"Wait a minute. I haven't thanked your father properly," she said. "You didn't have to offer your protection, Dr. Klimenko, but you did. When I read about you in the graduate catalog, I never dreamed that my choice of study would have such significance."

He leaned back in his chair and smiled the too-rare expression that transformed his face. "Remember what I said, Austin. Kind people helped me once upon a time, and one day you will aid someone in difficulty. Dealing with my troubles taught me the importance of being good and helping others." He pushed back his chair and stood. "Naturally, that's a simplification, but we can discuss other issues another time. Now run along. I have papers to grade."

Warmth spread through Austin. He seldom used her first name, and each time he did, she glowed.

The girls walked to the foyer. This time, instead of being overwhelmed by beauty, Austin was daunted by the sight of the towering stairway—steep, grand, and heavily carpeted. When Larissa skipped merrily up the stairs, Austin knew defeat. Although she was only two years older than Larissa, Austin felt middle-aged in comparison.

Larissa paused and glanced down at Austin. "What's wrong? Are you tired?"

"You bet I am." And she was, but it was the perfect excuse to not race up behind Larissa. She never admitted to anyone she was scared of stairs.

Larissa bounced back down. "Come on up, and we'll get you settled in your room. I'm dying to chat, but if you're tired, we can talk another time."

"Were you a cheerleader in high school?"

"No, why?"

"Just wondering where your energy comes from and how I can tap into its source. I've never felt so exhausted; I could sleep for days."

"You never had a husband accused of murder before," Larissa said. "That would make me crawl into bed and stay forever, but we won't let you do that. We'll keep you safe and help you find the killer. And if you want me to, I'll go with you to the scary old Don Jail when you see David."

"You don't have to do that."

"I want to. Besides, it'll be an adventure." Larissa bobbed up and down on a step as Austin climbed up to join her, carefully holding onto the bannister.

"Okay, you're on. We'll have adventures, but no catastrophes."

"That's right," Larissa said. "No catastrophes allowed."

CHAPTER FIFTEEN

Austin awoke Tuesday morning feeling refreshed for the first time since finding Reg's corpse. She'd had no nightmares and slept nine hours straight—a real luxury.

She examined the guest room in the bright light of morning. It was painted peacock blue, her favorite color, and located right next to Larissa's. *She* had probably been up for hours doing jumping jacks or running laps around her bed. Austin wished she could find Larissa's energy source.

As Austin swung her legs onto the floor, someone knocked at her door.

"Anyone awake in there? May I come in?"

Speak of the devil. Larissa walked in bearing a tray that held two large coffee mugs. She placed the tray on a dresser and carried a mug to Austin.

"Room service, madam."

Austin accepted the coffee and took a sip. "This is bliss. If it weren't for missing David so much, I could get used to treatment like this and never leave."

"Fine idea. We've got enough room here for you both, and then we could all have lots more adventures."

Austin flopped back on the pillows and whimpered. "Please don't remind me. Let's pretend today will be lovely, with nothing more complicated than finding the right dress at Holt Renfrew."

"With a little luck we can do that soon."

"Here's to luck." Austin raised her mug in a toast. "Let's make our date to go shopping one of the first things I do after I get David released from jail." Austin found it impossible to be discouraged around Larissa.

"And what's another first thing?"

"We'll drink champagne and toast the fairness of Canada's justice system."

"Here's to another splendid idea." Larissa raised her mug too. "Now, what's on your agenda today, and do you want help?"

"I better see McKinnon first." Austin wrinkled her nose. "Your father stressed that. Then I'll drop by the Royal York Hotel and try to find Senator Simpson. You're welcome to come along."

"Sure thing. Besides, you may need my help. At least I can be moral support."

"I need all the help I can get."

Austin phoned the homicide department and learned the earliest she could see McKinnon was two o'clock. She booked the time, then immediately began worrying how to approach Senator Simpson while she got ready to go downtown.

She unlocked her VW and watched Larissa insert herself elegantly into the small car. As a matter of principle, Austin rarely hung out with anyone petite and rarely even stood beside anyone short. Since Larissa surpassed all standards for dainty female perfection, Austin should've felt like an oaf. Yet Larissa's infectious enthusiasm and kindness overcame Austin's insecurities, and Austin found herself leaning on this tiny dynamo for encouragement.

She inched the car out of its parking spot, only to brake hard. She looked in the rear-view mirror, checked her side mirror, and twisted around to survey the neighborhood.

Larissa scooped her purse off the floor, where it fell during the jarring stop. "What're you doing?"

"Someone could be lurking out here, ready to follow us around town. Figured I'd better stop to see if the coast is clear, so to speak." She tried to sound bold and attempted to laugh, but the sound turned into a cough, spoiling the effect.

"I already checked." Larissa punched Austin's arm lightly. "Looks like we're safe for now."

"Let's hope so."

Austin drove in silence for a time. "Am I going the right way?"

"I'll let you know when we get close to the hotel." Larissa cleared her throat. "So, tell me, how do you plan to get the senator to talk?"

"I don't have a plan yet," Austin said. "I'll have to improvise on the spot."

"That's not wise."

"What do you suggest?" Austin's eyes looked sideways for a moment, then went back to the road ahead.

"Want to tell the truth or use a ruse? And how're we going to find him?"

"Ask the desk clerk for the senator's room number?"

"That's not how things work." Suddenly Larissa waved her hand to the left, startling Austin. "You need to turn here. There's the parking lot."

After finding a space to park, they made their way into the hotel lobby. The long, rectangular space was topped by a coffered ceiling two stories high, from which hung huge chandeliers. Columns marched along the walls and held up a mezzanine that ringed the room.

Austin gasped. "This place is so old and fancy that I bet Queen Victoria stayed here."

"She didn't, but her great-great-granddaughter Queen Elizabeth did. The Royal York is the largest hotel in the entire British Commonwealth." Larissa stood up straighter and puffed out her chest. Her father wasn't the only Klimenko who loved historical facts.

Austin basked in the surroundings. "And look at all this gold leaf and velvet. Now I understand why you worried about finding the senator. The hotel is enormous."

Suddenly Larissa grabbed her arm and pulled Austin close. "Hush, I need to eavesdrop."

Both girls froze in place.

A man's voice boomed from behind a Corinthian column. "A Chevrolet was fine for me last week, but not for my boss. The senator can't be driven around the city in a Chevy. He needs at least a Buick. A Cadillac's even better. Anything else is unacceptable. Got that?"

Austin leaned toward Larissa's ear. "You think he's talking about Senator Simpson?"

"Unless there's a senators' convention in town," Larissa whispered back. "Besides, he can't be an aide to one of *our* senators. Canadians aren't this noisy in public."

Austin suppressed a giggle.

"Call me back when you find a better car. And hurry. Senator Simpson has an appointment at noon."

Austin and Larissa exchanged triumphant smiles and peeked around the column. An athletic-looking man hung up the house phone and strode onto a waiting elevator. The door slid shut. They watched the elevator floor indicator light move until it stopped at number nine.

"Good grief, what luck," Austin said. "Let's wait a bit and then follow. We can wing it from there."

Larissa took a silver compact from her purse, checked her lipstick, and fluffed her hair with her fingers. "If that man says he's been in Toronto for a *week*, what's he been doing here all that time?"

"If he was here when Reg died, that's significant, to put it mildly." Austin slung her purse over her shoulder and set her jaw. "Let's go."

Two pairs of nervous knees trembled in front of the elevator on the ninth floor. Planning to improvise had been a bad idea. When the time came, neither Austin nor Larissa came up with any schemes.

While they deliberated what to do, a chambermaid pushed a service cart around a corner.

Larissa jerked away from Austin's side and rushed to the maid. "Can you help me?"

"*Mais oui*. I help." The maid had a Québécois accent.

Larissa replied in rapid French. Austin tried to follow their conversation, but her two years of high school French couldn't handle the job.

Austin waited with growing impatience while Larissa talked to the maid. Finally she finished and rejoined Austin.

We're all set." Larissa rubbed her hands together and adjusted her jacket, ready for action.

"What was that about?" Austin asked.

"I know where the senator's room is—right there." She pointed a short way down the hall, to door 920.

Austin's mouth fell open. "How do you know?"

"I told the maid that my very rich uncle was staying here and that his aide was in room nine fifteen and that we came to visit my uncle on his birthday and that I needed to know the room number." Larissa's words rushed out at breakneck speed.

Her eagerness never ceased to amaze Austin.

Larissa continued. "When the maid asked if my uncle took a suite, I said that he probably had, since he's so wealthy, and she said the only suite on this floor was right down there." She pointed to the door. "*Et voila, c'est parfait, oui?*"

"*Otlichno.*" Austin used the Russian word for excellent. "Now go back to plain old English. My brain cells are spinning already."

Larissa giggled and started to answer when they heard a door open. They turned in unison toward the sound. A man stood in the doorway of room 920. Austin judged him to be an older version of Reg Simpson—more than six feet tall, with a square face and thick, lustrous hair. His navy blue suit was obviously expensive, and he shot his cuffs as he looked down the hall, giving Austin a chance to admire his ornate gold cufflinks. Before she could decide what to do, Larissa grabbed center stage.

She fell against Austin and shrieked. "My ankle. I've hurt my ankle."

The tall man turned when he heard the noise and came toward them. "May I assist you, ladies?" He looked at Larissa, blinked, and looked again. For the first time, Austin experienced Larissa's effect on men, realizing instantly such scenes would repeat endlessly over the course of their friendship.

"I'm afraid I sprained my ankle." Larissa actually whimpered, a true damsel in distress.

"Are you able to walk to your room?" He offered his arm. She took it.

"We're leaving the hotel. We've been visiting a relative." Larissa gave him a brave smile, took a step, and winced. She leaned more heavily on his arm. "I'm afraid it hurts too much for me to walk. Whatever shall I do?" She addressed Austin, who was bowled over at the sudden change in her friend. Larissa sure knew how to deploy her assets.

"This really isn't proper, but why don't you come to my suite while I call for the hotel doctor?" He studied Larissa. "But let me introduce myself. My name is Reginald Simpson III. I'm a United States senator. You have nothing to fear from me." His chest seemed to grow by at least three inches.

Taking an instant dislike to the proud man, Austin glowered at him. "We don't want to inconvenience you."

"But my ankle hurts so much." Larissa tugged at Austin's sleeve. "Can't I go in and rest, just for a minute? After that I may be able to walk."

Austin suppressed a grin as she watched Larissa's award-worthy performance.

"We'll put ice on your ankle and give you something to drink," Senator Simpson said. "Then when you feel better, you can decide if I should call the doctor. How does that sound?"

"We accept your kind offer. My name is Larissa, and this is my

113

friend Austin."

He turned his attention to Austin for the first time. "What an unusual name. Are you by any chance from Texas? My closest colleague in the Senate is from there."

"I am a proud Texan."

Larissa jumped back into the conversation before Senator Simpson could reply. "I'm in pain. Can't we go to the senator's room and put some ice on this?"

They entered the suite, with Larissa limping and hanging on to the senator's arm. She flagged gracefully onto an overstuffed sofa in the sitting room, and Austin sat beside her to keep Simpson away.

The senator ordered ice, Cokes, and coffee from room service, allowing Austin time to organize her thoughts. Everything had unspooled so quickly, events were overtaking her. They were with the senator, but under false pretenses. She sat up straighter, stuck out her chin, and resolved to make the most of the opportunity. After all, the senator couldn't see that she wore an invisible Nancy Drew name tag.

A knock sounded on the door. The senator opened it, and the man from the hotel lobby strode into the room. "Hi, boss." His voice was loud and booming. The newcomer stopped in front of the sofa and stared at Larissa. Once he saw her, he looked at nothing else. "I see you have company." He gave a low whistle.

The senator made introductions. The loud man was Darrel Smith, his executive assistant. Smith was a little shorter than the senator and stocky, but he had a similar square jaw and shiny, thick hair. Within minutes he had announced that he was a Harvard graduate and that his father was a friend of Joseph Kennedy, the dead president's father.

What a showoff. He must be posturing for Larissa's benefit.

Austin noted, however, that the senator made no move to stop Smith's boasting, only listening and smiling benignly. Although tempted to mention David's Princeton fellowship to show that Darrel wasn't the only one with prestigious relatives, Austin gritted her teeth and didn't interrupt Darrel's résumé.

When room service arrived, Austin made sure to put the ice compress on Larissa's ankle herself. Watching the men grovel at her friend's feet would sicken her, although it might have made them more compliant once Larissa began asking questions.

A little voice in Austin's head urged that the time was now or never. "This is rather awkward, Senator Simp—"

"Yes, we understand," Darrel said. "Having you in the senator's suite wouldn't do much for his reputation either. Once your friend is up to it, I'll help her to the lobby, and you can be on your way." His eyes sought Larissa's, and she gave him a winsome smile.

"Darrel, what brings you to Canada?" Larissa asked.

Darrel looked at his boss.

The senator shook his head and replied slowly, "We're here on a family matter."

Larissa's hand flew to her mouth. "Gosh, you're the man whose son was murdered last week. The papers said the victim's father was a United States senator."

Simpson's face contorted, and he lowered his eyes for a moment before looking up again. "That's all true. My son was murdered."

"How awful for you," Austin said. "We're very sorry for your loss."

"And when did *you* come to Toronto?" Larissa stared boldly at Darrel and smiled slightly.

"Two weeks ago," Darrel said.

"Darrel." The senator's growl sounded like a reprimand.

"It's okay, sir. They've read the papers, so they must know already about your son, that he was a draft dodger."

Austin had never heard anyone use the term with such scorn.

Darrel turned to Larissa. "I came up to Toronto to track down the senator's son."

Every look Larissa gave Darrel seemed to act like a shot of

truth serum.

"That must've been so difficult for you, sir." Larissa looked up through fluttering eyelashes at the senator. "Your own service in World War Two was so outstanding."

Perhaps Austin didn't know her friend as well as she assumed. *Where did she get this act?*

"How did you hear about my military record?" The senator's face registered confusion and pride at the same time.

Larissa looked vague and airily waved a hand. "Must have read that in the newspaper too. You're famous here. Canadians always admire war heroes." Flutter-flutter went her thick eyelashes.

"Had you been in touch with your son before he was murdered?" Austin asked Senator Simpson.

"I bet you were able to find him fast," Larissa spoke to Darrel, who reddened.

"I managed to locate him, but he didn't realize it. Reg was—"

"Darrel, my appointment is at noon." Simpson's tone was sharp. "See about having my car brought around. I can't be late meeting with the police commissioner."

"Yes, sir." Darrel's manner changed, becoming formal and businesslike. "It was a pleasure meeting you, ladies, and I hope to see you again soon." He looked only at Larissa.

Like a countess in *War and Peace*, she held her hand out to him. "We might meet again. Who knows?"

"You can say that again," Austin mumbled. She half expected to watch Darrel kiss Larissa's fingers.

Larissa rose from the sofa and stood shakily. "We'll go downstairs with you, Darrel. I can walk if I can hold on to you." Flutter-flutter went the eyelashes. "The ice made my foot feel so much better."

Darrel's expression melted into a puddle of goo. "I'll be happy to help."

Goodbyes were said, and Darrel escorted the girls to the hotel lobby. He kept patting Larissa's hand, the one that gripped his arm.

"You sure you feel okay?"

"I'm much better now, thanks."

"When can I see you again?"

Larissa lowered her eyes. "Why, Mr. Smith, you must be at least fifteen years older than I am. Besides, you appear to be a married man." She scrutinized the wedding band on his left hand.

"Only wanted to make sure that your ankle is all right."

"Yes, you're concerned about *my ankle*." She smiled demurely. "Thanks for taking such good care of me, but we must be off. We also have an appointment, don't we, Austin?"

"Right, I'd almost forgotten. Shall I bring my car up so you won't have to walk too far on your sore foot?" Austin tried not to roll her eyes.

"Please, and then Mr. Smith and I can have a little chat," Larissa said. "Can you wait with me, Darrel?"

His answering smirk was enormous. "I'll have to see about the senator's car, but I'll stay with you, so long as your friend doesn't take too long."

"I'll hurry," said Austin. God forbid Darrel or the senator had to wait a moment longer than necessary. Austin stomped off to the parking lot.

Could Darrel be the killer? What a pleasing outcome that would be. She'd taken an instant dislike to him and suspected he'd done horrible deeds, even if those didn't include murder.

Still, she wouldn't be astonished if he had killed Reg. Never mind about the motive. She had a hunch, just a hunch.

CHAPTER SIXTEEN

Austin drove her Beetle under the hotel's porte cochère. Darrel Smith ushered Larissa outside and helped her into the car as if she were a porcelain figurine apt to break if handled roughly. Once he shut the door, Austin gunned the engine and roared onto York Street, heading north. She didn't want to show how irked she was, so she drove in silence.

"That went well, didn't it?" Larissa smoothed her skirt over her knees and settled deeper into the passenger seat. The coquette had vanished. "Men can be so stupid around women, and that makes them malleable. If I shocked you, I'm sorry. I play the helpless female when it's necessary."

"You didn't shock me."

Larissa looked sideways at Austin. "Oh, yeah?"

"Hmm, maybe a little." Austin barely suppressed a smile.

"Look, I'll explain something. I watched my aunt enthrall men for years, saw how easily she manipulated them, and learned how to do the same. It's not something I'm necessarily proud of, but it works. I try to keep it down to once a week."

Austin looked at her in horror. "Once a wee—"

"I'm kidding. Once a month, tops."

Austin couldn't help but laugh. "Enough of your damsel-in-distress stuff now. Let's get down to business and figure out what we'll do next."

"Right on." Larissa pumped her small fist in the air. "Okay, here's what we have so far. We confirmed the senator's aide was in

Toronto, looking for Reg right before he died."

"And we learned Darrel is a braggart, just like Reg. Darrel's also dishonest. His presence here at the time of the murder seems significant."

"He came on to me while you were getting the car. If we'd passed through a dark place, he would've put a hand up my skirt. Although, just because a married man acts like an ass, that doesn't mean he's a killer. "

"I suppose not," Austin admitted, "but here's an odd coincidence. The senator's son was the only guy who ever tried anything like that with me. Maybe the senator promotes that kind of thing." She'd hold the details of Reg's behavior at the party for another time. "What's your opinion of the senator?" she asked instead. Larissa must be an expert on men, something Austin never claimed or aspired to be.

"Oh, the senator doesn't seem so bad, better than Darrel anyway. Of course, a snake would be better too. However, Simpson doesn't act much like a grieving father." Larissa tapped her fingers on the door handle. "He's too brusque and business-like. I figure something besides his son's death could be bothering him."

"What will happen if the senator finds out who I am? I started to tell him but—"

"I saw that," Larissa said. "But it was worth the risk not to confess why we were in the hotel." She bit her lip and looked thoughtful. "Why didn't they ask what we were doing at the hotel in the first place?"

"You threw them off their game, Larissa. They weren't thinking straight near you."

"Hey, don't give me that. Maybe *you* had them flustered. You're not a homely old cow."

Austin flinched, remembering how her mother always criticized her appearance. "Maybe not, but you're breathtaking."

"I repeat—you don't realize how attractive you are. Don't run yourself down." Larissa fluffed her long brown hair with an exaggerated gesture. "As for my looks, I'll use whatever I've got to help find Reg's killer. I don't know your husband, but if you loved David enough to marry him, then he cannot be the murderer."

"Thanks. That's how I feel too." Austin's eyes blurred with tears, and she wiped at them with the back of one hand, keeping the other on the steering wheel. "It's so frustrating. I can't see him until he's completely processed into the prison system. I can't even call him." Better not imagine what he was doing right now in his cold and lonely cell. Instead, she focused on her driving and made an expert maneuver around a double-parked car.

"Where're we going next?" Larissa asked.

"To the church. We've got time before my appointment with McKinnon."

"Why go back there?"

"To talk to the janitor—although Mrs. Duncan said he's been sick ever since the murder. I'm hoping he'll be there. He could shed light on what went on at the church the night Reg died."

"I doubt that. If he's as feeble as you say, then his powers of observation won't be good."

"I suppose so, but my motto is 'leave no stone unturned.' He may be an old rock, but he's worth picking up and turning over."

When Austin stopped at the traffic light at King Street, Larissa waved her hand and pointed. "Turn left here. King goes over to Bathurst. Then all you do is drive north."

While Austin made the turn, she returned to a subject that had fired her curiosity. "Can we get back to your aunt? You made her sound like a femme fatale."

"Gosh, yes. She gloried in the role." Larissa's voice tightened, and she cleared her throat. "When I was only nine, Mama passed away, and then Aunt April began coming over so often that Papa said she was underfoot. They argued, but she insisted I needed a woman's influence. Young as I was, I still saw how different she was from my mother. Mama was beautiful but never traded on it. My aunt was a knockout and played on her looks every day of her life."

Larissa examined her dainty pink hands, turning them over and over in her lap. "Sometimes Aunt April disgusted me, but she fascinated me just as often. She maneuvered men so easily; her behavior was as natural as a river's flow. She never did anything for herself that a man could do for her."

"Did her charms work on your father?"

"Charms, hah." Larissa snorted. "You're talking like a character in a nineteenth-century novel. Papa had seen plenty of Russian women as strong and competent as any man. He knows we can take care of ourselves. He was never taken in by my aunt, and she respected him for that."

"Is she still around? She sounds like quite a character."

"Sadly, no. She died two years ago, right after I graduated from high school. She helped me prepare for my graduation parties but not long after that, she had a stroke and died."

Larissa paused, then drew out her next words slowly. "You probably can't tell, Austin, but I don't get along with most girls my age. It's unusual that I took to you so fast. Since my aunt died, I've had Papa and my studies, and that's about it."

She glanced over at Austin and then ducked her head shyly. "Aunt April always said what fun we'd have planning my wedding. Now maybe you can help me, when the time comes, eh?"

Austin was so overcome by Larissa's sweetness that she lost her concentration, letting the car sit at a stop sign while she and her new friend beamed at each other. Then she spotted, in the rear-view mirror, an impatient driver glaring at her. He hadn't honked his horn, though. Simply glared.

Only in Canada.

The church office was locked when they tried the door.

Larissa looked at her watch. "It's almost noon. Maybe everyone's at lunch."

Austin stared down the deserted hallway and saw Reg's corpse in her mind's eye. Her knees wobbled, and her voice wavered.

"Maybe we're too, too…"

"Are you okay?"

"It's nothing really." She swallowed hard. "I'm just having a little flashback. It's tough for me to be here again." In only five days Austin's life had flipped not only upside-down, but also backwards and sideways and inside out. All but one area of her life suffered. Now she had a friend, someone to talk to while her husband languished in jail. Poor David. She had to find the killer and do it fast.

Larissa placed her hands on her hips and squinted at the dark empty hall. "Okay, so where's your janitor? What'd you say his name is?"

"Ferguson. Can't recall his first name."

They walked farther down the hall and, as they walked, gradually became aware of a slapping sound.

"What's the weird noise?" Larissa asked.

"Not sure, but if it's Mr. Ferguson with his trusty mop, we need to be careful not to scare him. He's so old that he could have a heart attack on the spot."

They continued down the hall. When they turned a corner, they saw a man mopping the floor. He wore bedroom slippers, torn trousers, and a frayed cardigan. Austin's heart went out to the old janitor. He ought to be tucked up at home in a recliner, covered by an afghan, rather than pushing around a rag mop.

"Mr. Ferguson?" she called.

The man glanced at the girls and muttered something. His mopping never stopped.

They slowly walked up to him. "Can we talk to you, sir?" Austin said. "Can you stop for a minute?"

Slap slap. He kept mopping. *Slap slap.* The rhythm of the noise notched Austin's nerves up higher. She'd had no idea she was so strung out.

"Please, can you help us?" Larissa asked.

He looked up briefly but kept mopping. *Slap slap.*

Austin edged forward and touched his arm with caution. "I'm the one who found the body last week." She waited, hoping her words would have an effect. They did, but not what she'd expected.

The man threw down his mop and sank to the wet floor. He buried his head in his hands, moaned, and rocked back and forth.

Austin crouched beside him and placed her hand on his shoulder. He didn't shrink from her touch—a good sign. After a moment, she said, "Why don't we go to the kitchen and have some tea?" Austin glanced at Larissa and jerked her head toward the kitchen.

Larissa took the hint. She dashed off down the hall and disappeared from sight.

Austin stayed with Mr. Ferguson, waiting for him to calm down. Five minutes passed before he quieted. She helped him to his feet, he grabbed his mop, and together they shuffled toward the kitchen. Mr. Ferguson headed to a part of the large room that held tables and chairs. Relief washed over her when they avoided the area where she'd found the body.

By that time, Larissa had put a kettle of water on the stove to boil, although she was still opening drawers and looking for the tea. "Mr. Ferguson, do you know where the tea is kept?"

Ignoring her, the janitor leaned on his mop and sank onto a chair, breathing hard. He turned to Austin, appearing to recognize her for the first time. "I remember you." His voice shook. "You brought the blueberry muffins." He dropped his head and mumbled. "Smashed. They were smashed."

Austin was afraid he would get upset again. Instead, he carefully laid his mop beside the table and folded his hands in his lap. He looked like an obedient schoolboy. When the kettle whistled, he smiled. "Me mum makes tea after we finish our chores. Tea is nice."

Austin took a seat beside him. "Mr. Ferguson, this is my friend Larissa." Austin nodded in her direction. "She's half Russian, so she drinks her tea with jam. Did you know Russians do that?"

He glanced at Larissa and then turned back to Austin. "Your friend is a pretty little thing. Reminds me of my sweetheart, but last week she was killed in the Blitz."

The girls exchanged surprised looks, and an uneasy pause followed. Finally, Larissa opened her hand. "Look, I found the tea, and now we're all set."

Austin regained her composure. "I'm so sorry for your loss, Mr. Ferguson."

"I am sad, yes, I am." He blinked, then shut his eyes. When he opened them, he appeared to be in a trance, and his tone was hushed. "I went off to war, you see, in the other invasion, the one no one remembers. Everyone knows about D-Day, but our battles in Italy are just as hard and lasting longer." His gnarled fingers gripped a spoon. "The Germans left their best men here after the Italians quit. We've lost more men and had more casualties than anyplace else. Everybody in me unit is dead. Everybody but me." He gulped and rubbed his throat.

Larissa said, "But the Russian front was—"

Austin cut her off. "How did you—how have you—survived?" He was recounting his war experiences as if they were just unfolding and didn't seem to know the difference. She made a quick mental calculation and was flabbergasted to figure out his age was nowhere near eighty. More like mid-fifties. Life must have exhausted him, making him look ancient. Then again, anyone over forty seemed ancient to her. Her heart went out to the old man.

"Guess my number's not up," he said. "There's no rhyme or reason on a battlefield, lassie. We landed on the beach at Salerno in forty-three. A fellow in a tank didn't see me, ran right over me, squashed me into the sand. When the tank rolled on, I got up and kept fighting. We always keep fighting."

Larissa carried the teapot to the table. "My father fought his way out of Russia but won't talk about it. He says I'm too young for his stories."

Mr. Ferguson's face contorted. "Some memories should stay buried."

The ticking of the kitchen clock filled the room as Larissa poured three cups of tea. When a minute passed, a clock hand moved and clinked.

Mr. Ferguson swirled sugar into his tea. "Me son went to Korea and never left." When he picked up his cup, his hand shook. "Me mum brought me to Canada after the Great War, after me dad died in the trenches. She thought Canada would be safe." He paused, staring into his cup. "She was wrong."

"Do you want to talk about your son?" Austin spoke quietly, hardly above a whisper.

He began to recite as if reading from a list. "Five hundred Canadians died in the Korean War. Only five hundred. Me son had just turned twenty. I tried to stop him, but he wanted to follow in my footsteps. I couldn't make him see what war was like." He swallowed a sob. "At his age, you don't listen. No one listens. No one understands." He bent his head and rocked back and forth.

"Did you see the body of the dead boy, here in the kitchen?" Austin asked.

Larissa said, "I don't think you should—"

Austin persisted. "I'd never seen a dead body before, all bloody like that. I can't imagine seeing hundreds, even thousands of bodies. You must remember all that."

"I do. I remember. I remember all of them." Mr. Ferguson covered his face with his hands, and his voice escaped from between his fingers. "But I don't remember a body in this kitchen."

Austin was confused and had no idea what to say next. Even Larissa seemed at a loss for words. The girls drank their tea, the old man moaned, and the kitchen clock kept ticking.

CHAPTER SEVENTEEN

Austin was relieved to hear the clack of heels in the hallway.

Mrs. Duncan bustled into the kitchen and placed a package on the counter. She turned to the three tea drinkers. "May I join you, or is this a private party?"

Austin sprang to her feet. "I'm so glad to see you, Mrs. Duncan. Mr. Ferguson's been telling us—my friend Larissa and me—about his experiences during the war. I'm afraid he's a bit upset." She prayed the woman had skills she lacked, those to pull the old man out of his tailspin into sorrow.

Mrs. Duncan settled her comfortable bulk onto a chair, untied a scarf from her head, and smoothed her curly gray hair. "He always cheers up when he has one of my biscuits." She smiled at him, and Mr. Ferguson looked back at her, blinked, and started a monotonous hum.

She levered herself to her feet. "Indeed, this situation demands a good biscuit. I'll be right back."

Mr. Ferguson leapt out of his chair. When it scraped across the floor with a squeal, Austin and Larissa both jumped.

"Demands it. Demands it," he yelled. "The floor demands it. The floor is bloody. The stains won't come out."

He grabbed his mop and ran from the room. Soon slapping sounds once again echoed through the hallways.

His sudden speed and agility were confounding, but before Austin could say anything to Larissa, Mrs. Duncan returned, carrying her cookie tin. She set it on the table, dusted off her hands, and sank back onto her chair. Mr. Ferguson's absence didn't appear to surprise her.

"You wouldn't know it to look at him, but he's only sixty years old." She shook her head sadly. "Last week's murder shook his fragile hold on sanity. The doctor told his wife that it revived wartime memories and made them real again."

Talk about sanity. Austin was still reeling from the discovery that the old janitor wasn't all that old after all. "When he talked about serving in World War Two, he spoke as if it were happening right now."

"He told us about his son's death in Korea too," Larissa said.

"And he mentioned the London Blitz like it was last week," Austin added, "yet he denied knowing anything about the murder that really happened here last week."

"That dear man has been terribly disoriented since then," Mrs. Duncan said. "When the police interviewed him, all he could talk about was losing his friends in the Italian campaign. His mind's never really clear. He has good days and bad days, but his bad ones were never this awful before."

"He's only sixty?" Larissa said. "He looks ancient. I hope he has other children besides the lost son."

"That was their only child. His wife is a difficult woman to…well, to know. She often drops by, and we share recipes. Their lives have been grim since their son died, and that was fifteen years ago." Mrs. Duncan poured more tea. She got milk from the refrigerator and added some to her cup.

While she stirred her tea, she resumed her story. "His wife also looks older than her years." Mrs. Duncan ran a hand through her curls, making them bounce. "Gertrude Ferguson worries about her husband all the time, but she's a strong woman and seems able to withstand anything. While he was out sick, she stopped in to get his paycheck and talked about their problems. Reverend Baxter feels sorry for them and insists on keeping Mr. Ferguson on as long as he's willing. Mrs. Ferguson agrees her husband's better working here than staying home. All he does there is sit in his rocking chair, which drives her crazy. She's such a brisk, take-charge type, but I do feel bad for her." Mrs. Duncan played with a bracelet on her arm. "I feel so bad for both of them."

"Damn it." Larissa's cry astonished Austin. "When will there be women leaders who'll stop these dumb wars? War is nothing but senseless waste and tragedy." Larissa banged her fist on the table. Her hand was so petite that the effect was humorous.

"How old are you, Larissa, if I may ask?" The look Mrs. Duncan gave her was soft and compassionate.

"I'm twenty, old enough to know a few things. I know if women were in power, we'd avoid war. We'd keep our sons from running off to fight."

"I'd like to agree but can't. Human nature never changes. There have always been wars, and there always will be."

"But that would change if women led their nations. That hasn't happened yet, but it will someday."

Austin had never thought about stopping all wars and certainly had no idea if female leaders were the answer. She'd give the notion some thought, just as soon as David got out of jail. Right now all her brain power had to work on that.

Moving their conversation back on track, she said, "Do you think the war in Vietnam is related to Reg's murder? I mean, besides the fact that David and Reg both opposed the war. That's not quite the same thing, though."

"Where are you going with this?" Larissa said.

"I'm not sure." Austin spoke slowly, weighing her words. "We're running up against the subject of war and old soldiers, and if we factor in Senator Simpson's war heroism or lack thereof, well, there we are again. We're back to talking about more war."

Mrs. Duncan removed the lid of the cookie container. "I fear your theories are all way beyond me." She handed the tin to Larissa. "But please have more biscuits, dearies. If you're hunting for a killer, then you'll have to keep your strength up." She beamed sweetly. "I assume that's what you will end up doing."

Austin returned her smile. "I like your reasoning." She tasted an oatmeal cookie and almost smacked her lips. "Gosh, this is as good as your shortbread. Could I maybe get both recipes?"

"I'll bring them in tomorrow. You can pick them up any time."

Austin finished her cookie and took another. "Have you thought of anything else I should know, Mrs. Duncan, anything new since I was here before? We need more facts if we're going to get my husband out of jail."

"Well, goodness me, something did come up after you left. If only I could recall what it was. I'm sorry, but my memory isn't what it used to be."

Larissa said, "We were just downtown at the Royal York Hotel, where we ran into Senator Simpson and his aide. We thought maybe—"

Mrs. Duncan snapped her fingers. "Sorry to interrupt, but I need to say this before I forget again."

"Something about the senator?" Austin asked.

"About his aide. What's his name? Sam Slick?"

Larissa giggled. "Darrel Smith, actually, but Slick does fit." She helped herself to another cookie.

"Right, that's it. Thank you, dear," Mrs. Duncan said. "Darrel Smith dropped by yesterday. Said he was on a fact-finding mission for the senator. That's when I realized I'd seen him before."

Austin sat forward, and a trill of nerves ran down her back. "You remember when?"

"Last week, the afternoon of the murder." Mrs. Duncan narrowed her eyes in concentration. "It was Halloween."

"I *knew* he was a bad guy," Austin said, looking at Larissa. "What was Darrel up to, Mrs. Duncan?"

"Not sure," she replied, "but I *thought* he was waiting for the meeting to begin."

"What meeting?" Larissa asked.

"The one against the war, of course. In jeans and sloppy shirt, he looked like all the other draft resisters, but his hair is short, and he doesn't have a beard. I noticed him because he was neater than the rest. Yesterday he looked even more different in his navy blue suit."

"Did he say anything that suggested he'd been here before?" Austin asked.

"He didn't. He did mention, though, that he and the senator flew here after they learned of the murder." Mrs. Duncan drank more tea. "He looked familiar yesterday, but I couldn't remember where I'd seen him until after he'd left." She beamed. "My memory may take longer than it used to, but eventually it all comes to the surface."

Austin rubbed her forehead and blinked her eyes. "When the anti-war meeting began last week, were you still here, Mrs. Duncan?"

"I left around five, right before it started. Some of the young men always arrive early. They like to hang around and talk, and that's what they were doing when I left."

"What was Darrel doing then?" Larissa said.

"I remember him standing at the water cooler. He was by himself, dear. I'm sure of that."

"Sounds like Darrel Smith tried to see Reg last week." Austin drummed her fingers on the table. "Pete told me that Reg believed his family had no idea he was here in Toronto." An idea hit her with such force that she bounced in her chair. "Oh good heavens!"

"What? What?" Larissa cried.

"*Darrel Smith.* That didn't sink in earlier." Austin's voice rose. "His initials are *D S*, just like David's." Her voice slid into a whisper. "But I can't tell McKinnon that. I'd have to confess what we were up to when we cornered the senator."

"Will you please explain what you're talking about?" Larissa sounded whiney.

"I'm confused too," Mrs. Duncan said.

"Just thinking out loud. Sorry." "Austin turned to Larissa and said softly, "Tell you later." Then louder, "I wonder if Darrel actually saw Reg before he died."

"That's a good question," Larissa said. "Want to bet we can figure it out?"

"Now, girls," Mrs. Duncan said, "be careful. One murder is more than enough. Besides, I don't understand why you can't just let the police handle this."

"My husband is in jail, and the police show no interest in hunting for another suspect."

"But that's not right." Mrs. Duncan's face grew red, and she bristled with righteous anger.

"That's why we're doing our own digging," Larissa said.

Mrs. Duncan frowned and clasped her arms across her chest. "I see why you want to get involved, but your enthusiasm makes me anxious."

Austin brushed cookie crumbs off her hands and stood. "Then you'll be glad to hear that after we leave here, we're going straight to the police station to tell DS McKinnon everything we've learned."

"That makes me feel better, but take care, girls."

"We will," Austin said.

"We promise." Larissa placed her hand on her heart.

They said their goodbyes and left the church. Once outside, however, Austin realized she'd forgotten to leave her contact information. She dashed back inside, found Mrs. Duncan in the office, and wrote down an address and phone number on a slip of paper. "If you think of anything else, call me at Larissa's house. I don't feel safe staying at my apartment with all that's going on."

"I don't blame you one bit, dear." Mrs. Duncan stuck the paper to a bulletin board with a thumbtack and admired her handiwork. "Reverend Baxter says my organizational skills really help him. You might have made out that he's a little untidy." She turned and eyed Austin's jacket. "If you don't wear heavier clothes, you'll catch your death of cold. And get a toque, dear. It'll keep you warm."

"A what?"

"A toque. You know—a knit hat. Most of your body's warmth escapes from the top of your head unless it's covered up. You can't live here without a toque."

Curses, Austin thought. *I don't want to live in Canada, and I don't want a toque.* Aloud, she said, "I'll get one, but it'll have to wait until this calamity gets sorted out."

"Very good, dear. Now go on with you." She made a scooting motion. "Your husband needs rescuing."

Happy to obey, Austin rushed out and rejoined Larissa in the Beetle.

As they pulled onto the street, Larissa said, "I'm glad you've got a car. It saves so much time."

"David would just die if he knew I was driving it every day."

Larissa made a face. "You need to drop that expression. It's not appropriate right now."

"You're right." Austin chewed her lip. "Sometimes I forget how my life's changed. It had better change back. And soon."

And to herself she added, *I have to march into a foreign police headquarters, and the mere idea scares me. Last year at my wedding, whoever could've predicted this would land on my to-do list one day?"*

CHAPTER EIGHTEEN

While Austin parked the car near police headquarters, she began to hum.

Larissa looked at her quizzically. "What's that?"

"A Dylan song." Austin mimed strumming a guitar. "When I'm uptight and my mind's going in circles, I try to figure out what one of his songs means. His lyrics are impenetrable, but they haunt me anyway. This one, 'All Along the Watchtower,' starts with two riders outside in the howling wind."

"Wow, sounds ominous." Larissa paused and then spoke softly. "Bet I know why it popped into your head. We're the two riders, and can't you feel the winds of danger howling around us?"

Austin's eyes opened wide. "Oh gosh, maybe so."

Larissa continued, "I don't know much about Dylan. I'm into the Beatles myself."

"Everybody back home likes them, but Dylan's my guy. I learned to play the guitar just for his songs, but I had to leave it in Texas. Only so much can fit into a Beetle. " Austin twisted to face Larissa. "Look, I've simply got to say this. What we're doing could land us in real trouble, just like Mrs. Duncan said. You shouldn't put yourself in danger for me. After all, we've just met."

"But doesn't it feel like we've known each other forever? We're soul sisters."

"We're the wrong color for soul sisters," Austin said with a wry laugh. "Anyway, I know what you mean, and that's precisely why I can't be responsible for getting you hurt."

"Papa and I *want* to help you. You're all alone and battling injustice. That's an opportunity that doesn't come along every day." Larissa punched Austin playfully on her arm.

"Battling injustice? You make me sound like Wonder Woman."

"You're more powerful than a senator, faster than a VW Beetle, able to leap tall church towers in a single bound."

Austin choked. "That's enough. Seriously, though, remember you can drop out anytime."

"All right, but it ain't never gonna happen."

Detective Sergeant McKinnon wasn't free to meet with Austin yet, so an officer showed her and Larissa into a waiting room where they sat and thumbed through research publications about Canadian law enforcement. Austin concentrated on finding how-to tips on catching criminals. When approaching footsteps broke her concentration, she looked up and saw a strapping young policeman walk up to Larissa.

"Would you like something to drink?" he said. "Our coffee's really not bad, eh."

Larissa merely gave a half smile, reminiscent of the Mona Lisa, and shook her head. This appeared to be enough to enchant the young cop, who left looking dazed. In the next few minutes several more policemen passed, each turning toward Larissa the way a sunflower turns to face the sun.

Austin laughed softly.

"What's so funny?" Larissa said.

"You're going to cause a traffic jam. I've never seen anything like your ability to attract men, yet you don't seem to care, or even notice, for that matter."

An officer approached. "I bet you're Austin Starr, eh?" He looked hopefully at Larissa.

Austin stood. "Sorry to disappoint you, but I'm Austin." She tried to hide her irritation at the way he, like so many Canadians, added "eh" to the end of his sentences. Then she shook off the irritation. She knew she was in trouble when such a piddling thing set her teeth on edge.

"I'll wait here for you," Larissa said. "It's better if you see McKinnon alone."

"Only if you're sure."

"Go ahead, scram." Larissa waved her away.

And so Austin left her friend behind, confident in Larissa's ability to cope with all the smiles, coffee, and reading material the policemen were sure to offer. Austin imagined them tripping over each other, spilling drinks, and dropping magazines in their zeal to snare Larissa's favor.

DS McKinnon was on the phone when Austin entered his office. While he finished his conversation, she watched him intently. His face was drawn, his tie loose. His tweed jacket lay rumpled across a chair and dangled half on the floor.

When he hung up the phone, he got straight to the point. "Why are you here again so soon? Has something happened?"

"There's been a new development." Austin passed the anonymous note across the desk. "This was in my mailbox yesterday. Here, I've brought the envelope it came in too."

"I told you not to interfere in police business." The words exploded from his mouth. "What have you been up to? More to the point, what have you done to provoke this response?"

"Don't you see? This note means that you don't have Reg Simpson's killer in custody." *Just as I keep telling you.* Gosh, kind and temperate DS McKinnon was awfully crotchety today.

"That's possible, but you didn't answer my question. What've you been up to?"

"Not much. I went to the church to talk to the janitor, who's just tragic. I feel so sorry for him. Do you know he lost a son in the Korean War?" She was afraid to tell McKinnon she'd seen Senator Simpson at the Royal York, doubting he'd buy her explanation of how that happened, ostensibly by accident. But if she didn't tell him

135

she talked to the senator and McKinnon found out later, then he'd be furious. She feared losing his goodwill and wished she'd discussed this dilemma with Larissa.

"And what else?" McKinnon pursed his lips and eyed her with suspicion.

"After I received that note, I didn't feel safe in my apartment anymore. I'm staying with friends now. Dr. Klimenko and his daughter have taken me in."

"A sensible thing to do." He smiled for the first time.

Vast relief washed over her. Besides needing his help, she actually liked this man. In fact, she thought of him as her own personal policeman.

"One other thing I must tell you." But she didn't know exactly how to say it.

"Don't tell me you've done something really stupid. I've had a bad day, and that would be the last straw." He shoved his glasses on top of his head, forcing clumps of hair straight up.

Austin tipped her head to avoid looking at him, afraid she might giggle at his silly hairdo. "While I was at the church this morning," she said, "I talked to the secretary, Mrs. Duncan. She mentioned that Senator Simpson's in town. His aide, Darrel Smith, dropped by the church yesterday and was asking questions."

"So? Nothing wrong with that."

"But wait, sir, I'm not finished. Mrs. Duncan says Darrel was at the church before, last week, the day of the murder. Darrel was hanging around, waiting for the anti-war meeting when Mrs. Duncan left." Austin saw that McKinnon was ready to interrupt and rushed on. "Moreover, when Darrel saw Mrs. Duncan yesterday, he said he and the senator had only just arrived in Toronto. He alleged they came up here because of the murder. Now, honestly, don't you find that suspicious?" She sat back in her chair and allowed herself a smile of triumph.

"Let's get this straight," McKinnon said. "You're implying the senator's aide killed his boss's son. What's more, you want us to pursue Darrel Smith as a suspect. Did I get that right?"

"It's a reasonable line of inquiry."

He cocked his head. "Have you been reading our law enforcement journals in the lounge?"

Austin's mouth dropped open. "Look, I know more than you think. Have you met this aide, Darrel Smith? He's a real sleaze-bucket."

"What?"

Too late, Austin saw her error. "Well anyway, that's what my friend Larissa says. She happened to run into him."

"And just where did she *happen* to run into him, by total coincidence, no doubt?"

"I don't remember."

A loud puff of breath escaped from McKinnon's mouth. He closed his eyes. "You and your little friend were bothering the senator, weren't you?"

With great vigor, Austin shook her head. Noticing that the policeman's eyes were still closed, she said, "Not really, uh, sir."

McKinnon's eyes opened, and he glared at Austin. "If I find out that you were annoying the senator, young lady, then I will—"

"Sir, Larissa had to meet her aunt at the Royal York. I went along, and we ran into the senator."

"Hogwash." He stood and began pacing. "I should've laid down the law before. Do you know that Prime Minister Trudeau takes the senator's calls?" He whirled around to face Austin. "If you mess up this case, then my head will roll. Do you understand?"

Although shaken by his vehemence, Austin stood her ground. "Yes, sir, I do understand. But if you mess up this case, my husband could go to prison." Austin gasped, astounded at what she'd said. But she wouldn't take the words back. And when McKinnon only raised a brow at her outburst, she said, "And you haven't met Larissa. Men fall all over themselves when they see her. As a matter of fact, she's right outside, where your colleagues are finding every excuse to meet her." Austin hoped Larissa's attractiveness would dull McKinnon's senses, although he'd probably be the only man alive able to function rationally around her.

He held up his hand. "Stop, please stop. That's beside the point. Does Senator Simpson know you're related to his son's killer?"

"David did not kill Reg!"

"Let me rephrase that. Does the senator know who you are?"

"No."

McKinnon's shoulders sagged. "That's a small mercy. Now please, Austin, I beg you, stay out of my investigation. You realize that it's mine and not yours, don't you?"

"Yes, sir."

"And don't you forget it." He sighed loudly. "Now, where were we?" He glanced down at the cryptic typed note. He picked it up and brandished it in Austin's direction. "We'll analyze this to see if we can learn anything. It'll be a miracle if it holds any clues."

"But look at how the letter *O* smudged each time it was typed," she said. "Some typewriter out there makes that smudge consistently."

"I know, and our technicians will figure out the kind of machine that made the note. I rely on experts, and you must do the same. Leave these matters to us." He took the glasses off his head and tossed them on his desk, then rubbed the bridge of his nose.

"Look," he said, "I admire your spunk and determination to clear your husband's name. In fact, I wish some of my subordinates showed as much resourcefulness and courage as you do."

He paused to pick up his glasses and place them back on his head, allowing Austin a brief moment to bask in his praise.

Then he continued. "But in your zeal to get your husband out of jail, remember there are other elements to this situation, ones you appear to overlook. Perhaps I expect too much of you, since you are only, what, twenty-one or twenty-two?"

"Twenty-two, but I—"

"Let me finish." He began to pace again. "Sometimes matters

are too delicate to describe, especially when you have high government officials from two different nations involved. I can only hint at this complication, but I'm sure that if you ponder this after you leave headquarters, you'll understand what I'm trying to say."

"I do and I—"

"That's enough. I'm done. Now, if you've nothing else new to tell me from all your amateur sleuthing, then I have a job to do." He picked up a pile of papers and restacked them, then heaved a massive sigh.

"Yes, we're done." Austin felt like a whipped dog. If she'd had a tail, she would've tucked it between her legs. Instead, she rose and walked to the door, then paused and turned to face him. "I'm sorry I made your hard day worse."

"Apology accepted. Now go back to university and quit playing at cops and robbers." He made a pretend gun out of his fingers, pointed it at her, and winked.

He winked at me. A strong desire to hug DS McKinnon swept over Austin.

CHAPTER NINETEEN

After leaving police headquarters, Austin and Larissa spent the rest of the afternoon in the library at U of T. Feeling overwhelmed, Austin needed quiet time for contemplation. Had they made progress in finding Reg's killer? She couldn't be sure. Her quest seemed even less attainable when the enormity of the undertaking hit her.

McKinnon's warning crept into her thoughts, but she brushed aside his demand to quit playing the sleuth. No one could ever be as intent on proving David's innocence as she was. She would solve the mystery. *She would.* And then he could come back home to her and they would snuggle their way through the onslaught of the terrifying Canadian winter.

Neither girl talked on the drive back to the Klimenko home. When they entered the front hall, the professor emerged from his study, tapping a pen against the knuckles on his gloved hand. The pen made a hollow sound.

With wrinkled brow he regarded Austin solemnly. "A woman named Duncan called for you, Mrs. Starr. She wants you to meet her at the church tomorrow."

Austin froze. "Did she say why?"

"Only that she needed to talk in person. She sounded upset."

"This is so neat. I bet she remembered a big fat clue." Larissa hopped up and down with excitement, then stopped jumping and slumped against the wall. "Darn it. I can't go with you tomorrow, Austin. I've got a class I can't miss."

"Don't worry. I'll fill you in later." Austin slid off her jacket and brushed away a blotch of dirt. Where had it come from? Probably police headquarters or maybe the library. Certainly not the church. Mr. Ferguson kept everything there spotless.

Austin knew her mind was wandering; she was so tired. She snapped back into the moment to say, "I wonder what Mrs. Duncan wanted. What could be too important to say over the phone? I won't sleep tonight, trying to guess what she'll say."

"Whatever it is, she clearly thinks it is significant." Dr. Klimenko walked to a table and placed his pen carefully on it. Returning to them, he said, "Let's make dinner, and you can tell me about your day."

The girls followed him into the kitchen, happy to give lavish details about their interviews with the senator, his aide, the janitor, Mrs. Duncan, and DS McKinnon. Klimenko expressed amazement at the number of people who talked to them, but he showed no undue concern for their safety.

He might've acted disturbed, however, if Larissa had mentioned Darrel's lascivious behavior. News of his lechery surely would've angered the professor. Austin didn't envy him having a daughter who brought out the beast in men.

As she predicted, Austin spent a restless night. Visions of murder and military carnage danced in her head, only to be pushed aside by scenes of David huddled behind bars.

The day had finally dawned when she could visit him in jail. So what if she had to skip class? The jail's visiting hours started later in the day, leaving her time to meet with Mrs. Duncan before finally being able to see her husband.

In the bedroom mirror, Austin frowned at the dark circles under her eyes. She swabbed make-up over the blue skin and hoped that neither Mrs. Duncan nor David would spot how exhausted she was. David had more than he could handle and didn't need to worry about her. In fact, she didn't want anyone worrying about her when all efforts should center on getting him released from jail.

Her head sagged to her chest, and she shut her eyes. She was sorry the Klimenkos had already left for campus. She could've used some moral support before starting her day.

Outside in the nippy November air, decaying leaves lay in bunches, sodden with rain. She walked through heaps of them to get to her car and by the time she got inside the Beetle, her shoes were wet. Chilled from her feet up, she felt miserable.

And surprised at how much she missed having Larissa beside her.

Yesterday, Larissa's charm and energy had helped mask the growing negative bent of Austin's own thoughts. When she was by herself, Austin recognized how scared she was. Putting up a good front was easier when someone else was around. Alone in the car, she only heard her own thoughts, and they were not entertaining.

Austin switched on the radio, wanting loud music to drown out her worries. She punched the button to her favorite station, CHUM 1050. While the car warmed up, she listened to Paul McCartney advising Jude against carrying the whole world on his shoulders.

"Hey, Jude, I know how you feel," Austin lamented as she pulled away from the curb.

A riff about overcoming pain might be apt for her circumstances but didn't work to blast away her fears. Still, the interminable "na na na na" of the chorus sucked her in and held her mesmerized. By the time the lengthy song ended, she'd almost reached her destination.

Two blocks south of the church, however, her car came to a standstill. Getting stuck in traffic always bored her, so Austin took the opportunity to run through the rest of her pre-programmed buttons on the radio. After going through them three times, she observed that the traffic hadn't moved at all.

She turned off the radio, rolled her window down, and listened to sirens screaming past on a cross street. People rushed down the sidewalk toward the commotion. She asked a passerby what had happened and was told someone had been run over. Austin pulled into a parking space, left her car, and joined the throng walking north toward the accident. Not only was she anxious to meet Mrs. Duncan, but she had to confess, if only to herself, that she was also curious about what was causing the uproar.

Her height gave her an advantage; over people's heads she could see that police had barricaded the intersection of Lennox and Bathurst and were holding the crowd back. An ambulance waited nearby, and emergency workers prepared a stretcher.

The crowd gave a collective gasp when workers picked up a body from the pavement, placed it on the stretcher, and covered it with a blanket.

Austin caught the briefest glimpse of familiar curly gray hair. Her knees buckled, and she grabbed the arm of a man standing beside her.

"Are you all right, miss?" he asked.

"I think I know that woman," she said. "I must talk to the police."

"They won't let you anywhere near them. They're too busy," the man said. "Why don't you sit down over there? You don't want to fall down in this crowd, eh."

With the chatter of strangers sounding ghoulish in her ears, Austin scrambled over to an empty storefront. She leaned on the door for a moment and then sagged to the step, grateful for the stability.

Her pounding brain felt too immense for her skull

Austin sat staring at the forest of legs planted in front of her as the crowd watched the police work the accident site. Part of Austin was glad that Larissa wasn't with her while another piece desperately wished for her presence. She speculated when her life would return to some semblance of normalcy—or if it ever would.

Austin willed herself to calm down. She breathed in and out

slowly. As her head cleared, she realized how awful her mid-section felt, slithery, as though frenzied minnows darted around inside her stomach. She stood, clutched her purse to her chest, and began to bulldoze her way through the crowd. When people grumbled at her pushing, she explained that she knew the victim.

She overheard two women talking.

One said, "The driver didn't even stop. That unfortunate lady worked at the church over there."

The second replied, "What's this world coming to?"

Others in the crowd muttered their agreement.

Austin stopped pushing forward. The stranger's words confirmed her fear that the victim was Mrs. Duncan. Instantly, other fears jostled Austin.

Two deaths on the same block within one week seemed suspiciously coincidental.

What if someone had run over her not by accident but on purpose? And if that were true, then Mrs. Duncan had been murdered, and her death could be tied to Reg's. Following that line of reasoning, Austin felt hope take hold.

No one could blame her husband for *this* murder. From his cell in the Don Jail, David did not cause a so-called hit-and-run accident.

Perhaps David was better off in jail. She was probably the one in danger, nosing around in someone else's business. How ironic that she'd left the supposed wildness of Texas for the purported tranquility of Toronto, only to find violence. Murder and mayhem. Homicide and havoc.

Austin needed to talk to the police, but officers at the scene were too busy. Some took statements from witnesses, and others engaged in crowd control. No one had time to listen to Austin's theories.

She crossed to the west side of Bathurst and managed to push her way inside the church, looking around for Reverend Baxter. Unable to find him, she reasoned that if he'd been in the church when the accident occurred, surely he'd have gone outside when he heard the uproar.

She stood beside Mrs. Duncan's desk and stared at her things. The cookie tin under the desk, a small make-up bag beside it. An umbrella. A pair of dress pumps reminding her that Mrs. Duncan had worn high heels each time she'd seen her.

Austin's eyes misted over as she recalled the woman's kindness. She sniffled, wiped away her tears, and continued scrutinizing the desk. Mimeographed church bulletins lay neatly stacked in Mrs. Duncan's in-basket. Who would type up the bulletin for next Sunday?

Austin fixed on a notepad with her name written on it. Startled, she seized the pad and saw the Klimenko telephone number. What had Mrs. Duncan needed to tell her? How would she ever find out now?

On the bulletin board beside the desk was tacked a card labeled "my shortbread recipe," but the slip of paper with Austin's address and phone number was no longer there. Perhaps Reverend Baxter had borrowed it for his own use. When she found nothing else of interest, Austin sat in Mrs. Duncan's chair and meditated on what to do next.

Despite DS McKinnon's demand that she stop sleuthing, she needed to tell him her theory about the hit-and-run. Austin rummaged through her messy purse and found the scrap of paper with McKinnon's phone number.

Footsteps sounded in the hall. She turned to glance at the door as Mr. Ferguson walked in, holding his ever-present mop. "What's going on? I was in the boiler room and kept hearing sirens. What's happening?"

Austin didn't know how to answer, not wanting to increase the wretched man's pain or send him flashing back to scenes of old bloodshed. Let the police tell him who the traffic victim was. She had more than enough to handle already.

"Someone was run over," she said, "and the police have put up barriers to keep the scene secure. I came in looking for Reverend Baxter." When Mr. Ferguson's expression didn't change, Austin guessed that her news didn't faze him.

He scratched his head and looked around the office. "The reverend went off to see someone in hospital. Mrs. Duncan was here a while ago, but she went out to buy tea. She's good about that." He paused and then added in what she assumed was an afterthought, "I hope no one was badly hurt."

Austin felt unable to elaborate on the accident and instead said, "Do you think Mrs. Duncan would mind if I borrowed her phone? My call won't be long."

"Of course she wouldn't mind, lassie. She'll be back soon, and you can stay and have tea with us again." His smile transformed his face, giving her an inkling of what he must've looked like as a handsome young soldier. "I enjoyed our talk the other day."

Austin lowered her head to hide her surprise and sorrow. "I enjoyed our conversation too." She looked up and managed to meet his kind eyes. "I'm a naturally curious person, Mr. Ferguson, and I like learning about people's lives. Forgive me if I ask too many questions."

"Not many young people care what happened in the past, Mrs. Starr. It's good you're interested. My son was like that. He's gone now, you know."

"I'm so sorry."

Every part of his face appeared to shrivel. One eye twitched, and he licked his lips. He seemed to consider saying something else about his son, but instead reached out to shake her hand. "I must say goodbye now. I've got work to do." Hugging his mop, he turned and shuffled into the hall.

Austin began to dial McKinnon's phone number. Halfway through, however, she put down the receiver, deciding she should stop and reflect before leaping into action. He'd been a bit put out when she'd taken her last theory to him; perhaps the detective sergeant would conclude that Mrs. Duncan's death was no accident without her help. Still, if she didn't talk to McKinnon, she did need to discuss this new death with someone.

Visiting David was next on her agenda. She'd tell him about the hit-and-run, and later she could tell the Klimenkos. That should suffice.

Austin tried to get up, but her legs were too weak to hold her. She collapsed back in the chair and then laid her head down. Her mind whirled. She'd just talked with someone who'd been run over by a tank, lived to tell the tale, and now exhibited craziness. Moreover, she was now sitting at the desk of a woman run down in the street. And all this after she stumbled upon a corpse just days ago. This was more reality than she could cope with after twenty-two years of coddled life.

One day she'd hunt down all the people who'd told her how stable and calm Canada was. Boy oh boy, did she have a thing or two to tell them. Regaining her pleasant existence in Texas seemed like an unattainable dream. Nevertheless, it was one she was bent on pursuing.

Kay Kendall

CHAPTER TWENTY

Austin slipped out of the church and into the crowd on the sidewalk. The crowd was smaller now, but little groups still gossiped about the accident. She threaded her way back to her parking space and was relieved to unlock the Beetle and crawl inside. After turning on the motor and checking her side mirror, she was overwhelmed by fatigue and sorrow and fear. She thought she'd pushed off the emotions in Mrs. Duncan's office, but after seeing the street, she lost it. She put her foot on the brake and her head on the steering wheel and wept.

"Don't bite off more than you can chew." Her grandmother's favorite axiom floated around the closed space. Well, it was too late now. Austin had indigestion from the full-course meal she had chosen—managing a new marriage, living in a foreign country, and now searching for a killer. Burdened with woes, stretched beyond her capacity, and intermittently nauseated, Austin realized she was in no condition to visit David. She wiped her eyes with the back of her hand.

But this was the first day he could have visitors, and she had to see him. Needed to see him. The wait had been too long already. Maybe after this first trip, future visits would be easier.

The jail was east of the Don River and the Don Valley Parkway. That area of Toronto was uncharted territory, but she assumed she could find her way. She opened the glove compartment, took out her map of the city, and plotted the route. After thirty minutes of driving, however, Austin was hopelessly

148

lost. She pulled into a gas station.

"This your first time visiting the Don, eh?" the gas jockey asked after he gave directions.

"Yes, first time."

"Nasty old place. I wouldn't go unless I really had to."

"My husband's there. I have to go."

The man scratched his chest and peered at her through dirty glasses. "Miserable bastard. The Don's overcrowded. The food's lousy, and the prisoners get hardly no time out of their cells. My cousin was there a while back, eh, back when two men was hanged for murder. Right there in the Don Jail."

Austin's stomach vibrated. She thanked the man for his help and raced away. She had planned to get a sandwich somewhere, but the idea of lunch sickened her now.

Following the man's directions, Austin found the Don Jail Roadway. With a growing sense of apprehension, she parked the car and walked up to the imposing entrance of the old building. A grotesque head of a man sneered down from his carved stone perch above the door, looking like the Norse god Thor, ready to hurl a thunderbolt for any infraction of the law.

She stumbled into the atrium, where the space soared several stories. Cast-iron snakes and dragons decorated the stairs with alarming effect. The place was like something from a Dickens novel. The association made her wince, but she kept moving forward, found a guard, and asked him how to visit an inmate.

"Lucky you came on a weekday, miss," he replied. "Our lines are real bad on weekends. Today you won't wait long to see your loved one, eh?"

Only fifteen minutes later, there he was—the brilliant mathematician, political activist, and love of her life. Dressed in prison overalls, wearing a grim expression, David sat behind thick glass. His beard was gone, and his hair was cut. Once shoulder-length, now it didn't even cover his ears. Austin was taken aback to find she missed his old hippie look.

David nodded as he picked up the telephone next to him. She tried to read his face, but his expression was exceptionally closed. She hesitated to pick up the receiver on her side of the glass. What was she going to say? She pasted a fake smile on her face, prepared to lie and lie and lie—to dish out cheer and cups full of hope to her husband when she had none for herself. She imagined bashing through the glass and falling into his arms, but that wasn't going to happen. A guard stood watch nearby.

"How are you?" How stupid. She could've kicked herself. She knew the answer.

"Hanging in, I guess. What choice do I have?" His fingers clenched the phone so hard they turned white. "I've missed you so much, babe."

"Oh, David, I can't sleep without you beside me. It's been hell not being able to see you or even call." No, no, she mustn't complain. She brightened her tone. "But I've been busy, working hard to get you free. Got to get you out of here and back home where you belong."

Painful emotions flickered across David's face, and he appeared to struggle for composure. "Been dealing with my lawyer? Something new on my case?"

"Nothing new from the police, and your lawyer isn't very active. I met with him once and exchanged a few calls, but that's it. Remember, he's from Legal Aid and not paid by us. You know what they say: you get what you pay for." She shook her head, trying to concentrate on the important issues. "But please, honey, how are you doing really? I've been so worried." Austin gazed around and observed how morose the other visitors looked. Her nose quivered at the smell of too much disinfectant. She sneezed.

"If I knew I'd get out soon, it wouldn't be so bad. Not knowing is hard, and being away from you and worrying about how you're doing…well, I feel guilty. You're alone somewhere that's not congenial. You only moved here for me, and now I can't be with you."

For once, David's words rushed out, crashing into each other. Austin had never heard him talk so fast.

"You'll be out soon." She managed a thin smile, trying to look chipper. Not her best acting effort.

"Don't know about that, but sure as hell hope you're right. You got an inside line to the Almighty?"

"Don't I wish." Her grin was so forced that it felt lopsided. "Actually, the minister at the United Church wants me to join his congregation. Can you believe it? As if I'd ever worship where I tripped over a corpse."

They brooded over that absurdity in silence.

"Something's been preying on my mind," Austin said at last, "ever since McKinnon took you away that horrific night."

David shifted in his chair. "Oh?"

"Remember when McKinnon said someone came forward and said he'd seen you at the church around the time of the murder?" This time it was Austin's turn to wiggle uncomfortably in her seat. "Well, I was wondering, how do you explain that?"

"I can't, can't do it. Wasn't there. I told you the truth. Someone is either mistaken or lying and trying to do me in. Maybe someone who really believes that I killed Reg." He shrugged his shoulders, and his posture sagged. "Can't explain it any better than that."

"Witnesses aren't always dependable, I guess. But I believe you. I do, David. Don't ever doubt that for one second, okay?"

His answering smile melted her soul into a puddle of mush. She wanted to smash through the stupid glass and kiss the daylights out of him. Now wouldn't that just frost that nasty guard watching from the corner?

For several moments Austin and David gazed longingly at each other. Finally, he broke the silence.

"I'd be doing a little better if only I had stuff to read. Can you bring books next time?"

"I'm so, so sorry. I didn't know what was allowed, so I came empty-handed."

"I've got nothing to do but brood. Do you know brooding's a great way to pass the time?" David passed his free hand over his face and scowled. "Now, tell me, who won the election?"

"I don't know. It slipped my mind, with all that's going on." She hung her head.

He gripped the edge of the table that separated them. "What's wrong with you, Austin? Don't you know how important this election is?"

She bit her tongue and calmed herself with an effort. "I'm worried about bigger things than the election, like getting you out of jail. Ask one of the guards. Somebody here will know who won."

David glanced at the guard and lowered his voice. "These numskulls only follow the hockey scores. And how can *you* get me out when my lawyer can't?"

Austin needed to change the subject so they wouldn't argue. She remembered the reporter who'd called and seized on him as a diversion. "Guess what?" she began. "A journalist wants to interview me about your case. A man from the *Star*. Somebody named Campbell."

David shot her a look that would've withered a head of lettuce. "Of course you refused. Right?"

"Of course. I only wanted to bring you up to date on everything that's gone down." When his facial features softened, she began detailing her efforts to find the killer, talking non-stop into the telephone. When she finished, David was silent. She wasn't sure if he looked impressed or not.

"Everything you've discovered is useful," he said at last. "If a piece of information doesn't rule something out, maybe it can rule something in. Good job, honey."

Austin flushed.

"But can you trust this professor and his daughter? You don't know them that well."

"David! With you bottled up here, I need support from

152

someone, somewhere. I flipped out when that anonymous note showed up in our mailbox."

"Don't get me wrong; I appreciate that you're looking for Reg's murderer. But I don't want you hurt."

David pressed his hand to the pane of glass, and she pressed hers back. They stayed that way for a long moment.

Other couples were doing the same thing. Displays of emotion seemed to soften the air. She thought about other women who'd sat at these tables during the past century, heartbroken to see their men incarcerated but proud of them for holding up, for not giving in to despair. Surely some of the men had been innocent, like David. The place could have inspired Dylan's song "Desolation Row."

"What're you thinking about?" David's face was pinched with worry.

"Thinking I'll come back tomorrow and bring some books. Maybe I'll even bring some good news." She reached into her purse and pulled out pencil and paper. "You've had plenty of time to remember everything you know about Reg. What are your theories about who killed him, given all I've told you?"

David thought the question over for a long time before answering, reverting to his usual pattern after a talking jag. Austin was used to this, but now it bothered her. If their feet hadn't been separated by a partition, she would have kicked him under the table and demanded that he hurry up.

Where was her patience today? She felt held together with bits of fraying string, about to fall apart any minute.

"I've thought about this a lot," David said in his slow, deliberate way, "and there's no obvious answer. The only idea I have seems farfetched. Actually, I have two ideas."

"Tell me, for heaven's sake, and I'll check them out." Austin was ashamed she sounded annoyed.

He looked up from examining his fingers when he heard her tone. "Easy. I'm getting to that."

"Sorry," she mumbled.

His expression grew tender. "I know this is hard on you too, Austin. You didn't sign up for this."

She was such a jerk. Now he was apologizing to her when it should be the other way around. "We'll muddle through this together. Don't worry."

A grin lit up his face. "Hey, aren't you the girl who always says that 'Worry' is her middle name?"

"Yeah, I know. Figured this place could use a few good jokes." They shared a true smile, and she relaxed.

"Ideas," he began. "First, find out where Pete was at the time of the murder."

"But Pete was Reg's best friend. Besides, I told you I already talked to him. He seemed really upset that Reg died."

"Naturally he acted upset, but maybe that's all it was, an act. Maybe even Pete got sick of Reg and his boasting. I know I was."

"Then I'll check Pete out again." She wrote "see Pete" at the top of her to-do list. "What else have you got?"

"I wondered about his main girlfriend, Dulcie."

"But she seems really devoted to him. And harmless. It can't be Dulcie."

"Why not? Reg always stepped out on her, so maybe she got tired of his philandering. I'll admit these aren't great ideas, but they're all I've got. There are no obvious suspects—other than me, I suppose." David tried to look jaunty but couldn't pull it off. Instead, he looked like a scared ten-year-old.

"Doesn't Darrel Smith need more scrutiny?"

"Yeah, although that's a tough one. His connection to the senator protects him." David stared hard at Austin. "You need to be careful there. Anyway, your friend McKinnon sounds like he's losing patience with you. You don't want him against us."

"Believe me, I know." The mere idea made her ill. "The church secretary could've helped me, but now she's dead and I'll never learn what she wanted to tell me. If I had a hundred bucks, I'd bet it all on her death being a murder. That was no ordinary hit-

and-run. I feel it in my bones, as my grandmother used to say."

He chuckled and shook his head. "You've brought a fresh perspective into this hellhole. I sure miss you, honey." His voice got husky, and he ducked his head.

Austin yearned to hold him, and her skin craved his touch.

"Good lord, David, I miss you so much my stomach hurts. Still, we've got to keep our thoughts positive. I'll be back tomorrow, and I promise to get you out of here if it's the last thing I do." He started to protest, but she cut him off. "Only kidding. I promise to be careful."

It was hard to leave without kissing him goodbye. As a substitute, Austin examined her husband through a glass nasty with smudged fingerprints and what could have been lipstick smears. He looked shrunken and scared and very ordinary. She might never have loved him as much as she did now. Emotions flooded her— care and compassion and simple worry.

There was no doubt that she loved him. This was her man, for better or worse. And she was more than ready to experience the *better* part any day now.

CHAPTER TWENTY-ONE

Austin left the stuffy, overheated jail expecting to rejoice in freedom and crisp air. Instead, a cold rain had whipped down from the north and blasted with damp force. Her jacket, adequate for Texas winters, was no match for autumn in Ontario.

She bent her head, plowed into the wind, and reached her car quickly, only to be slowed by her inability to find her car key. Torrents of rain poured down on her head as she clawed through her jam-packed purse. When items fell out and into puddles, she soundly cursed her luck. After minutes of frantic searching, Austin finally found her key, and then she reclaimed the fallen objects from the dirty rainwater swirling at her feet.

The odor of wet wool and the reek of the crowded jail entered the car with her, the stench clinging to her like bugs on flypaper. In her head, her mother's voice declared Austin looked like a wet dog.

She sat in the parking lot, watched the rain as it wept against the car windows, and pondered what to do next. Once again Lenin's infamous *chto delyat* demanded an answer. When she'd studied his political tract, she'd never dreamed his words would become her personal mantra. Repeating it now kept her from teetering on the brink of the abyss, from getting too close to real terror, the possibility of David's conviction for murder.

Whenever she put one foot in front of another, deciding with each step what was to be done, then her mind stayed focused and didn't whirl into the infinity of anxiety that loomed when she lost control. Honestly, she was doing the best she could possibly do.

Those books featuring Nancy Drew and Miss Marple had only taught her so much.

Despite the deluge outside, thoughts of the teenaged sleuth and the nosy spinster lifted her spirits. How would her skills compare to a teen with few resources and a woman with decades of life experience? Somewhere in the middle, she guessed. Which should be good enough. Her thinking grew rueful, however, when she remembered the CIA recruiter who'd promised adventure and intrigue. She'd passed all that up for marriage. How could she have known that safe choices could so easily prove deadly?

Was it only one year ago?

Look at what had become of her, how far she'd fallen. She didn't even know who'd won the American presidential election. That was unbelievable when once—most of her life, in fact—she'd been a current affairs maven. Now even her obsession with one of the candidates wasn't enough to keep her mind on the election.

She'd loathed Richard Nixon since she was six years old. During the first-ever televised presidential convention, when Nixon spoke, a miasma of slime slithered off the screen. Her dislike was compounded by the fact that she'd been dusting the living room for her mother. She abhorred dusting.

Ever since then, her personal sleaze-o-meter zoomed off the charts whenever she thought about Nixon, let alone saw him on television. His nickname suited him, although *Tricky Dick* didn't seem harsh enough to capture his true nature. Really, when she gave the subject more thought, she realized her whiplash-quick dislike of Nixon was akin to her instantaneous aversion to Darrel. Unable to point to particular characteristics that made her leap to those judgments, she was satisfied that the clichéd *snake oil salesman* covered both of them.

Would it matter to her own plight—or rather to David, since he was the one in jail—if the vile Nixon ended up beating Hubert Humphrey, the candidate of the Democratic Party?

No. But she still needed to find out who won the election.

What a pity Lyndon Johnson would soon quit pulling the strings of presidential power. He'd worked them better than anyone until he was tripped up by the Vietnam War. Her uncle in Dallas was a crony of LBJ's, and that connection might've been helpful if LBJ remained president, if worse came to worst with David's case. But now the possibility of Johnson's help was only a pipe dream. And even if he exercised power as a former president, would he do it for a protestor to *his* war?

She searched for a news program on the radio. The rain still fell in icy sheets as Austin raced around the radio dial. She hoped for news on the hour, having waited in the car so long already that she might as well hang on ten minutes longer.

Her forced incarceration in the bug-like car was oppressive, making her think how much worse David's confinement must be. After ten minutes of Janis Joplin, Otis Redding, and the Doors, she switched to the CBC.

At three o'clock the news report opened with the American election result. The announcer explained that only four hours earlier Humphrey had conceded defeat. Richard Milhous Nixon was the next President of the United States.

Score one for Tricky Dick.

Five minutes later the rain stopped temporarily, but Austin's pain over Nixon's victory was not ameliorated. Muttering about the cruelties of politics and history, she put the car in gear and headed to the U of T campus, where her studies demanded attention. Her rotten day couldn't get any worse

Austin was studying in her library carrel when someone walked up behind her. She twisted around to find Darrel Smith peering over her shoulder. She already distrusted him, and now he was trying to read her notebook.

She shut the book. "What're you doing here?"

"We need to talk," he said.

"What about?"

"Lots of things, but this isn't a good place for a conversation." Darrel's eyes flickered around the library stacks. He'd exchanged his business suit for the academic garb of tweed jacket and corduroy pants.

"Can you be more specific?"Austin let her voice register annoyance.

"I can, but let's get out of here so we can talk in private. Where can we go?"

"If you absolutely insist, then the foyer will have to do. I'm not going outside again in this rain." She straightened papers and grabbed her purse. "Let's get this over with; I've got lots of work to do."

In the foyer Austin stood with her back against the wall, glaring at Darrel. He glared back. "So what's on your mind?" she asked. "I need to study, so spit it out."

"You're certainly nothing like your friend Larissa." Darrel jeered at her, exposing notably long canine teeth. "Why does she hang around with you anyway?"

"Funny, but that's what I was thinking about you and your wife."

Darrel stepped toward her with menace, but Austin stood her ground. She refused to back up even the few inches that separated her from the wall. She disliked this man and wouldn't let him bully her. Why, he was absolutely Nixon-esque.

"How'd you find me?" she asked. She knew she should feign politeness but couldn't do it. Her loathing was instinctual and too strong.

He smirked. "I have my methods."

"You're kidding, right? You can't come up with anything better than cheesy movie dialogue?"

His smirk mutated into a glare.

"Well, if you're not going to tell me what you want or how you found me, then I'm going back to work." She stepped forward and was delighted when he backed up to get out of her way. She paused when they were nose to nose. Their height was roughly the same. Score one for her.

"If you'll calm down, then I'll deliver my message and be on my way." His tone became almost conciliatory. Or perhaps only smarmy.

"So, shoot." Oh dear, ugly choice of words. "Have you been talking to people at the church? Is that how you found me?"

Again he ignored her questions. "Senator Simpson has powerful friends, both in Washington and Ottawa. You don't want to cross him." Hostility marred his handsome face.

"Never dream of it. In fact, I'm on his side. I want to discover who killed his son as much as he does." She manufactured a smile but couldn't bring herself to flutter her eyelashes, à la Larissa.

"But that's the problem. You and the senator disagree fundamentally. The senator is satisfied that your husband is the killer and thinks you should butt out of his business. You have to quit poking around the Simpsons, father and son, or, or—"

"Or what?" she demanded.

"Or else," he said.

Although Darrel's words sounded lame, they still set off an alarm in Austin's head. His threat was suspiciously like the written one she'd received. Her mistrust of him soared, and her guard went up even higher.

"That's rich. You're threatening *me*, a mere student with no money and no influential friends in Canada. How could I possibly hurt the esteemed senior senator from New Jersey? Why's he so easily intimidated?"

Darrel choked. "I didn't say that; you don't intimidate Senator Simpson. He just wants you to leave him alone to grieve in peace."

"All right, I can respect that, but know this: I'll never rest until my husband is out of jail. He doesn't belong there. If I'm the only one left standing to pursue the murderer, well then, I'll stand and pursue. You should respect my feelings about that in return." Austin folded her arms across her chest. "But you should know that you make me question what the senator is afraid of."

Darrel shoved his face so close to hers that she could feel his breath. She refused to flinch.

"You've been warned. If you keep on in your pigheaded way, then you'll regret it." Darrel whirled around and stomped to the main exit. He flung open the door so violently that it whacked an incoming student in the arm. Darrel didn't stop as the boy hurled insults at his back.

When Darrel had been standing in front of her, Austin had felt brave. Once she was alone, however, her spine wilted to the consistency of a fragile flower stalk. She sank back against the wall, needing the support. Acid rose in her throat, and she started to gag. She searched frantically for a trash can.

Later, back in the library stacks, she tried to resume her studies, but her thoughts kept returning to Darrel's words, raking them over and over. This was the second threat she'd received in forty-eight hours.

Would there be a third? Was the same person responsible for each threat, or were multiple parties pressuring her?

A vision of Mrs. Duncan rose before her. It reached out to Austin and offered her a plate of cookies. Then it lay down on the floor and was magically covered by a blanket, the way the twittering blue birds had covered Disney's Cinderella with a new garment.

Except Cinderella found her happy ending and Mrs. Duncan would never have one.

A tear rolled down Austin's cheek and splashed onto her book about the Russian Revolution. She hoped she wasn't responsible for that nice woman's death. She must find out if DS McKinnon believed her death had been an accident or another murder. If her death had been deemed an ordinary hit-and-run, would he have even heard about it?

Austin had lost track of how many times she'd cried since finding Reg's body. It had to be an all-time record for her. She disgusted herself, but at least she was no quitter. She wouldn't give up until David was out of jail, free of all charges and suspicions.

Concentrating on her studies was impossible now. Austin gathered her things and left the library. She planned to stop at her apartment to check her mail before going to the Klimenkos' for dinner. She dreaded opening her mailbox.

CHAPTER TWENTY-TWO

Austin's hands shook as she pulled everything out of her mailbox. Not one piece of mail looked sinister. Her relief was only beginning to blossom when she heard someone enter the lobby behind her. She turned to see a female hippie who, despite the inclement weather, wore a gauzy see-through dress and sandals. The stranger jangled when she walked, her feet adorned with toe rings and ankle bracelets.

The woman shook her damp, scraggly hair, wiped her sandals on a mat, and strode toward Austin. "Do you know where the Starrs are? We're sick of hanging around waiting for them to show up."

Austin was so thunderstruck that she stuttered. "I don't know. I-I-uh, why do you need to find them?"

"We're going to crash at their pad." She stamped her foot and jangled. "Do you know them or not?"

What a brash woman.

Then Austin recognized the problem. This woman was the advance unit of the draft resisters, their so-called guests, who were scheduled to stay in their apartment. She and David had quarreled about them the morning after the murder. As she was deciding what to say, the front door flew open.

A disheveled man who held a crying baby lumbered in. When he caught sight of the woman, he stomped over and thrust the baby at her. "Here, Meadow. You better take Moonjava now."

Austin's mouth fell open. Girl or boy—she couldn't tell with a name like that. Then she saw that the child wore no diaper and that it was a girl.

Freed from holding his daughter, the man searched the pockets of his long, hooded jacket and pulled out a joint. When he lit up, Austin erupted.

"You can't smoke that in here. Put it out."

The man looked daggers her way, stubbed the joint out carefully on the heel of his work boot, and pocketed it.

His obedience gave her courage. "I'm Austin Starr. I forgot you were coming, but you can't possibly stay here now."

The man and woman looked flabbergasted and began to sputter. He punched the wall, but the woman found her voice first. "God damn it, we're counting on you, aren't we, Doug?" She turned to her husband. "Now what're we supposed to do?" She held her child at arm's length. "Shut up, Moonjava. I can't think when you yell in my ear."

"Meadow's right." The man named Doug frowned at Austin through strings of greasy hair that hung nearly to his nose. "You can't let us down like this."

Austin raised her chin and planted her feet about a foot apart, securing her base. "The situation's changed since we agreed you could stay with us. My husband's in jail, and someone's sending me threats. I'm not even staying in my own apartment right now."

"Well then, that's great for us. We can stay in your place," Meadow said.

"She didn't mean that the way it sounded," Doug said.

"It doesn't matter." Austin assumed her sternest expression. "You can't stay here. I mean, it wouldn't be safe for you either." She decided to stretch the truth. "And besides, the police keep coming around to check on our place. You wouldn't like that, would you?"

Meadow and Doug shuffled their feet and muttered.

Austin felt in control for a nice change, and her rising confidence led her to make a kind gesture. "I'll drive you over to see the organizing committee's leader. He'll figure out where you can stay."

With no better offer, the couple agreed, and in short order Austin got all three of them and their gear into her car. She was driving out the driveway when Meadow said, "Can we stop at a grocery store? I need to get formula for Moonjava."

"Sure thing; happy to help." Austin turned the car around to head for the nearest Dominion supermarket.

While Austin drove, Meadow chattered. "Toronto's like dullsville. There aren't any cool dance places like back in Philly."

Austin stifled her views about Toronto. Instead she said, "I don't know about night spots, but there are plenty of cheap apartments, and the grocery stores are okay."

"Big deal. All the stores we've seen are pitiful. They don't have the stuff we're used to."

"Why's your husband in jail?" Doug interrupted his wife's complaints. "How'd he get nailed? What'd he do?"

Austin pretended not to hear him, disinclined to share David's jailhouse woes with these bizarre strangers. "Here's the grocery store where I shop." She pulled into the Dominion parking lot. "Maybe you'll like it, Meadow."

They were in an Italian area, Austin's favorite part of the city, not far from the university. Merely walking down the street, she could smell basil, rosemary, and garlic—lots of garlic. The Dominion supermarket attracted ex-patriots. She often heard Massachusetts accents in the fish aisle and North Carolina over by the produce.

Moonjava and her dad remained in the car, and Meadow went with Austin into the store. She continued to whine. "Back in Philly we have great bread, but I bet it's awful here."

If Austin loved anything in Ontario, it was the bread. The surge of Italians who moved to Toronto after World War II brought along their baking skills. Forgetting about the formula for Moonjava, she proudly dragged Meadow to the bakery department.

That fan of Philadelphia, however, was unimpressed. "Jeez Louise, this dump doesn't even have hoagie rolls. Hey, you," Meadow brayed at a store clerk. "Where're your hoagie rolls?"

"Sorry, miss. What do you want?"

"Hoagie rolls. Back home in Philly we have lots to choose from."

Austin died on the spot. She might not love her new home, but thought it rude to run down Toronto to its own citizens. "All right, let's skip the bread and get the formula." Mentally, Austin threw up her hands. "I've got an appointment and need to hurry." She thought of her refuge, the Klimenko home, and wanted to return as fast as possible.

Back at the car, Meadow put her grocery bag down and took her daughter from her husband. Doug eyed his wet jeans in disgust and began to spray Austin with questions again.

"So what gives with your husband? Why's he in jail? Is he innocent? If he didn't commit a crime, then why was he arrested? Because he's a draft resister?"

The barrage weakened Austin's resolve. She patiently went through the basics of David's case until, halfway through her explanation, Doug interrupted. "Did you know Senator Simpson's in trouble? Yeah, politics sure are a nasty business, man."

Austin swiveled to look back at him so quickly that her hands turned the steering wheel too. The car swerved, but she regained control easily, although Moonjava shrieked.

"Sorry about that," Austin said. "Doug, tell me everything you know about the senator. What kind of trouble?"

"From what I read, Simpson's fame came from his World War Two service," Doug said. "He won medals on Okinawa and served in Korea too. His whole political career's based on his alleged brilliant military record, and he talks about it all the time. Now someone's come forward saying two of his medals are frauds. We're in the middle of a war, and the old vets are pretty twitchy about patriotism, you know? They don't like it when a guy lies about his military record. They think it tarnishes the memory of their buddies who served and died."

He cleared his throat. "My old man fought in the Battle of the Bulge. He still gets choked up when he thinks about his friends' deaths and gets mad when anyone criticizes our military. Obviously, that happens all the time now. That's made it tough for me to come up here, but I couldn't fight in 'Nam." He twisted a lock of his stringy hair, reminding Austin of David. "My dad doesn't understand that my war is not like his was. It's tough on both of us, just tough."

Meadow reached back and grabbed her husband's hand. "It'll be okay, sugar. You'll see."

Austin waited for what she hoped was a respectful amount of time before quizzing him again. "Can you spell out exactly what 'political trouble' means for the senator?"

"Sure," Doug said. "New Jersey newspaper editors are blasting him, and vets are writing letters to the papers. So far it's only local. It'll die down soon enough, probably."

"I don't think so," Meadow chimed in. "The scandal's gonna blow up and bring him down, down, down." She cackled.

"Oh, come on, cupcake." He gently chucked his wife on her arm. "You don't like him, so you're ready to see him fall. I bet he weathers this."

"We'll just wait and see." Sulking, Meadow added, "I'm gonna be right."

Austin dropped Moonjava and her parents off at the paint store where the head of the anti-war committee worked. After that, she drove in circles around the city as she chewed over what she'd learned about Senator Simpson.

His political problems tantalized her, but what they might mean for David was unclear. It *was* clear, however, that the senator was under loads of stress. And when people were stressed, their dark sides often came out to play.

Reg had told Pete that his dad's medals weren't earned. The hubbub in the press back in New Jersey certainly seemed to validate that. She couldn't see the senator as the killer of his own son, however, or even the instigator of the crime. But his sidekick, Darrel, was another matter. Whenever she thought about him, a vision of Nixon loomed in her mind. In other words, she figured Darrel would consort with the devil.

Austin also reflected on Meadow's behavior. While she and Austin were both displaced persons, Meadow's negativity gave Austin an ugly example to avoid. If she was an unhappy foreigner, she should keep it to herself.

Her mother would've been proud to hear that conclusion.

Austin imagined she'd run into Meadow in the months to come, always hearing her before she came into sight. When "back in Philly" blasted down the store aisles, Austin would know that Meadow had grabbed another unlucky clerk.

Austin sat at a traffic light, tapping her nails on the steering wheel. The driver behind her finally honked his car horn, and her reverie broke. She waved a hand in apology and tallied the honk as only the second she'd heard in Toronto.

She flashed back to driving the crowded freeways in Houston, where horns sounded routinely. Austin recognized her thoughts—getting homesick for those notorious roads—for the diversion they were. Sighing, she concluded she'd had enough driving around and thinking and worrying. She turned the car toward the Klimenkos' part of town and her new sanctuary.

"May I use your phone to make a long distance call?" Austin asked Larissa after dinner. "It might be expensive, so I'll reimburse you."

"Don't be silly," Larissa said. "Make the call. What's up?"

"I want my friend Earleen to dig into the controversy over Senator Simpson's medals. Her military connections could help. She just started work for the Veterans Administration in Houston, and her husband's serving in Vietnam."

"Sounds tough." Larissa's lips turned down, and her eyebrows rose. "You don't really think the senator had his own son killed, do you?"

"I'm not sure, although I do think the senator and Darrel are connected to the death somehow. The storm over Simpson's medals could be what ties them to the murder. I need more information and hope that Earleen can help."

"So do you want me to try to meet up with Darrel?"

Austin wrinkled her nose at the thought of the senator's aide. "Let's see what Earleen finds out before we throw you into that particular lion's den."

"Fine with me," Larissa said. "If I never see him again, it'll be too soon."

"You got that right." Austin stood and crossed to the bookcase that filled an entire wall of the Klimenko living room. She studied the shelves, chose two volumes, and showed them to Larissa. "May I borrow these for David?"

"Feel free. The books Papa uses for his research are in his study, so anything in this room is fine."

"I'm going back to the jail tomorrow. I promised David I'd bring books, but I don't have time to go to a bookstore."

"Want me to come with you?"

"Not yet, thanks. I do want you to meet him, though. He's curious about you and a little suspicious of why you and your father are being so nice to me. At this point, he suspects everyone of wanting to do us in." Austin put the books down, pulled a tissue out of her pocket, and blew her nose. She was afraid she was going to cry again and didn't want to appear weak in front of anyone, not even Larissa.

Larissa averted her gaze. "Papa's been in prison, so I'm not prejudiced against anyone in jail. I also stand by my earlier judgment. If you married David, then I'm sure he's a decent person. I only want to meet him, that's all."

"Thank you," Austin said simply. "Now I'm going to call Earleen."

The next day was Thursday, marking a week since Reg's murder. To Austin it felt like a year. So much had happened in those seven days that she dreaded what the next week would bring.

She attended class in the morning and afterward went to her apartment to examine the mail. She scoped out the lobby for Moonjava's parents or anyone else who could waylay her. Seeing no one, she opened the mailbox and found it brimming with paper. She decided to read through the mail before going to see David. She climbed the stairs, holding her breath all the way. These stairs weren't treacherous and she'd gotten used to them soon after they'd moved in. What she *was* worried about was meeting up with someone unsavory or dangerous.

She made it up without meeting anyone, not even a neighbor. The apartment looked forlorn. Her one plant, a dieffenbachia, was as droopy as she felt. She was tending to the plant when she realized she was dragging her feet, not wanting to see the Don Jail again. She missed David desperately but hated seeing him locked up, languishing behind smudged glass.

She went through the mail, putting aside bills for David to pay. Beneath a flyer from Canadian Tire lay an envelope that looked appallingly familiar. Once again her name was typed on the front in capital letters.

She got a pair of tongs from the kitchen and used them to pick up the envelope. She slit it open with a paring knife, pulled the single sheet of paper out with the tongs, and stared at the short message.

YOU WERE WARNED. BE PREPARED TO DIE.

Her stomach dropped to her feet.

She couldn't take her eyes off the page that she still gripped with kitchen tongs.

This was ludicrous. Who would want to kill her? Darrel was

evil, perhaps, but she couldn't imagine that he wanted her dead. Why would he?

Why would anyone?

Austin returned to the kitchen and found a roll of wax paper. She cut off a length and wrapped it around the envelope and note paper. Next, she put the entire package inside a copy of *Time* magazine she found on the kitchen counter, then placed the package in her purse with the books for David.

Satisfied, she went to the telephone hanging on the wall and dialed the number for the Metropolitan Toronto Police. When told that DS McKinnon was out at a crime scene, she left a message for him to call that evening, giving the Klimenkos' phone number.

She hung up the phone and bleakly surveyed the scene. Austin was methodical, not wanting to rush through her panic and forget anything important. She picked up the mail for David and her purse holding the magazine with its malicious insert. She took it as a good omen that the dieffenbachia was already showing signs of improvement. Aware that she was desperate to find portents of good luck in order to bolster her nerve, she let herself out of the apartment, locked up, and hurried from the building.

Her exit was more troubled than her entry had been—anyone she encountered could have left the threat. Since there were no likely suspects, everyone was suspect.

Anyone could be the killer.

CHAPTER TWENTY-THREE

"Honey, you don't look so good." David's voice over the jail's phone was low, and his face through the dirty glass showed concern.

"My secret admirer struck again. This time the message said, 'You were warned. Be prepared to die.' The note was short and punchy, so it wasn't hard to memorize." Austin tried to sound brisk and businesslike, but couldn't quite pull it off.

David flinched. "That's a real death threat. Did you tell the police?"

"I called McKinnon. He wasn't in, so I left a message."

David ran his fingers through his newly cropped hair. "You've got to stop playing detective. Promise me you will." His voice was loud now. The prison guard looked their way, seeing if he needed to intervene.

"If I stop, then chances are you'll stay in jail until you face trial. I'm sure they'd consider you a flight risk. But never mind." She made a waving motion with an imaginary eraser. "I will *not* let you stay cooped up in this horrid place."

"There's got to be another way to help me, other than putting your life on the line. Maybe we could hire a detective or something." His voice trailed off into hopelessness. "Needless to say we don't have the money, but still..." David leaned forward. "Did the second note look like the first?"

"Right down to smudges on the letter *O*. I took care to handle the thing properly and used kitchen tongs, not my fingers. I left the note in the car, wrapped up in wax paper. I'll give it to McKinnon."

David smiled. "That's my girl. You're keeping your wits about you."

Austin lowered her head, embarrassed. Her purse lay beside her on the floor with the borrowed books sticking out. "Before I forget, I brought you two books. How do I get them to you?" In irritation, she pointed at the wall of glass that separated them.

"Give them to the guard, but you're trying to change the subject. Will you please quit digging for clues? This isn't funny anymore."

"It never was particularly funny and yes, I am changing the subject." Austin held up the books so he could read the titles: *Tales of the South Pacific* and *Advise and Consent*. "These came from Dr. Klimenko. See how they relate to Senator Simpson? He served in the Pacific campaign and now he's in the U.S. Senate. Who knows, maybe you can find something helpful reading these books." She noticed his sour expression and added hastily, "I'm kidding. *Mostly*."

"You're like a dog with a bone. You're not going to stop snooping, are you?"

"So let's talk about something else."

For the next twenty minutes, David described his life in jail and Austin detailed her growing friendship with the Klimenkos. Then the prison guard moved toward them.

"Time's almost up," he said. "Five minutes."

"Quick. Tell me all you know about Reg." Austin's resolve showed in her jutting chin. "You hinted before that he'd done bad things but refused to tell me the details."

"You're supposed to quit nosing around."

Austin laughed. "Are you sure *you* didn't write that note?" She saw his expression and changed her tone. "Fine, I promise to be careful, so quit nagging. But I've got to say this. If my own husband won't help me, how can I expect other people to help you?"

"I don't like this. I think you're crazy."

"That's funny, coming from you. Look at the crazy things I've done since I married you. Moving to Canada out of the blue tops the list, and that's nuttier than trying to get you out of jail. Come on, tell me about Reg."

"All right, I give up." David shifted in his seat. "A few weeks back, one of the guys accused Reg of stealing money from the group, and then Reg accused him of spying for the Mounties."

"Wow. Any of that true?"

"Both charges were being looked into when I was jailed, so I don't know what's gone down since. Maybe Reg was trying to get even with his accuser. Obviously, with him dead, it's all moot now."

"Why didn't you tell me this before?"

"I don't know, but probably because it didn't seem fair to Reg since it was only a rumor. The first time you asked about Reg, I hadn't been arrested yet. After that, those details got lost in the ballooning catastrophe."

"David, honestly." Austin shook her head. "Did you tell anyone else about this after you were arrested?

"I did, but the cops seemed to think these details only strengthened my motive—that I was angry at Reg for hurting the group, so I killed him."

"That logic escapes me."

"Because there is no logic. It's just a stupid way to look at things."

"Then how about the possibility of an RCMP plant? Who did Reg accuse, by the way? I wish you'd told me this before. I should talk to this guy."

David shoved his face nearer the glass that separated them, glaring. "Now, Austin—"

"You know I should talk to him. Who is he?"

"Pete's older brother, Phil."

Austin's mouth fell open. "I didn't know Pete had a brother up here. Did I meet him?"

"Phil's only been here since August, and he and Pete don't get along. Pete's support of Reg was a sticking point."

"Then I need to get back to Pete right away; through him I can find Phil."

"Look, one of these guys might be the one who's threatening you. This isn't a lark."

She leveled a long look at David. "Someone is trying to scare me off and frame my husband for murder. I won't be intimidated."

"Like Mrs. Duncan? She's not intimidated; she's dead."

Austin slunk down in her chair, and her stomach fluttered at the reminder. "Yeah, well, maybe that was an accident. I'll ask McKinnon when he calls. I'd better start keeping notes so I don't forget anything."

"You're a trip, Austin, you really are."

"Time's up," the guard announced.

Austin and David pressed their hands together against the glass. After performing their new ritual, she rose from her chair and turned away.

Austin drove back to campus as fast as she dared. Once at U of T, she dashed about, trying to find Dulcie as a way to get to Pete. She had no luck locating her, however, and ended up studying in the library. All afternoon Austin stayed on the lookout for suspicious characters.

The death threat felt unreal, but still she was rattled.

That evening at dinner, Austin told the Klimenkos about the latest warning she'd received, and they erupted with frantic questions. She was patiently responding when the telephone rang. Larissa left to answer the call, returning moments later.

"For you, Austin. It's Earleen."

Austin ran to the phone. "What's up, Earleen?" She tried not to yell from excitement. "Did you dig up anything on the senator?"

"I'll say. Guess whose scandal made the front page of today's *New York Times*?"

"Are you kidding me?"

"Nope. The story about Simpson's bogus medals has hit the big time." Earleen snickered. "His disgrace was all anyone could talk about at the VA today. And dig this…" Earleen cleared her throat. "My boss told me about meeting Simpson once in Washington. Said the senator acts like the sun comes up just to hear him crow."

Austin laughed. "But aren't most bigwigs full of themselves?"

"Might could be, but my boss says Simpson was the worst he's seen. That's why he's not unhappy to see Senator Simpson land in trouble."

"Ah yes, there's a case of good old *schadenfreude* for you."

"Darn it, girl, you're right. And right about now Simpson's probably sweatin' like a turkey the day before Thanksgiving."

"Earleen! I sure miss talking to you."

"So when are you comin' back to Texas, where you belong?"

"Maybe I can come for a visit once David gets out of jail. If he gets out of jail, that is."

"You gotta think positive. If David's not guilty, then he'll get out. You'll see. And I'm gonna do all I can to help."

After talking a few more minutes and hearing a few more details about the senator, Austin rang off. When she returned to the dining room, she was too wound up to sit at the table.

Larissa was excited too and couldn't wait to let her speak. "What was all that about?" she demanded. "Did Earleen come up with anything on Simpson?"

"She said his scandal is all over the national news now."

"What're you talking about?" Dr. Klimenko said.

Austin turned to him. "I'm sorry, sir. The scandal over Senator Simpson's medals from the battle of Okinawa jumped from local papers to the *New York Times* today."

"Only the most important paper in America, Papa."

"I am aware of that, Larochka." Klimenko smiled indulgently.

"Earleen said that after this morning's *Times* came out and the wire services started spreading the story, Democratic Party leaders demanded Simpson's resignation from the Senate Armed Services

Committee. Simpson is scheduled to become the ranking Republican on the committee when the Senate begins its new session in January."

"No wonder Simpson seemed edgy when we saw him at the hotel," Larissa said. "Bet he was worried this story would blow up in his face."

"But just wait," Austin said. "Earleen dug up even more. This morning's *Times* also broke the news that his only son was a draft dodger in Toronto and that he'd been murdered. Evidently the senator covered up his son's flight to Canada, so now the whole thing's huge news."

Dr. Klimenko, eyes narrowed, began to rub his gloved hand. "But surely the senator could have gotten preferential treatment for his son so he didn't have to evade the draft. Isn't that how it usually works in Washington?"

"Maybe his son didn't want him to try. Maybe Reg wanted to make his own kind of political statement." Austin held onto the back of a chair and rocked with agitation. "Now I really need to find Pete. He's bound to know more about this than anyone else—that is, from Reg's point of view. Maybe I could go out tonight." She turned to Larissa. "Want to go to Grad's and see if we can find Pete? If we hurry, we'll get there before it closes."

Larissa and her father exchanged worried glances. "I don't think that's a good idea," she said. "Daytime is one thing. Night-time, well…"

Her father nodded his agreement. "You both need to stay here where I ca—"

The doorbell rang, and he looked at his watch. "It's rather late for someone to visit."

Larissa rose, but he stopped her with his gloved hand. "Stay here, Larochka. I'll see who is at the door." He left, closing the dining room door firmly behind him.

Larissa got up and ran to the window. When she looked outside, she whooped in excitement. "A cop car's out front. What do you want to bet it's your policeman?"

Both girls were huddled at the window when the dining room door opened and Dr. Klimenko returned. Following him was Detective Sergeant McKinnon.

The policeman wore a full-length trench coat. Austin liked this new look, an improvement over his usual tweed sport coat. Now he looked like a real detective.

McKinnon said, "I'm sorry to bother you so late, but my desk sergeant said you sounded frantic, Austin, when you called this afternoon. What's happened?" He sat down in the seat Klimenko offered him at the table.

An awkward pause followed.

Larissa finally asked if anyone wanted tea or coffee.

"Perhaps you would like a whisky?" her father suggested. "I have a bottle of single malt that I would like your opinion about. I'm told it is good, but I'm not an expert on Scotch, only vodka."

McKinnon agreed, and Klimenko got four glasses. He poured whisky for himself and McKinnon, sherry for the girls.

Austin took a sip of the sherry and tried not to make a face at the too-sweet flavor.

"Excuse me for a moment," she said. "I have to get something to show Detective Sergeant McKinnon." She hurried from the room and returned quickly, carrying her copy of *Time* magazine.

McKinnon started to speak, but Larissa leaned forward and put a hand on his arm. "Wait. You'll see why this is important."

To Austin's surprise, he barely looked at Larissa, concentrating instead on the magazine. At least there was one man who retained control of his mental faculties around her alluring friend.

Austin took out the wax paper package, opened it carefully, and showed the envelope and note to McKinnon. She made sure she didn't touch the papers with her bare fingers. The wax paper covered the parts that she touched.

"This was in my mailbox this morning, and that's why I called you. I wouldn't have bothered you unless I had a good reason."

McKinnon took the note and eyed it gravely. "This appears to be made on the same machine as the first note, doesn't it?" He didn't wait for an answer. "The first note and envelope had one other person's fingerprints on it besides yours, Austin, but those weren't in our files. Our lab people say that the original note was made on an IBM Selectric typewriter, probably one of the earliest models, produced in 1962. Do you or your husband have access to such a machine?"

Austin's face flushed in anger. Her mouth fell open, but no words came out.

Professor Klimenko answered for her. "Let us give the young lady a moment to collect herself. She's had a trying day, and we're very concerned about her welfare. My daughter and I are sincere in our devotion to keep her from harm, and that includes anything that is said to her that would upset her unduly. I'm sorry to say that your question falls in that category. Now, would you care to rephrase it, or shall we discuss the merits or lack thereof for this single malt whisky?"

After this lecture, Klimenko sat back in his chair, studied McKinnon's face, and then grasped his glass in his good hand. He took a large swallow. "I find it difficult to sip whisky. You must know that we Russians toss back shots of our vodka neat."

McKinnon tasted his own whisky and appeared to consider the chastisement. At last he looked over at Austin and said, "I gather I sounded obtuse. Actually, I wanted to rule out your ability to type and send the notes to yourself, not to accuse you of doing it yourself. I see now that my meaning was unclear, and I beg your pardon."

Austin found her voice. "A little insensitive, yes, but I forgive you, especially since you used that fantastic word *obtuse*."

When she and McKinnon smiled at each other, both Klimenkos looked puzzled.

"What just happened?" Larissa asked.

"My policeman and I share a love of words," Austin said, and then she ducked her head in sudden embarrassment. "Oh gosh, now you know my secret, Detective Sergeant McKinnon. I think of you, along with Larissa and her father, as my protector."

She gazed across the table at these people who had been strangers so recently. Yet in the last week each had become a trusted confidante. Her mind flashed, seeing a vision that had them coalescing into a formidable army, ready to back her up for the battles that were sure to lie ahead.

CHAPTER TWENTY-FOUR

One bottle of single malt and one of vodka stood depleted on the table. The policeman pronounced the whisky excellent. The professor said he agreed, yet returned to his vodka. When they stopped dancing around the details of the murder case and began dissecting World War II battles, the girls slipped out of the dining room.

At the top of the stairs, Larissa whispered, "Get ready for bed and then come see me. We need to talk."

Austin changed into her nightgown and joined Larissa in her room, where Larissa sat cross-legged in bed, humming with energy.

"I'm so wide awake, I can't possibly go to sleep right now," she said, brushing her hair.

"Me too. My head's buzzing with details about the murder." Austin curled into an armchair and tucked her feet under her. "Do you think McKinnon finally understands that Simpson and Darrel are somehow connected to Reg's death?"

"I'm not sure. McKinnon seems sympathetic to the idea, but he knows that tackling a United States senator will put his own job on the line. I feel sorry for McKinnon. He'll have a huge political problem to deal with if the senator is involved."

"I'm sure there's a link somewhere, but what it is, I don't know yet," Austin said.

"I'm not as convinced as you are." Larissa examined a fingernail and peeled off a strip of polish. "Granted, the senator and his underling act like something's fishy, but I doubt if the senator has the stomach to order the murder of his own son."

Austin whimpered. "Please, don't talk about stomachs. From the moment I found Reg's body, mine has been in knots. I feel nauseated every time I think about all that blood."

"And now some psycho's sending you death threats."

"My list of fun just keeps on growing." Austin looked down, rubbed her tummy, and spoke to it. "There, there. Why can't you just behave?" She rolled her eyes at Larissa. "My stomach says it wants to go back to Texas and fill up on enchiladas and tamales."

"I've never had Mexican food, but from what I've heard, it doesn't sound like it's gentle on the digestion."

"If you were raised on chile con queso, then you'd understand. I can't drink vodka straight, but you Russians sure knock back the stuff."

Larissa beamed. "Wasn't Papa clever, how he introduced the whisky and loosened up McKinnon? I bet he's under a lot of stress and needed to unwind. Without the alcohol, I'm sure McKinnon wouldn't have said a word about the investigation into Mrs. Duncan's death."

"You're probably right, but he disappointed me. The police haven't found any evidence that her death was anything but a hit-and-run." Austin made a face and released a deep sigh. "But I don't care. I'm sure Mrs. Duncan was murdered. I just have to prove I'm right, and I will—I will."

"Maybe you *want* a connection?" Larissa's voice grew gentle. "I'm being objective here, not critical. Hunches can only go so far."

"You think I'm crazy too. That's what David called me this afternoon. Crazy." Austin uncurled her feet and sat forward in the chair. "There's a pattern here, but we can't see it yet. Whoever killed Reg wanted that sweet woman dead too. Needed her dead. Whatever she wanted to tell me got her killed. And her secret went with her to the grave. If I'm crazy, then that's why." She rose and stomped to the door.

"All right, all right, calm down. You sure do get worked up

when you're on a case." Larissa pointed at the arm chair. "Now come back here and sit. You know I support you."

Austin remained defiant for a moment, and then her resolution softened. "I'm sorry, Larissa. I didn't realize I was so tense." She took a deep gulp of air and returned to the chair.

"It's no surprise that you're tense." Larissa stretched her legs in front of her on the bed and wiggled her toes. "Okay, let's do something constructive now. Let's figure out what we'll do tomorrow. If we make a plan of attack, then you'll feel better."

"Only real progress will cheer me up." Austin glanced at a calendar hanging over Larissa's desk. "A week ago tonight I found Reg's body. Even after all our digging, so far there's no obvious alternative to David as the killer. It's all so depressing." Austin began messaging her temples, then rolled her shoulders. "All right, tomorrow I want to find Dulcie and ask her how to get hold of Pete. And his brother Phil too. I've never met him. He could pass me on the street, and I wouldn't recognize him."

"And what about Darrel?"

"I don't know what to do about him. If anyone scares me, it's the senator's sidekick."

"But you faced him down once already," Larissa said.

"Sure, but that was before I got a death threat."

"My offer to talk to him still stands. I'll get more out of Darrel than you can. What's more, McKinnon said the senator's flying back to Washington on the weekend, so we need to act fast."

"Asking you to meet with Darrel is really throwing you to the wolves, Larissa. Even the senator doesn't bother me as much as Darrel does." Austin pursed her lips, but she relaxed them when she imagined the same expression on the face of her disapproving mother.

"Darrel plays the bad guy so his boss can look good. Darrel's the enforcer."

"Hadn't thought of that, but you're probably right." Austin scrunched up her face again. "It boggles the mind that the senator might've wanted to kill his son."

"Agreed, so how about trying this on for a theory? Why couldn't Darrel have snapped? Or maybe Darrel killed Reg in a fit of misplaced zeal?"

"Maybe, but if Darrel really is the killer, then it's too dangerous for you to question him."

"I can handle Darrel, as long as it's in a public place." Larissa grinned. "Just don't tell Papa about it."

Snow was falling the next morning when Austin and Larissa set off across campus, catching Austin unprepared. Neither the flats she wore nor her jacket were up to the weather, but she refused to stop at her apartment to change clothes. She was too bent on finding Dulcie to delay that goal by even a few minutes.

And so she shivered and suffered.

They spent an hour scouring the campus without any luck. Then, just as they were heading to the Junior Common Room to warm up, Dulcie appeared, running toward them with her coat flapping open and her long hair streaming out behind her.

"Thank heavens I found you. Pete's got to talk to you, Austin." Dulcie's breath escaped her mouth in icy gasps. "He's at work now but can meet you at Grad's at noon. He didn't know how to find you, so I offered to help." She stopped and coughed, then rewound her scarf around her bare throat. "He's upset, maybe even a little scared."

"This is so weird." Austin couldn't believe her good luck. "I was coming to find you so *I* could talk to Pete again. What's happened? The last time I saw him, Pete wouldn't tell me anything."

"My mom always said I had ESP," Dulcie gushed. "I remember one time when I was little and the neigh—"

"Dulcie, pay attention," Austin said. "We were talking about Pete, right?"

"Right, sorry. I was going to tell you about Pete." Dulcie

narrowed her eyes, making an obvious effort to remember. "Something bad went down, and now Pete's changed his mind. I don't know why, but he's desperate to see you. He said, 'Austin will help me.' " Dulcie buttoned up her coat, pulled a knit cap out of her pocket, and jammed it on her head. Her clothes were askew, adding to her frazzled look.

Larissa stepped forward and thrust her hand out. "I'm Larissa Klimenko. Austin's been staying at my house since David went to jail."

Dulcie ignored her outstretched hand and enveloped Larissa in a hug, following up with another one for Austin. They all began stamping their feet in an attempt to warm up.

"I'm freezing," Larissa said. "Dulcie, we're on our way to the JCR for something hot to drink. Why don't you come too?"

In the Junior Common Room of University College, outdoor clothes were piled on tables and chairs and hung from pegs on the wall. The number of coats, hats, mufflers, and gloves was startling, the smell of soggy wool overpowering. *This must be what wandering into a café in Siberia was like*, Austin mused. Everyone besides her wore winter boots in this prelude to the challenging winter that lay ahead.

The girls unwrapped themselves and settled down for a round of hot drinks.

"Dulcie, what're the guys from the group saying now about Reg's murder?" Austin asked. "Do they think David's guilty?" She paused while the waitress served their drinks. "And do you know Pete's brother, Phil? I need to talk to him. He may be able to put some of the puzzle together for me."

"I know him, but you're too late," Dulcie said. "Phil left for Calgary two days ago. Everyone's talking about whether Phil spied for the Mounties. He's made your husband old news."

"Calgary? How come?" Austin was dumbfounded. Now she'd never get to talk to him, just like with Mrs. Duncan. Not alike exactly, since presumably Phil was still breathing and walking around. But still...

"Nobody knows why Phil ran off to Calgary, although rumor says he told a girl at the commune where he was crashing that his days playing double agent were over. When I saw Pete, I wanted to ask him about the rumor but didn't because he was already so upset about Reg."

"I'll have to forget about Phil then," Austin said, "and concentrate on Pete. Do either of you want to come along to Grad's when I see him?" She looked at Larissa. "I know you're trying to meet up with someone else." She didn't want to say Darrell's name aloud. He was her secret. "How about you, Dulcie? Would Pete feel better if you came too?"

"It won't matter one way or the other. Besides, I've got a class," she said.

Austin crossed her ankles and looked down at her legs, checking for goose bumps. She was so cold. "I feel as if I'm either about to break this case wide open or else I'm going to lose my momentum. If that happens, then it'll be game over for David."

"Come on, take heart, girl," Larissa said. "He doesn't even have a court date yet. It's not over till it's over."

"I'm not going to give up; don't get me wrong. It'll be a mighty big job to find Reg's killer, and so I just hope I'm ready for the long-distance race ahead." Austin finished the rest of her coffee. "All right. See you tonight, Larissa, and thanks again, Dulcie."

Austin put on her jacket and prepared to leave. Dulcie hugged her again, and Larissa gave her a thumbs-up.

Having unburdened herself about the hardships facing her, Austin headed back into the storm. She sensed even bigger struggles lay ahead.

By the time Austin walked four blocks to her car, she was shivering non-stop. Now she had no choice; if she didn't stop at her apartment for warmer clothes, she might get a nasty case of frostbite. She knew nothing about the condition, but it didn't sound pleasant.

The snow was piling up, making driving difficult. She'd never driven in more than a fluff of snow before and realized she didn't know the basics. She turned one corner too fast and spun into a curb. No harm was done to the car, only to her jangled nerves.

When she reached her building, she was a wreck. She ran, skidding, into the lobby, blowing on her hands. Once again she dreaded opening her mailbox.

Yet when she unlocked the box with shaking hands, she saw only one lone sales flyer from the Hudson's Bay Company. Relief flooded through her. The flyer seemed to shine with beauty and promise, and she allowed herself a moment to savor the tiny victory.

Upstairs in the apartment, she found two sweaters and a heavier jacket, plus one of David's wool scarves. She needed to buy winter clothes at the Bay as soon as possible. That store had just gained a warm spot in her heart.

Better prepared to face the cold, Austin returned to her car. She drove carefully to Grad's, where she found Pete waiting in a booth. His mouth was pressed into a straight, grim line, and he didn't smile when she joined him. She scooted onto the bench across from his and immediately noted a large bruise on his cheek.

"Dulcie said you had to see me."

Pete cracked his knuckles. "Last night," he began and then stopped. "Last night," he tried again and stopped again.

"What is it, Pete? What's happened?"

He drew a pack of cigarettes out of his jacket and fiddled with it. Then he lifted his face to Austin. Was it her imagination, or did he look spooked?

"Last night I had a run-in with a man named Darrel Smith."

"Is that why your face is bruised?"

Pete's hand flew to his cheek. "Yeah, he hit me, but I, uh, I ran. I'm fast, and I know the streets, so I got away from him." He looked sheepish. "I shouldn't have run. Makes me sound yellow, but he's a hefty guy, and he's mean."

To herself, Austin said, *I knew it!* To Pete, she said, "So you two clashed. How did that happen?"

"I was here at Grad's, same as usual," he said. "I left around ten and was walking home when this guy comes up. He knew my name and everything. At first I didn't recognize him, and then I remembered seeing him before."

"When?"

Pete waved off her question. "Darrel told me Reg's dad sent him. I didn't believe him and kept walking. Then he grabbed me, and I couldn't get away. He started out nice and calm, but the longer he talked, the louder he got. He ended up yelling in my face."

She'd been certain Darrel was a bad operator and was delighted to have one of her theories confirmed. "So what did he say?"

"He accused me and Reg of trying to ruin the senator's career. He said we'd started up an ugly rumor about the senator's military service." Pete stopped to drink some coffee and light a cigarette.

"That's right," Austin said. "The last time we talked, you mentioned Reg believed his dad had cheated on his military record. Is that what Darrel was referring to?"

"Yeah, sort of. Only Reg and me, we never started no rumor. Reg said his dad cheated, but I never told no one, until I told you, and that was just days ago."

Austin looked up at the ceiling and scrunched her eyes. "Sounds to me like they're looking for someone to blame for the senator's political troubles."

"Maybe that's it, but all I know for sure is the senator and Darrel are plenty mad at me. Darrel even warned me to drop out of sight. He demanded I stop going to our group meetings." Pete laughed nervously. "And get this. He said if they hear I've gone to the police, I'll never walk or talk again."

Austin's eyebrows lifted and her heart raced.

Pete pointed at her face. "You look shook up, but those were his exact words." Pete dragged on his cigarette and leaned forward. "And Darrel says they'll know if I go to the cops because the senator has contacts high up in the government, here and in the States. I believe him, and he's got me, uh, well, running scared." He took another pull on his cigarette. "That's when I thought of you. I figured we could team up, work together. The vibes are getting real scary."

Austin couldn't help herself, remembering how Pete had behaved before. "And so you thought I'd be thrilled to help you, is that it?" Her tone was sarcastic. Even though she needed Pete's help, it was still hard to overlook his gauche behavior the last time they'd been together.

"We have the same enemies now."

"That might could be, as we say in Texas." At last Austin smiled at Pete, and he relaxed visibly.

"Okay then." Pete put out his cigarette and laid his hands flat on the table. "There's even more stuff to tell you. Just wanted to make sure we was going to get along all right on this."

"I understand."

A waitress arrived, and Austin ordered tea. After the interruption, Pete said, "So you've gone native, drinking tea."

"Too much coffee's hard on my stomach. Tea I can handle." She toyed with Pete's ashtray for a moment. "So what else can you tell me?"

"You want to hear about the first time I saw Darrel?"

Damned straight she did. "Sure. When was that?"

"Last week, the night Reg was killed." Pete hunched back in the booth, then leaned forward again. "And that wasn't a fun talk either."

"Damn it, Pete. Why didn't you tell me before?" She banged the ashtray on the table, and ash flew everywhere. "Sorry." She picked up a napkin and started to clean the mess.

189

Pete grabbed her wrist. "Stop it. You need to listen real hard to what I'm gonna say next."

Austin wrenched her hand free and dropped it in her lap. "I'm listening."

"It went down like this: Reg and I got to the meeting at the church right when it was starting up. Then somebody rushed in and told us about the demonstration over at Queen's Park. We all left to go over there, and that's when Darrel came up to me and Reg. He'd been there all along, but we hadn't spotted him. Darrel was dressed like everybody else, kind of camouflaged." Pete puffed on a new cigarette and eyed a waitress walking by. "Okay, so Darrel stopped us from going off with the rest of the guys. He said Reg's dad found out Reg was in Toronto and sent Darrel to talk to him. When Reg heard this, he freaked and started yelling at Darrel."

"What was Reg yelling?"

"Besides all the curses and stuff? Reg kept swearing he had nothing to do with no leak about his dad's war record. But Darrel kept insisting he did. Then Reg said to leave him alone and quit bugging him. I'd never seen Reg so angry, and that's really saying something."

Austin tried to be patient while Pete stubbed out his cigarette and lit another.

"Here's what's really weird." He leaned across the table. "When they was yelling at each other, I realized how much alike they looked, like they was cousins or something. They even moved the same way. I wasn't going to say nothing though, but then I heard Darrel slip up and say something about his dad." He swallowed hard. "The thing is, Darrel was talking about the senator. Reg was so upset that he didn't notice, but I did. I called Darrel on it, and that's when he got real mean."

"Wait. You're saying that Darrel is the senator's son?"

"Yeah, pretty sure he is. Things got real hairy after that though, so it gets confused in my mind. Reg and Darrel was shouting back and forth about who was closer to the senator, and then this old janitor comes in the room, and they chill out a little."

"Mr. Ferguson?"

"Whoever. It was like they wouldn't air dirty family laundry in front of no one. I guess I didn't count, but a real outsider was a problem. So the janitor comes in to see what's causing all the noise, they calm down, and the janitor walks Darrel out and down the hall. When he's leaving, Darrel says something to Reg like 'you're not done with me yet,' or 'I'm coming back for you.' Something like that."

"And then what happened?"

"Then it's me and Reg in the meeting room, staring at each other. He says he wants to check out the demo, so we leave the church and start walking to Queen's Park. But we're all agitated like, from all the yelling. After we go a few blocks, Reg says he's left his fancy suede jacket in the church. Says he's going back to get it. He tells me he'll catch up with me at Queen's Park. And that's the last time I ever seen Reg."

Austin's eyes felt as big and round as the upended ashtray. When the waitress finally bustled over with Austin's tea, apologizing for the delay, the air was thick with more than just cigarette smoke.

Austin broke the tension to say, "That's a lot to take in."

"No shit. But here's what I figure. What with Darrel threatening me again last night, that's got to give the cops something to go on. I mean, your husband shouldn't be the only suspect in Reg's murder."

Austin laughed and felt hysteria take hold. She sipped tea to calm down. "I've said that all along, only no one believed me." She toyed with the ashtray. "Have you told the police any of what you just told me?"

"Nope. 'Course not."

"Why not?"

"Come on, you know why. Darrel scared me, and I wasn't gonna talk to no cops about nothing. You never know who you can trust." Pete leaned back in the booth and glared at Austin. "When Darrel popped up again yesterday, that's when I thought of you. In spite of the way you brushed me off last time."

Austin chose to ignore his remark. If she wanted to work with Pete, she had to.

"After all you've just told me, Pete, do you think Darrel killed Reg?"

Pete stared at her and drew hard on his cigarette. "I don't know. If Darrel was still at the church when Reg went back, then, yeah, maybe so. They really got down and dirty." He stubbed out his cigarette and lit yet another one. "So where's your head at now, Austin?"

She wiggled on the bench, then rubbed her hands together. "All right, here's where I'm at. We need a game plan, one that won't get back to the senator. It's tough, though, his being tight with the authorities."

"Sure, but I figure you can come up with something. You're the smart one, in grad school and all." He looked at his watch. "Gotta get back to work, but I'll pay for your tea, don't worry about it." He stood up and put some change on the table.

She put out a hand. "Wait. How can I find you?"

"I work at Sam the Record Man on Yonge and—"

"Right, it's just north of Dundas." Austin was glad to know the place. That was a first. "I'll try to drop by the store later today. When do you close?"

"At seven, and if you don't come," Pete said, "then I'll see you here at Grad's this evening. How's that?"

Austin nodded. "By then I'll have talked things over with two people I trust. I want to hear their ideas about what you've told me and what we should do. One's a professor who's already been kind of, hmm...something like a prisoner of war, and he'll have good advice. I'm staying with him and his daughter at their house over on Maple Avenue."

Pete whistled. "Outta sight. That's Rosedale."

Damn. Why had she let that slip? She hoped that wasn't a mistake. "I don't know the area, but it's a nice place on a quiet street, very homey." She paused, searching for the right words. "Listen, Pete, thanks for confiding in me. I'm beginning to see a glimmer of hope."

It was only after Pete left that Austin recalled the old joke about the light at the end of the tunnel being an oncoming train.

CHAPTER TWENTY-FIVE

The mosaic of the murder pieces had shifted. Austin needed to fix the new layout in her mind before taking action, before plunging ahead. Alone in the booth at Grad's, she stared at the table, visualizing chunks of her mystery, moving them around like domino tiles.

The newest piece was Darrel's relationship to the senator. If he were Simpson's son, did that make him a more likely murder suspect? She shouldn't rush to a conclusion. Without a doubt, however, this new possibility could alter how both Simpson and Darrel related to Reg's death.

Reg probably hadn't known that Darrel was his half-brother, but perhaps he'd had inklings. And how jealous was Darrel of Reg, the acknowledged son? Now Austin could understand why Darrel was so committed to the senator and protective of his interests. Did this apparent devotion constitute a motive for murder, though? She couldn't see her way clear to that, not yet anyway.

For the first time, however, Austin did see a potential motive for the senator to have his son killed. Reg had disappointed him, while the illegitimate Darrel seemed a chip off the proverbial old block. Perhaps Senator Simpson wanted to substitute the illegitimate son for the legitimate one. People had killed for flimsier reasons.

She wasn't convinced, but at least she had an embryonic theory.

And what about the puzzle piece with Phil's name on it? Pete had swamped her with so much information that she'd forgotten to ask him about his brother. And Phil might not even belong to the puzzle she was trying to solve, yet she still wanted to talk to him. But doubted if she could track him down in Calgary.

She was lost in thought when the waitress returned.

"You want anything else? My shift's ending."

Austin hesitated, dazed. A moment later the waitress's words registered. "Nothing else, thanks."

The waitress thrust a mimeographed sheet of paper at Austin. "The owner wants our customers to get these. Our new menu starts next week. Hope you'll like it, eh."

Austin inspected the paper. *Not a good mimeo job, not as good as the church bulletins.* Mrs. Duncan did such a meticulous job.

Thinking about her made Austin's heart ache and her conscience hurt.

Then an almost-thought nudged at the back of her mind, something about the bulletins. The vision fluttered just out of reach.

Oh man, she was confused. Nothing was clear, only dim shapes shimmering in the distance. She had no signposts to guide her, only will-o'-the-wisps intent on luring her to return to the church.

She'd promised David that she'd talk to Dulcie again and also to Pete's brother Phil. She'd already forgotten to question Dulcie and completely ignored the matter of Phil when she'd had his brother Pete right in front of her.

Too many variables clogged her brain. She felt she was either losing it or that data would soon start slopping out of her head and onto the table. A sudden yearning for the quiet of Cuero swept over her.

"Damn it," Austin said out loud. The elderly woman sitting at the table opposite her muttered something about "these young people nowadays."

"Damn it," Austin swore again, this time whispering. She

hadn't talked to her mother in days. Had she even remembered to tell her parents she was staying at the Klimenko home? Mother probably thought she'd gone to ground on purpose, especially after Austin hung up on her.

That wasn't the case, but not a bad idea either. She didn't intend to cause them undue worry—just solve the murder before listening again to the sour notes of her mother's demands.

In her mind's eye, Austin drew up a list entitled *Shoulds*. She should chat with Dulcie again—probe for more information, that is. She should find Phil in Calgary and talk to him by phone. She should call her parents and let them know she was fine. Do the same for David's parents.

Yet she wanted to do none of those things. They all could wait.

Rather, she had to return to the church. She had to get a look at Mrs. Duncan's mimeographed church bulletins. The will-o-the wisps might be trying to lead her astray, but they were quite insistent.

"Watch where you're going," the old woman snarled.

"I'm sorry," Austin said. "I didn't see you."

"My point exactly." The woman in her fur-trimmed coat spoke with diction so precise and distinguished, she sounded like Queen Elizabeth.

The lady adjusted her fur hat and hurried down the side steps at the United Church. Her gate was brisk and remarkably spry. She navigated the slippery sidewalk in her galoshes with ease, a skill Austin envied. Austin watched until the woman turned the corner at Bathurst and disappeared from view.

In Austin's admittedly short experience in Toronto, few people had ever spoken so forcefully. Maybe that was what snagged her curiosity.

Who was that harridan? Probably a member of the congregation. Austin shrugged and entered the church.

Once inside, she encountered the minister. He carried a briefcase stuffed full of papers and was trying without success to close its tab. Austin remembered his messy desk.

"Can you spare a minute?" she asked.

"Yes, but only a minute." Despite his harried look, Reverend Baxter managed to give her a warm smile.

"I was sorry to hear about Mrs. Duncan's death," she said. "What a great loss for your church."

"This church has begun to feel like a charnel house."

My goodness, that makes two outspoken comments in a row. "Would you mind if I go into the office and look at some old church bulletins?"

"Sure, go right ahead. Is that all you need?"

"There is one other little thing. I just ran into a woman wearing a fur hat who was in a big hurry. I wondered who she was."

"You must mean Mrs. Ferguson." He wrinkled his brow. "I hope you didn't literally run into her, or you would've gotten an earful."

"I bumped into her all right, and she wasn't pleased. She made quite an impression on me."

He bobbed his head in apparent understanding, then looked at his watch. "I'm sorry, but I really must be going. Will we see you at Mrs. Duncan's funeral?"

"When will it be?"

"Not until next Wednesday. Her family needs time to come from Scotland."

The minister dashed away, leaving Austin alone in the church, not her favorite place. Indeed he was correct—it was beginning to feel like a death house to her as well.

Austin squared her shoulders and, consciously imitating Mrs. Ferguson, strode down the hall and into the office. On a table behind Mrs. Duncan's desk, she located stacks of church bulletins. She flipped through them, not quite knowing what she was looking for. Only when she quit reading the words and concentrated on the overall look of each page did she find what she needed.

All the bulletins, regardless of their dates, had something unusual in common.

Each had been typed on a machine that smeared the upper case letter *O*.

Her hand flew to her mouth. Her breathing constricted. She stood transfixed, staring at the bulletins for several minutes. She'd found what she'd been half expecting to see, but the revelation overwhelmed her.

Her eyes sought Mrs. Duncan's desk and focused on the typewriter, an IBM Selectric. Her unsteady legs were barely able to carry her over to it.

DS McKinnon's technical experts had hypothesized that the threatening notes left in Austin's mailbox were made on an early model of this type. Judging from the nicks on this machine, she guessed it wasn't new.

Austin dropped into Mrs. Duncan's desk chair. Her hand shook as she flicked the switch to turn on the machine. She found a blank sheet of typing paper, rolled it into the carriage, and typed a handful of upper case *O*s. Each one appeared smudged.

She typed several sentences, all in capital letters. Each letter was perfect except for the *O*s. Success.

Now she had the answer to one mystery. This was the machine that produced the threatening notes that had appeared in her mailbox.

"Oh my God." Tingles went up her spine. And then a tremor shook her from head to toe. Twisting to look over her right shoulder, she saw no one and breathed easier.

What now?

So many people could have had access to this typewriter. Reverend Baxter worked in an adjacent room. Darrel had visited the church at least two times. And a host of people unknown to Austin must have stopped by to see either the minister or his secretary. Any of them could have grabbed a second to type a short note.

How she wished she could consult Mrs. Duncan about this. Why had she called the Klimenkos and asked to talk to her? Austin couldn't help thinking that she had discovered some clue that everyone else had overlooked.

Austin's stomach was upset again, so she walked into the hall and found a water fountain. She'd eaten nothing all day, and all the coffee and tea were burning inside her.

While she drank, she heard familiar sounds coming from down the hall. Mr. Ferguson was mopping again, but she had no desire to talk to him. She was so disconcerted now that if she tried to converse, she would talk as much gibberish as he sometimes did.

Wiping her mouth with the back of her hand, she returned to Mrs. Duncan's desk and shoved a sampling of church bulletins into her purse. The best thing to do was show them to McKinnon. But first she had to talk to the Klimenkos.

Her hands wouldn't stop shaking. Her legs were wobbly too, although they managed to carry her out of the church unscathed. Still, visions of doom assailed her. A wreck lay ahead if she wasn't careful driving.

Or perhaps she faced something even worse.

When Austin arrived at the Klimenko home half an hour later, Larissa noticed the look on her face at once and then ran to her from across the room.

"Tell me," Larissa demanded. "What's happened?"

Austin filled her in. When every detail had been divulged and then repeated, she plopped onto a chair and dropped her head into her hands. After a few minutes, Larissa took charge.

"All right, that's enough." Larissa pulled Austin's hands from her face. "Everything you said shows you're making progress. You've uncovered more clues, just like you needed to. So why're you upset?"

"I don't know. It's just that, it's just...there's too much to take in and process, emotionally, I mean. And it's all so, so *real*. This isn't fun, not a bit like reading a murder mystery."

"That goes without saying since these are real dead people, not fictional ones." Larissa put her hands on her hips. "However, that's no excuse for paralysis."

For the first time all day, Austin smiled. "You're absolutely right. I need to get a grip, and I need to call McKinnon and tell him everything I discovered today."

"You haven't called him yet?"

"I didn't want to stay in the church long enough to use the phone. Easier to drive here and use yours. That church freaks me out."

"The telephone." Larissa rolled her eyes. "I almost forgot to mention that someone called for you."

"Oh no."

"Nothing to worry about, just some reporter from the *Star*. He said he's been trying to find you for days."

"A guy from the *Star* called earlier in the week, but I wouldn't talk to him. How did he learn I'm staying here?" Austin locked eyes with Larissa. "I don't like everyone knowing my business. The last thing I want is to talk to a reporter. He's awfully pushy."

"It's his job."

"I don't care. I don't like it."

Larissa gave Austin a hard look. "Better go lie down for a bit," she said. "You look wiped out."

Moments later, Austin was obediently mounting the stairs to the guest room when the phone rang. She heard Larissa answer and announce that Austin wasn't available.

Austin came back down the stairs. "The reporter again?"

"A woman, but she hung up before I got her name." Larissa held out her hand. "You might as well come into the kitchen. Bet you haven't eaten all day. Maybe a snack will do you more good than a lie-down."

Dutifully, Austin took her friend's hand and followed her into the kitchen.

Hmm, maybe there are Russian dumplings left over from last night's dinner. Her stomach growled at the memory of *piroshki* eaten during her summer in Moscow, and Larissa's homemade ones were even better.

Austin sat at the kitchen table and watched Larissa take *piroshki* from the refrigerator, but then her thoughts returned to the mystery of the female caller.

Who knows I'm here? The only woman who had known is dead, and I don't like people tracking me down. No, not one little bit!

When Larissa set a bowl of steaming dumplings in front of her, Austin was surprised that she was unable to concentrate on their flavor. Her mind kept churning—it would not stop. If she didn't figure out who called and what she wanted, then Austin had no business calling herself a sleuth.

CHAPTER TWENTY-SIX

Austin parked across from the United Church and watched sleet pepper the windshield, waiting for it to subside before she left the car's warmth. She'd been in a rush and forgotten her gloves, and her hands were stiff with cold. She tucked them inside her coat, relieved she no longer had to hold the chilly steering wheel.

Austin's spirits drooped, bruised from her first fight with Larissa. When Austin announced her intention to return to the church right after finishing her snack, Larissa had attacked the idea with all the force and persuasion she could muster. And once Larissa saw that Austin was leaving despite her predictions of dire consequences, Larissa refused to speak to her, turning her back and busying herself in the kitchen.

When Larissa heard Austin go out the front door, she called out one final warning. "Mark my words. You *will* find trouble."

Austin replayed the scene in her mind and regretted upsetting her friend. And for what? To follow a premonition that one more visit to the scene of the crime would help solve the mystery of Reg's murder? How absurd.

"You're acting on a thoughtless impulse—not an inspired hunch," Larissa had yelled.

Austin now understood their quarrel was mostly a case of nerves. Both girls were keyed up. Larissa had wanted Austin to wait until daylight to return to the church since Larissa was due to meet Darrel at a restaurant near the Royal York later that evening and couldn't go with her.

Austin checked her watch. Five o'clock. Outside in the dark, passersby rushed home from work, clutching their coat collars around their necks to ward off the cold. Most coats sported red flowers—artificial poppies, made and sold by disabled Canadian veterans. The irony of the blood-red poppies and what they represented was not lost on Austin—bright flowers, cheery on drab winter clothes, but somber in their intent. Remembrance Day was only three days away.

War was haunting her. Alone in the car she recited, "In Flanders fields the poppies blow between the crosses row on row," all she recalled from the World War I poem. Back home the American Legion distributed poppies too, but the Canadians succeeded in blanketing their population with them. Her mind jumped—she worried how her father would mark Veterans Day, never a happy time for him. Like Senator Simpson, he'd fought in the Pacific during World War II, and he mourned many friends lost in battle. He never talked about his wartime experiences, however, no matter how often she asked, putting her off just as Dr. Klimenko did to Larissa.

Down a block from her car, just visible through the windshield, was the spot where Mrs. Duncan had perished. The memory of her kindness haunted Austin. Now she wanted to avenge her death as well as spring David from jail.

What a pity she'd been unable to reach DS McKinnon before she left the Klimenko home. McKinnon was out on a case when she'd called, so she left a message that she'd come to his office in the morning and bring important news. Leaving more details hadn't seemed a wise option. Maybe someone at police headquarters was feeding information to the senator.

Austin buttoned up her coat and wound David's warm scarf around her neck—both a talisman to ward off danger and a guard against the cold. In Toronto, the cold and danger were beginning to feel related. She longed for the mild, dry spells that were a pleasant treat in Cuero in the late fall.

Only a few lights were on inside when Austin entered the church through the side door. Seeing no one, she walked straight down the hall, turned the corner, and passed the area where Mr. Ferguson liked to mop the floor. She went into the kitchen, passed to the far wall, and flipped the light switch. As they had the night of the murder, florescent flights crackled and illuminated the sterile room.

Austin stood in the middle of the floor and turned slowly in a complete circle. She wasn't sure what she expected to see. Certainly she wasn't dopey enough to expect an overlooked clue to lie right there in front of her.

Indeed, nothing suspicious met her eyes. No dirt, no clutter. Surveying the immaculate kitchen, she wished her own were this perfect. This level of cleanliness met her mother's sky-high standards, no mean accomplishment for Mr. Ferguson.

She examined the spot where Reg's body had lain when she stumbled upon it, saw in her mind's eye the fringed suede jacket streaked with blood and littered with her crushed blueberry muffins. Their effect called to mind the remembrance poppies—splashy, cheerful colors representing terror and death.

A shudder ran the length of her body.

Then she flinched again when a noise came from the hallway. Because she'd returned to the church expecting something to happen, the sound seemed to be her destiny calling. Austin left the kitchen, moving as if in a dream.

She was taken aback, however, at what fate presented. Walking toward her was the brusque woman she'd run into earlier. Mrs. Ferguson moved like a military commander reviewing her troops. When she reached Austin, she stopped and inspected her.

"I could use your help." She spoke with a steely conviction and not a trace of pleading. "I came here seeking someone who could help my husband, and you will do nicely, very nicely indeed. He likes you." She took off her fur hat and shook out her gray hair.

So like the dear, departed Mrs. Duncan, Austin thought. But

only the hair, however. Only the hair.

"Do excuse me," the woman continued. "I have forgotten my manners. I am Mrs. Ferguson, the wife of the church caretaker. You surely must be the young woman known as, umm, Austin Starr." Mrs. Ferguson coughed politely into her hand and made a face.

Austin didn't know what to make of this encounter, hesitating to commit to helping Mr. Ferguson without more information. "What's wrong with your husband, and how do you think I can help?"

Mrs. Ferguson shook melting snowflakes from her fur hat, then held it away from her. "This is the worst time of the year for him."

"Because of Remembrance Day, you mean?" Austin was proud she knew to use the Canadian name.

"My, my, you are a bright little thing, aren't you?" Mrs. Ferguson snapped. Then she squinted, looking Austin up and down. "In fact, you aren't little, but you are indeed young, so very young."

Tall for her generation, perhaps only two inches shorter than Austin, Mrs. Ferguson had an erect carriage that enhanced her imposing presence. Austin automatically stood taller.

Mrs. Ferguson shook her head. Austin couldn't tell if it was in astonishment or disgust. Perhaps a mix of both. The woman didn't seem to approve of her, so why would she want her help?

"The church secretary used to help when my husband got into one of his moods; Mrs. Duncan always had a calming effect on him." Mrs. Ferguson rotated to look down the hall and then back at Austin. "Needless to say, that's not an option now, so I hope you can spare the time to come to our home and talk with him. I assure you, it shouldn't take long. Company almost always makes him easier to manage when he's like this."

"You want me to go to your house?" Austin swallowed hard, dumbfounded.

"It's only a short drive. I promise not to take much of your time."

"And how is your husband right now? I've seen him distressed before, you know, very agitated and confused."

"Have you indeed?" Mrs. Ferguson's words slashed at Austin with cold precision.

"Your diction is beautiful. You speak so elegantly."

Mrs. Ferguson's face softened, ever so slightly, before it resumed its general haughtiness. "I did study drama in school and was on the stage in London, although only for a brief time. At the age of ten, in school back in Scotland, I was given a Shakespeare speech to memorize." She became almost chatty. "It was a turning point in my life, and I still recall every line. It was splendid, quite splendid."

Mrs. Ferguson had assumed the aura of a stately queen. Austin was entranced by the change. "What speech was that?"

Mrs. Ferguson adjusted her posture. Her height seemed to grow by inches. " 'Things without all remedy should be without regard: what's done is done.' " She stared straight at Austin, and while her lips smiled, her expression contained no joy or humor.

Austin's stomach did a back flip. "Why, that's...isn't that from—"

"Lady Macbeth says those lines. She said other notable things too, and many are my favorites." She assumed the pose of a school teacher and shook a finger in Austin's face. "You must never say the name of that play out loud. It is bad luck to do so. We thespians refer to it only as the Scottish play."

"An unlikely choice for a school child, isn't it?"

Mrs. Ferguson raised a penciled brow. "Not strange at all. Nothing in Shakespeare is strange." She shifted her purse from one hand to another. "Now, will you please accompany me to my home? I must return to my husband." She folded her arms across her majestic chest.

Austin's curiosity got the better of her. "If you think I can help..."

"I do indeed, and my car is right outside."

"But mine is too and I—"

"How kind of you to offer." Mrs. Ferguson's voice dripped with a fake sweetness. "However, I know the way, and I can run you back here as soon as we've cheered him up." She took Austin's arm and propelled her toward the side exit. "So it's decided then."

"It would appear to be," Austin said. Although she agreed out loud, inwardly she was of two minds.

One part of her brain shrieked: *Why are you doing this? It's a distraction. Weren't you here on a mission?* The other half replied: *Nothing new at the church, except this peculiar woman. Might as well go with her and see if she holds the key to the mystery.* Maybe she could ask her husband a few questions. In the comfort of his home, he might relax enough to answer her. He might even remember something from the night of the murder that he hadn't been able to recall.

The first voice backed down, uttering only one last whimper.

Time will tell.

Meanwhile, Austin's feet kept tramping out the door after Mrs. Ferguson.

Kay Kendall

CHAPTER TWENTY-SEVEN

When they reached the sidewalk, Austin asserted herself. "Mrs. Ferguson, I really must drive my own car. It's right over there." She indicated her Volkswagen, parked across the street from the Ford Falcon that Mrs. Ferguson had unlocked. "I'll take my car and follow you home, and then I can—"

"Get in, Mrs. Starr. You do not want to catch your death of cold."

Austin did as she was told. She'd been taught to obey her elders, and this one was formidable. The older woman demanded deference with every breath she took, every word she said.

Watching Mrs. Ferguson drive, Austin marveled at how skillfully she maneuvered the Ford. Her driving was decisive, and she never mashed the gears when she shifted. Not bad for an old lady.

Keeping track of their route was impossible. The sleet had become a dense snow, covering the street signs and making them unreadable. Traffic was slow. Cars crept along the slippery streets. Perhaps it was better she hadn't driven her own car.

Mrs. Ferguson turned right off the main thoroughfare. That much Austin could follow, but then she lost her sense of place. "Where are we now?"

"Have you ever seen Casa Loma?" The schoolmarm resurfaced.

"What is it? Sounds Spanish."

"I assure you the place has nothing to do with Spain. A Canadian industrialist built the mansion right before the start of the

Great War. Casa Loma always reminds me of Culzean Castle. You won't know this either, but it's near my old home in Scotland. I drive past Casa Loma when I get homesick—or when I need to summon up extra courage."

Courage for what? Austin wondered. Was Mr. Ferguson's condition that overwhelming?

"I guessed you had not seen Casa Loma and assumed you would like to. Look up. See the largest mansion ever built in this country."

Barely visible through the falling snow towered an enormous gray stone building. Austin agreed it looked like a castle even though the time for building them was long past. It had crenellated walls and turrets that loomed over the street below.

"Imagine walking those ramparts," Mrs. Ferguson mused. " 'But screw your courage to the sticking-place, and we'll not fail.' "

"What did you say?" Had she heard correctly? The woman might be formidable, but Austin was guessing that she, and not only her husband, struggled with emotional issues.

"Nothing, Mrs. Starr, nothing." Mrs. Ferguson drove past the castle and stopped at a traffic sign. She twisted toward Austin. "Your name is unusual. It makes you sound like a movie cowboy."

"My parents didn't select my unusual name. My married name is Starr."

"So I assumed." Mrs. Ferguson's tone was sharp enough to slice meat. Through gristle and bone too. "Your parents did choose to call you Austin, isn't that correct? I myself would not have done that." She shifted into low gear and drove across the intersection.

"My family is from Texas, and Austin is a family name."

"Nevertheless, it is not suitable for a young lady," Mrs. Ferguson said, adding under her breath, " 'Unsex me here.' "

"Are you still quoting Shakespeare?"

"Yes, obviously. I told you already. Casa Loma takes me back to my youth, and Shakespeare was an important piece of it."

"Especially the part of Lady Macbeth?"

Mrs. Ferguson took her eyes off the road to look at Austin. "I learned many parts from Shakespeare, not just Lady Macbeth. Shall I recite something else? I like a challenge, so name any play. I can vanquish any feeble effort you make to, as they say, get my goat." The sound of her laughter was chilling in the already frigid evening air.

"If we're close to your home, then we won't have time for games." Austin tried to keep her voice from betraying her growing anxiety. She had no sense of where they were now or where they were headed.

"My home is ten minutes away, perhaps a trifle more in this weather. So you see, there is ample time for you to test me and for me to respond. You cannot stump me. Choose any female character from Shakespeare, and I can recite at least one appropriate speech."

Austin mind was blank. She sighed and felt an intense desire to count something. That might help her focus. They were driving down a tree-lined street, and it provided the distraction.

One tree. Two. Three. Four. Oh, dang, this isn't working.

She might as well play the silly game. Maybe it would keep her mind busy and alarming fears about the woman's sanity at bay. Except try as she might, all she could think of was Ophelia, and Austin was tired of tragedies. She wished now that she'd paid more attention to Shakespeare's comedies.

"How about quoting something from one of the comedies?"

Mrs. Ferguson grunted, surprising Austin with the unladylike sound. "Such silly females in the comedies; they never get soliloquies. They are like froth on a wave, and their lines are as short-lived. Listen, here is Cleopatra: 'My salad days, when I was green in judgment, cold in blood, to say as I said then!' "

She clamped her lips closed and drove in silence for several blocks.

Austin was afraid to broach a subject, not knowing what else might irritate this difficult woman. Maybe the experience of living with her sad husband had unhinged her.

The Ford paused at a corner and then turned slowly onto a street whose name Austin could barely make out. Lappin Avenue—a street and location foreign to her. She repeated the name several times, picturing a rabbit—*lapin* in French—with a jaunty beret.

Mrs. Ferguson drove up a block, pulled into a driveway beside a small house, and turned off the motor. She fixed Austin with a piercing look.

"I can indeed fulfill your request with lines from a comedy. In *All's Well That Ends Well*, Helena says this in the first act: 'Our remedies oft in ourselves do lie, which we ascribe to Heaven.'"

"*All's Well That Ends Well*? I like the title. I hope it rings true." Austin's smile wavered.

Without replying, Mrs. Ferguson reached across Austin and opened the passenger door. "Get out."

Austin obeyed.

The house was less than half the size of the Klimenkos', but otherwise much the same, made of red brick and built at the beginning of the century. There were three stories, with a few front steps going up to a covered porch. The Klimenko home was imposing, but this smaller version looked bleak. The autumn leaves that had made Austin's first view of the house on Maple Avenue a delight were absent here. Only unadorned branches framed the house, looking like witches' talons.

Austin stood beside the Ford, noting its dented right front bumper. She looked closer and ran one finger along the dent.

She stiffened. And then she shook herself. No, this couldn't be the vehicle that ran over Mrs. Duncan. Plenty of people had dents in their cars. She was being overly dramatic simply because Mrs. Ferguson was.

Mrs. Ferguson walked in front of the car and joined her.

Austin pointed at the bumper. "Your car's banged up. Did you have an accident?" She was proud of her cool response.

Mrs. Ferguson sniffed, disdain evident in every movement. "A

211

nephew borrowed it. He had a small mishap, nothing serious." She clomped over in her old lady galoshes and grabbed Austin's elbow.

Austin was tiring of this disagreeable habit. She tried to shrug off the clutching hand, but Mrs. Ferguson only gripped harder. A brief skirmish followed, which the older woman won. Her galoshes gave her traction on the slippery pavement, and Austin's shoes weren't worth a damn on ice.

How weird. We're both playing parts, as if we don't know anything unusual is going on.

But then Mr. Jones wandered into her skull and whispered advice: *You've got two options. You can take her down and then split, or you can see where this farce takes you. It's bound to be interesting, and you can take care of yourself. I recommend option number two.*

Interesting sounded promising. Austin hoped it would prove beneficial as well.

She allowed Mrs. Ferguson to hurry her inside.

They passed through the front door and into a small vestibule. While Mrs. Ferguson hung up their coats, Austin peeked into the living room. It was crowded with furniture, and objects covered every surface, reminding Austin of photos from the Victorian era. Her nose began to tickle, and she sneezed three times. Evidently no one had dusted in ages.

Mrs. Ferguson waved her inside. "Please go into the living room and for heaven's sake, blow your nose."

Austin managed not to sneeze again and crossed to the mantel to admire a pair of ceramic spaniels. She was wondering where Mr. Ferguson was when his wife came up and stood so close that Austin moved away for the sake of her own peace of mind.

"You have a good eye," Mrs. Ferguson said. "Those Staffordshire pieces are the most valuable objects here. They belonged to my grandparents. They had a lovely country home, but little is left from that time in my family's history, and more's the pity."

"Do you like living in Canada?" Matching the frankness of her hostess might be a mistake, but she wanted to distract this woman. Austin needed to find out what mysteries brought her to this house and then make a quick getaway.

"Why would I not enjoy living in Canada?"

"Let's see: the climate is different, and the people are too, I imagine—that is, different from where you lived before." Austin's words trailed off into lameness as she lost her confidence.

"I have become accustomed to living here."

"In other words, what's done is done?"

Mrs. Ferguson cocked her head and then nodded. "Precisely. Now then, let me show you some other mementos from my past." She took Austin's elbow again and steered her toward a corner of the living room.

They stood before an area swathed in wine-colored curtains. Mrs. Ferguson opened them by pulling on a gold cord, and a collection of memorabilia was revealed. There were sepia photographs of men wearing military uniforms, of a beautiful woman wearing a Grecian-style gown and heavy theatrical make-up, and of two caskets covered by cloths with military insignia. Above the photographs, a gleaming silver saber hung beside two revolvers.

The effect was ominous. Austin's nose twitched. She sneezed again. Mrs. Duncan frowned but said nothing.

These larger items were not what drew Mrs. Ferguson's attention, however. Instead she pointed to another collection of photographs, simply framed, that showed a young boy. "Here is my son, Charles, such a handsome little lad. Just look at those curls." Her breath caught in her throat. "I could never have another child, Mrs. Starr. Charles was very precious to us."

While Austin wanted to see where this soliloquy from the erstwhile lady of the stage was going, she feared upsetting her. The woman was prickly to a fault.

And perhaps deadly too, although there seemed no rationale for that conjecture.

Was Austin's imagination simply running unfettered?

Mrs. Ferguson picked up a wooden box and opened its lid. "Here are the emblems that I sewed onto my son's first Boy Scout uniform. I have nothing from his military uniform. He was blown to pieces in his tent in Korea, all his gear destroyed. His death destroyed my husband as well."

Austin had to speak. "I'm sorry for your loss and can't imagine how much your son's death devastated you both." She'd been doing this for days, expressing sympathy to people for the loss of their loved ones. When would it stop?

"My only consolation is that Charles died an honorable death. I do *not* expect you to understand. How could you—you, whose husband betrayed his country by fleeing the fight?"

Mrs. Ferguson gripped the box in her hands so hard that Austin feared it might break.

"Are you not ashamed to be married to a draft dodger? I would be—I'd want to hide my face—and yet you came with him to Canada." She returned the box to its shelf, thumping it down so hard that the saber above it swung out from the wall.

The verbal assault unnerved Austin. She froze and watched the saber swing until it finally slowed and stopped. The old woman breathed in and out, slowly and audibly, the process appearing to stabilize her. When she spoke again, her tone was unperturbed.

"And here is my husband in his uniform. This photograph was taken in 1941, the day he sailed for England with the Lord Strathcona's Horse Regiment. He did not return to Toronto, to me and our son, for five years." She spun around to face Austin and glared with fierce, unblinking eyes. "Five years he was away at war, Mrs. Starr, and you cannot imagine what that felt like either."

Austin hastily backed up so that they wouldn't touch. The heat from Mrs. Ferguson's anger was coming off her in waves, and Austin feared it would scorch her.

Mrs. Ferguson was breathing heavily again, almost panting. "By the time I received his letters, it was months after he had written them. I never had any idea if he were still alive or very much dead when I read his words. Every time soldiers came onto our street to deliver bad news, all the women watched out their windows, fearful, wondering whose house the officers would visit. They never stopped at mine. When my husband did return home, however, he was not the same man who had left."

Where in the hell was Mr. Ferguson? Austin needed to see him, help calm him if she could, and get out of this house so haunted by war and death. She didn't want to get in the car with Mrs. Ferguson again; she'd walk to a bus stop and find her way home. And then she'd call McKinnon and tell him all about her surreal adventure. Especially the detail of the dented fender.

"Where is your husband, Mrs. Ferguson?"

"My Gordon had nightmares for years. He was so nervous that he sometimes frightened our son, but Charles loved his father and wanted to be like him. When Gordon was finally calming down, some six years after his war ended, another one began. Charles was twenty and wanted to serve in the Korean War. He wanted to live up to his father's legacy. No matter how hard we tried, we could not discourage him. And you know the rest. We lost our Charles, and Gordon has never been the same."

"Where is your husband, Mrs. Ferguson?" Austin repeated. "Remember, I'm here to help him. Shouldn't we see about him now?"

Mrs. Ferguson's eyes darted sideways, and her eyelids fluttered. She appeared to be momentarily confused. "Gordon, yes, of course. I quite forgot about his present difficulties." She passed a hand across her face. "Yes, I shall find him while you wait here. I will not be gone long."

After she disappeared through a doorway, Austin walked over to a window and peered out at the street.

Why not take this opportunity to escape?

But too many questions whirled through her head, and she wanted answers for them.

Why was she here? Was it happenstance that the janitor's wife had found her in the church, or—and here was a thought so dreadful that her heart raced—had Mrs. Ferguson sought her out?

If so, then why?

This place felt like a madhouse, and she hadn't even seen Mr. Ferguson yet. When he arrived on the scene, she wasn't sure she'd be able to handle the emotional overload.

Why had she agreed to come here in the first place? Someday soon she must learn to override the good manners drummed into her by her mother. Good manners could lead to servility, into not standing up for your own best interests. Austin was sure this was one of those times.

A grandfather clock chimed six, startling her into a yelp; she was more uptight than she'd realized. She wondered if Larissa would worry about her. But no, she was probably still in a huff since they'd parted on bad terms. Oh, fudge. She should have listened to Larissa and stayed safely in the kitchen with her.

Lost in thought, Austin only slowly became aware of someone walking at a brisk clip toward the living room. That would be the lady of the house, certainly not Mr. Ferguson, who rarely moved faster than a shuffle.

Austin prepared for another strange encounter.

Nothing could have prepared her, however, for the nature of Mrs. Ferguson's entrance.

She wore a silky blue gown that reached down to her toes. No housecoat, it fell in waves like a robe on a Grecian statue. Austin checked the photo of the beautiful young woman on the wall. *Mrs. Ferguson.* Pictured, apparently, in her salad days.

Mrs. Ferguson swished her gown grandly as she paraded into the room, and Austin admired her ability to make an entrance.

"I have located my husband," she announced, "and he is eager to see you."

What could Austin say to that? She'd been thrust into a walk-on part in this crazy family drama, and now the lead actress was

216

insisting she play a bigger role. At least Austin hoped it would remain a drama and not veer into tragedy. If that were to happen, then she swore she'd run howling out of the house, and the devil could take the consequences. In fact, she felt as if the devil were indeed lurking about.

"Well?"

How could the woman sound so demanding when asking for a favor?

"Where is your husband? I agreed to talk to him, but I have to leave soon. We're running out of time. My friends will be worried about me. In fact, they're probably ready to send out a search party by now."

"Don't be concerned about that." Mrs. Ferguson's voice was unctuous. "Later you can phone to say you're running late. Now, come with me." She held out her hand to Austin.

Austin didn't move. "Where are we going?"

"My husband insists on your coming up to his room. He does not feel well enough to come downstairs, so he asked me to escort you."

Austin's sense of peril warred with her curiosity. A tiny voice in her head, sounding like Larissa, told her to grab her coat and leave, yet she simply had to learn what was going on with the Fergusons. There was a mystery here, and she needed to solve it, even if it had nothing to do with Reg's death and David's incarceration. While Mrs. Ferguson was decidedly odd, Austin doubted she had anything to do with Reg's murder. She hadn't the strength. And what was her motive? No, plenty of others were stronger suspects. Austin was just letting the woman's eccentricities drive her emotions.

Walking toward Mrs. Ferguson, Austin assured herself she was only creeped out, not threatened. Yet she didn't accept the other woman's grasping hand. "Let's see your husband, and then I really must go. Remember you said you'd drive me back to the church?"

"Mrs. Starr, I shall be happy to drive you there once my

husband is calm again. I remain convinced, however, that you will help solve his problem."

"I'm baffled by your confidence in me, but I'll give it a shot."

"Very good." Mrs. Ferguson's smile was large and triumphant, reminding Austin uncomfortably of Lewis Carroll's Cheshire cat. She hoped her own adventures would end up the same as Alice's, unsettling but interesting, with no harm done.

But the malicious glint in Mrs. Ferguson's eyes worried her.

This adventure was far from over.

CHAPTER TWENTY-EIGHT

Mrs. Ferguson led Austin into the hall and up a flight of stairs, small and serviceable, not grand like the Klimenko central stairway. When they reached the second floor, Austin expected to be shown into a bedroom.

Instead, Mrs. Ferguson advanced toward a second flight of stairs.

"My husband is up there." She pointed to the third floor.

Austin had managed to cope with the first flight by hanging on tight to the railing, but navigating a second was too much to demand of her anxious body. These stairs were steep and slippery, unlike the carpeted Klimenko stairs. On these slick wooden stairs, she could easily break her neck.

Whoa. Better rein in that imagination.

Still, after Mrs. Ferguson's odd behavior, Austin didn't know what to expect next. She couldn't imagine why Mr. Ferguson would hide on the third floor of his home. But maybe he wanted to stay away from his wife, which was totally understandable to Austin.

Or, dear God, was he hiding in some old army trunk or something, reliving bombings and life in a tank unit? What if she and Mrs. Ferguson didn't have the strength between them to lift him out? The crazed woman should have called a neighbor for help.

"Come along now." Mrs. Ferguson remained motionless midway to the third floor, swirling her long skirt and scoffing at Austin. "You cannot possibly be tired from mounting a short flight

219

of stairs. I must be forty years your senior, and I'm not even breathing hard."

Austin began to climb. There was no overhead light fixture in the stairway; what light there was came up from the second floor. With each step she took, her surroundings grew darker. By the time she reached the third floor landing, Austin couldn't see her own feet.

Not only was it dark, it was also silent.

Where could the man be? Did he have hobbies he practiced on the third floor?

Don't be an idiot, she told herself. *That's not what's going on here.* As her eyes adjusted to the dimness, she realized there was only one door ahead. This was not a third floor. It was an attic.

"Now up you go, Mrs. Starr, just a few more feet. You're almost done." Mrs. Ferguson opened the door and stood aside, motioning for Austin to enter.

"It's dark in there, and I can't see a thing. Where's your husband, Mrs. Ferguson? Surely not in there." As she turned to retreat down the stairs, pivoting on one foot, Austin was caught off balance as Mrs. Ferguson shoved her through the open door.

Austin fell to the floor. The door thwacked shut behind her; a key turned in the lock. She lay in darkness, trying to figure out what had happened and what to do about it.

"Mrs. Ferguson? Are you out there?" She expected no answer and wasn't unduly concerned when none came. Still, she'd had to try.

Her hostess had mutated into a captor, a move Austin had not anticipated. The evidence that Mrs. Ferguson was unbalanced had mounted without Austin ever fearing much of a deception. Well, there would be a logical way out of this mess and vexed as she was, Austin vowed to work her way out.

She got on her knees and crawled carefully across the bare floorboards. A crack of light pushed through the far wall, and she moved toward it. Her straight wool skirt rode up, and a protruding nail gouged her knee. She reached down and felt blood. If she made it out alive, then she'd worry about dying from tetanus. She continued creeping toward the light.

Austin reached the wall and stood to inspect it. A heavy blanket hung over a window, allowing in a sliver of light. The blanket felt scratchy, like her father's khaki-colored one from his military service, a reassuring thought. She tried to unhook the blanket, wanting to look outside and understand her situation better.

After a few minutes, the blanket was down and draped around her shoulders. That was some comfort, but seeing out was impossible. There was no streetlight for illumination, and a tree stood near the house, further obscuring any chance of a view.

Austin pushed on the glass and the sash, but felt no give. Could she break the glass and yell for help? If no one was out there, would that do any good?

Austin slid down the wall and slumped to the floor.

She had nothing with her. Her coat and purse were downstairs. She drew her knees up to her chest for warmth and made sure that the blanket covered her completely.

Almost as puzzled as she was scared, Austin considered how Mrs. Ferguson's actions had grown from odd to even stranger as time passed. Why had she been pushed into the attic? There was no rationale for her capture, other than her original suspicion that living with a demented husband had caused the old woman's sanity to falter.

Was Mrs. Ferguson the one who ran over Mrs. Duncan? Perhaps it wasn't murder after all. Maybe the janitor's wife was only afraid to come forward and confess that she'd caused the accident.

Austin shivered. How could she escape? How could someone rescue her?

If Mrs. Ferguson didn't release her, eventually the Klimenkos would miss her and worry. They'd go to the church, her last known location, and find her Volkswagen sitting across the street. Then they'd scour the area looking for her. In due course either Larissa or her father would think of calling McKinnon. Then the police would find her.

This logic calmed her.

Wait.

Surely she was getting ahead of herself. Circumstances wouldn't get so out of hand. As soon as she saw the old janitor, he'd talk sense into his wife, and then Austin could leave.

She heard the key turn in the lock and scrambled up, still clutching the blanket.

Light flared, and seconds later Mrs. Ferguson walked in the door. When Austin's eyes adjusted to the sudden light, she saw that her jailer was carrying a tray with tea things.

The sight of the tray transfixed Austin. Was this to be a Lewis Carroll story after all? The woman was quite obviously mad. And much more evil than the Mad Hatter at his goofy tea party.

"I brought you something to eat and drink. My shortbread is not as good as Mrs. Duncan's, but then, hers isn't available anymore." Mrs. Ferguson's cackle was shrill. "Such a pity. Mine must suffice." She flashed the smile that Austin was learning to read as malicious. "I see you found a way to keep warm, using that filthy old blanket. How clever of you. I'd forgotten how cold it gets up here."

Austin thought of rushing the old woman, knocking her over, and running out the door and down the stairs; however, Mrs. Ferguson seemed to read her mind. She set the tray down on a packing box and returned to the doorway, bracing herself in its frame.

All Austin's senses blazed to attention. She'd have to stay alert to catch the perfect opportunity to make her break. Her whole body hummed with energy. Or was it sheer nerves?

"What's going on? I want to go home." Austin tried to sound firm and resolute. Believing that she succeeded cheered her. She wasn't losing her cool, not yet anyway.

"You're here to see my husband, but he's sleeping. I knew you wanted to leave and was afraid you wouldn't agree to stay longer. Locking you up keeps you from leaving. I would've thought that a sharp brain like yours could've figured that out."

"That's absurd. I want to go home, Mrs. Ferguson. *Now.*"

"You have no home."

"What?" Austin felt the verbal slug in her solar plexus. "Certainly I have a home."

"You do not, and I don't feel sorry for you. You made your choice. Now you're left to wander the world like a waif. Your husband is in jail and will no doubt be found guilty of killing that other horrible person, Mr. Simpson, who also shirked his military duty. Your husband will be executed for that crime. In the end, all three of you will be punished for being untrustworthy. God rebukes the treacherous, like you young people."

The tirade astonished Austin. True, Mrs. Ferguson had made similar comments earlier, but this new outburst was ludicrous.

An idea flashed in her head. "Why did Mrs. Duncan deserve to die?"

Mrs. Ferguson rolled her eyes. "She was the single nosiest person I ever met. She was also sanctimonious. She insinuated that I don't take adequate care of my husband, urged me to show more sympathy for what he had endured in the war. She told me to mollycoddle him. I disagreed." She sniffed, making her derision clear.

"And that's why she needed to be killed?"

"I didn't say that. I merely gave you an assessment of her character. I did grow very tired, however, of everyone at the church exclaiming what a marvelous and caring person she was." Again she sniffed. "Here, drink your tea and eat some cookies. When my husband wakes up, I'll return and take you to him."

An emotional appeal wouldn't help her case with this hardhearted woman. Maybe something practical. "I'd appreciate your leaving the light on. It'll be easier to have my tea."

"That's a reasonable request. And now, Mrs. Starr, I bid you adieu. I'll come for you later." She exited with a final twirl of her skirt.

The overhead light stayed on, but the key turned in the lock, just as Austin had known it would. Nonetheless, she'd harbored a shred of hope that the woman would forget. Unfortunately, her jailer remembered details even though her sanity was questionable.

Austin wanted to eat the cookies and drink the tea but was worried they might be poisoned. She had been led, step by step, into something that had all the earmarks of a trap. But why did she need to be trapped? Nothing made any sense.

Could Mrs. Ferguson have had something to do with the murder of Reg Simpson? Implausible as that seemed, the idea was worth consideration. Her anger at American draft resisters seemed powerful enough to provide a motive, but did she have the means and opportunity to kill a young, vigorous male? Moreover, no one had seen her in the church the night of the murder.

Sounds coming from the roof made Austin jump. All the scratching and scraping probably indicated some rodent was overhead—a squirrel, a mouse, or worse yet, a rat. She giggled nervously. Maybe she should invite the critter down for tea and cookies, then sit back to see if the little thing expired. If not, she could finish the snack herself.

Wow, was *she* also going daft? Whatever was wrong with the Fergusons might be catching. She giggled again and worried she might be nearing hysteria. She wished she could talk to David and compare notes on their respective prisons. At least his had rules; she suspected that hers did not.

Again the key turned in the lock. Mrs. Ferguson entered carrying another tray. This one was covered with a lace doily and held a tea pot and a second teacup. Against Austin's better judgment, hope took hold in a tiny corner of her heart, and she dared to imagine Mrs. Ferguson would find a shred of sanity and let her go.

The woman's first words, however, caused more anxiety about her mental state.

"Where are my manners? I cannot abandon a guest in my home to take tea alone." Mrs. Ferguson set the new tray down, shut the door, and returned to the crate she was using as a table. With careful attention, she moved all the china pieces to the new tray.

As she placed the empty tray on the floor, her focus was so intense that Austin saw an opportunity to risk an escape attempt. Hesitant at first—not wanting to harm the older and clearly loopy woman—Austin feinted in one direction, then backtracked and lunged toward the door. Mrs. Ferguson, with magisterial grace and calm, swung the tray and tripped her. Austin fell against the chest holding the tea things, and a cup and saucer clattered to the floor, close to where Austin landed on her back.

Mrs. Ferguson screamed. The high, sharp sound lasted a long time, puncturing the air like an air raid siren.

And then the shrieking stopped. Just stopped.

Mrs. Ferguson bent to pick up the broken bits of china and dumped them into an empty box. "Be careful, Mrs. Starr. You don't want to cut yourself."

Her composure was eerie. Austin guessed that her captor was playing a variety of roles for some as yet unexplained reason. She remained on the floor for a moment. Her back felt bruised, and she needed to recover her equilibrium in order to attempt to escape again.

Mrs. Ferguson surveyed what remained on the tray. "We can each have a shortbread biscuit, but one of us will not be able to drink tea. That will be you, the younger, inferior one."

Mrs. Ferguson kicked at a few bits of broken china with her foot, nudging them under a chair. "It pains me to see my favorite cup and saucer smashed to bits. Did you recognize they commemorated Queen Elizabeth's coronation? Let's see, that was back in 1953, although she had become queen on her father's death in 1952." She gave a triumphant smile, glided across the room, careful to avoid Austin, and picked up a folding chair. She carried it back to the packing crate and sat down.

Austin glimpsed the handle of a revolver sticking out of the pocket of Mrs. Ferguson's gown. It looked like the one that had been on display downstairs.

Austin's heart pumped hard, and it was difficult to draw breath. She felt suffocated.

She was trapped.

Trapped with a mad woman or a murderer.

CHAPTER TWENTY-NINE

"Mrs. Starr, please take a biscuit." Mrs. Ferguson thrust the plate of cookies toward Austin. "Here. I insist."

Austin feared that either the cookies or tea could cause her premature demise. Not to be needlessly histrionic, she thought, but evidence was now conclusive that this old woman was bonkers.

Decision time.

She would pretend to eat a cookie and then get Mrs. Ferguson lost in conversation and memories of her past, whereupon she would ditch the uneaten sweet. Austin rose clumsily from the floor and walked carefully over to the plate and selected one cookie, then inched backwards, not turning her back on Mrs. Ferguson.

Mrs. Ferguson picked up the remaining teacup and drank. "You're not suitably attired to partake of tea, but then, our surroundings aren't as we'd wish either." She set down the cup and raised her long skirt, peeking at her shoes, admiring them. "What shall we talk about? Have you read any good books lately?" She laughed, and her face turned bright pink, making her appear feverish.

Austin's nerves prickled. She remained silent and waited for her so-called hostess to speak again. She would take cues from her, but had to remain focused on the gun in the woman's pocket. She had a vain hope it wasn't loaded, but she couldn't count on vain hopes.

"I'm reading John le Carré's novel, *The Spy Who Came in from the Cold*." Mrs. Ferguson nibbled daintily at a cookie. "I love stories

227

about spies and derring-do. Everything is so deliciously thrilling."

That was the same book Austin had read several times the summer before marrying David. Austin refused to discuss the book with her tormentor, but the title gave her an idea. "Speaking of spies…"

"Yes, do you know any?" Again Mrs. Ferguson cackled.

"Actually, I know one, so don't laugh."

"Do please tell me all about it. I lead a boring life and could use a spot of intrigue."

Austin cringed at the flat-out lie.

Mrs. Ferguson drank more tea. "Your story will distract us while we wait in this cold and dismal attic."

Austin didn't like the sound of that. "You'll be interested to know," she began, "that a spy infiltrated the anti-war group that meets at your husband's church."

"My goodness, a spy for whom?"

"Rumor says the RCMP."

"Bosh, spying for the Mounties doesn't count. That's not exciting. Here I thought the man was spying for the Russians. That would be exhilarating." Mrs. Ferguson set her teacup down and took another cookie. "Come to think of it, Gordon told me he overheard something about a spy for the Mounties. Those awful radicals in your husband's group were very worried about it too. Why, the night my Gordon came home after killing Reginald Simpson—"

A coughing fit burst from Austin, lasting at least a minute, while all the time her mind raced. Mrs. Ferguson even looked concerned.

Austin conquered the spasm in her throat. "Pardon me please. What were you saying before? Something about your husband and the spy in the anti-war group?"

"Why, yes, he said the group's members were upset. Are you okay?"

"I'm fine, thank you." Austin felt dampness at the base of her neck; despite the cold, she was sweating. "When did Mr. Ferguson tell you all of this?"

"Last week, the night he killed Reginald Simpson."

"Ah yes, I see."

And suddenly Austin did see. She understood that if the janitor had killed Reg, then his wife must have run over Mrs. Duncan on purpose. The inquisitive church secretary must have learned too much.

Austin knew that Mr. Ferguson could not have driven the car that hit Mrs. Duncan. The old man couldn't have run over Mrs. Duncan, parked the car, and sprinted inside the church in time to see Austin there. Most of the time, the man moved like a snail. A very slow snail at that.

Things were beginning to make sense. But what was that kind old man's motive for killing Reg? She still didn't understand that. And how did he manage to do it? He was infirm, and Reg had been so vigorous.

Perhaps she could get Mrs. Ferguson to tell her. Austin had confidence in her ability to get to the bottom of that secret, but no faith in her ability to escape from the attic unharmed. She must worry about that next.

Well, two people could play at madness. Austin began to hum and then to sing aloud. She thought it was strange how her subconscious unearthed relevant lyrics by Dylan when she needed them most. To paraphrase her hero, when you have nothing, you have nothing to lose.

She increased the intensity of her singing. She couldn't recall when she'd sung so loudly, felt like she was singing for her life. Perhaps she was at that.

"Cease that infernal squawking at once." Mrs. Ferguson's eyes were pinched shut. "What is that awful song? I've never heard anything so unpleasant."

"Obviously you know nothing about the greatness of Bob Dylan's music. You're too old to enjoy it anyway." Austin couldn't resist making that nasty flourish.

"Don't be impertinent, young woman. Your manners are disgraceful. And after I have been kindness itself, opening my home to you and serving you my best Earl Grey tea." Mrs. Ferguson's face tightened into a hard mask. "Furthermore, when I was your age..."

Austin silently applauded. Just as she'd hoped, the old woman railed on, venting her anger and paying scant attention to the prey she had captured.

Austin tuned out the woman's harangue and looked inward, trying to find a strategy for escape. Gradually, however, she became aware of sounds coming from the staircase. Slowly, ever so slowly, one wooden step after another uttered a slight but discernible creak. Mrs. Ferguson, lost in her rant against modern youth, appeared to take no notice.

The door opened.

To her relief, Austin saw Mr. Ferguson. He was dressed in dirty pajamas and was panting so hard that he clutched at the doorframe.

How had this skeleton of a man overpowered and killed Reg? And why? Austin wanted answers and vowed to get them if it was the last thing she did. She glanced at Lady Macbeth Ferguson. Bad turn of phrase.

"Gertrude, what are you doing up here? And why is she here?" Mr. Ferguson croaked out his questions and pointed at Austin. Then wheezing overwhelmed him.

Austin was considering the dustiness of the attic and its effects on their lungs when Mrs. Ferguson leapt to her feet, sending the second teacup crashing to the wooden floor. Once again she screamed, but this episode was brief, unlike her earlier shriek.

Mr. Ferguson ignored his wife, obviously used to her lunacy. He hobbled over to Austin. He peered at the blanket around her shoulders, then reached out to the rough woolen fabric.

"That blanket made it through the war with me." He stroked it with a veined and spotted hand. "It kept me warm in Italy during our drive up the boot. It lay in the snow and mud during the Battle of the Bulge. Yes, Belgium was even worse than Italy. My blanket finally dried out in Germany. I'm glad it's doing you some good now."

He smiled at her, appeared to lose interest in the blanket, and edged over to the window. Glancing outside, he said, "Remembrance Day is coming. I remember. I remember too damned much."

Taking his arm, Mrs. Ferguson said, "Now, Gordon, you must not—"

"The CBC says Prime Minister Trudeau will lay a wreath at the National War Memorial in Ottawa." With a sudden fury, he wrenched his arm away from his wife. "Having Trudeau at that ceremony is a travesty." He was yelling now. "That man never served in the war and mocks those who did serve. Instead of being ashamed, he's cocky. He thinks he's so smart. Got a law degree here and then another hare-brained one at Harvard while other men fought for freedom and democracy against the Nazis." He began to wheeze again, and spittle hung from his mouth.

The Fergusons stood with their backs to Austin, and she got another peek at the gun in the pocket of the blue gown. She inched toward the door, hoping it was unlocked.

Mrs. Ferguson swung around. "Stop right there, young lady. My husband was trained to kill by the British Empire's best men, so I advise that you reconsider. Who knows how many Italian and German lives he took, and adding one more, a traitorous American, would mean nothing to him. Nothing."

Mr. Ferguson rubbed his forehead and eased down on an old trunk. The effort seemed to exhaust him. "Gertrude, what're you saying? What's going on? Why is she here?"

Mrs. Ferguson didn't answer. Instead she swept over to the tea tray, picked up the plate of cookies, and carried it to her husband. "Here, Gordon, have a cookie. You'll feel better. These are from Mrs. Duncan's recipe, the shortbread you like so much."

A synapse jumped in Austin's head.

"Were you jealous of her, Mrs. Ferguson? Did your husband like Mrs. Duncan too much? Is that why you killed her? Is that why you ran over her and made it look like an accident?"

"You nasty little bitch!" Mrs. Ferguson ran to Austin and slapped her. "That's none of your business."

"Gertrude," Mr. Ferguson wailed, "what have you done?" He hoisted himself awkwardly and stood on shaky legs, staring in horror at his wife.

"Why, Gordon, I'm doing what I always do. I'm taking care of you. This youngster insists on prying into our affairs, and she's even more persistent than Mrs. Duncan. You know what I did to take care of her."

"Her death was an accident." Mr. Ferguson's mouth dropped open.

For the first time, doubt, or perhaps confusion, appeared on Mrs. Ferguson's face.

"Why, Gordon, I'm sure I mentioned it to you." She blinked. "I came home from picking up your paycheck, crazed with worry. Remember? I'd slipped up chatting with Mrs. Duncan. When she asked how you were recovering from the horror of the murder, I dismissed your feelings, said you were used to killing people, that to you one dead body was just like another. When she looked shocked, I laughed and said I was kidding."

Mrs. Ferguson paused and rubbed her forehead before she continued. "Although she seemed to believe me, I couldn't trust her not to brood over my response. I was careless, so used to being cavalier and haughty with her that I got carried away. I had to kill her, don't you see? I couldn't take the risk that she would tell the police."

"Oh, Gertrude!" The man's words were one long wail.

"Never mind. What's done is done. Nothing can be helped now." She sat down only to spring up again almost instantly.

"No, no, no. There is something else to do. I must take care of little missy here. Once she's out of the way, our lives can return to normal."

Normal? *Normal?*

The Fergusons hadn't lived in that state for years.

CHAPTER THIRTY

The three of them remained motionless, as if on a stage waiting for the curtain to go up on a bizarre final act. Austin was so tense she feared she'd be sick. She had to keep cool and outsmart Lady Macbeth's stand-in. She expected to see Mrs. Ferguson swish her blue skirt in preparation for some bold move.

And sure enough, Mrs. Ferguson did not disappoint. She reached into her pocket and drew out the revolver. With a hand that stayed quite steady, she pointed the gun at Austin.

"I play fair, Mrs. Starr. When you paid no attention to my first warning, I sent a second. My note told you to prepare to die. I hope you did so. I regret that events have gotten us to this stage, but here we are. There is no turning back."

"What's done is done," Austin whispered.

"Wait, Gertrude. This is crazy." Mr. Ferguson moved toward his wife. "Give me the gun."

"Get back, Gordon." She gripped the gun now with both hands. "I have everything under control."

"You don't. Killing is never the answer."

"No? Then why did you kill Reginald Simpson?"

"You know I didn't mean to."

He looked so pitiful and forlorn that despite the circumstances, Austin's heart went out to him. He wasn't a bad man. She couldn't see him that way, despite what he evidently had done to Reg—in rage perhaps?

"Did Reg remind you of Trudeau?" Austin asked. "Did he

belittle your military service?"

Mr. Ferguson stiffened, and he turned to look at Austin. "He did, he certainly did. And my son's too. When I went into the kitchen to turn off the lights, that boy Reg was there. He was upset already, talking to himself, digging through the pockets of his jacket. And then when I came in, he turned on me. He treated me like the enemy."

"No need to distress yourself, Gordon. I said I would take care of everything, and I will."

Mrs. Ferguson's face was suffused with gentleness and pity. Austin was struck by her compassion. But was it real or phony? She couldn't tell. Perhaps this woman would've been a great stage actress, given the opportunity.

Sobs began to rack Mr. Ferguson's body. Through his tears, he managed to utter a few words. "He goaded me. He said awful things about soldiers. I had to make him be quiet. Had to. Had to. Pleaded with him, pleaded, but he kept on and on and on." He rocked back and forth, back and forth.

The women watched as Mr. Ferguson tried without success to regain his composure. Austin again wondered how such a shambles of a man could overpower and kill a vital young one. Perhaps his wife was right. He was a trained killer, good at his task, but with a skill that he took no pleasure in exercising.

His wife was another matter. She appeared to have no compunction about killing one or even, God forbid, two people. At least Mrs. Duncan hadn't recognized she was about to meet her death.

Which scenario was worse, looking death in the face or not knowing it was coming?

Mrs. Ferguson again pointed the gun at Austin. "Now see what you've done, you young hussy. You upset him more than he was already." She snapped her fingers. "Look, Gordon, let's wrap her body up in the army blanket. It'll soak up any blood before it drips. Later tonight, we'll move her body out and dispose of it."

Mr. Ferguson exploded. "No! That blanket is for comfort, not for evil. You will not kill her, Gertrude. Give me that gun." He approached his wife with outstretched hands.

Mr. Ferguson became another person. His concentration was intense. His steps were solid.

Adrenalin must be flooding his body, Austin thought. *This must've been what happened when he tackled Reg.*

Mrs. Ferguson looked baffled. When her husband moved toward her, she backed up but kept hold of the gun. Finally, she was cornered against the packing crate where the tea things sat.

Her husband loomed over her, inches away.

Trying to break the tension, Austin began to babble nonsense about the commemorative teacup, but Mr. Ferguson took control of the stage.

"Give me the gun." His tone was commanding. He reached out his hand, but his wife jerked the gun away. He grabbed for it, and the gun fired twice. The first bullet went into the wall and the second into Austin.

The room erupted in noise.

Mr. Ferguson grunted with exertion.

Mrs. Ferguson shrieked in fright.

Austin yelled in agony.

Fire and ice engulfed her. Her shoulder burned. She clutched the old blanket to the wound, hoping to staunch the blood.

The gun went off a third time, and Mr. Ferguson sank to the floor.

"Gordon! Gordon? My God, what have I done?"

With a piteous shriek, Mrs. Ferguson fell on her husband, grabbed him, and cradled him in her arms. Blood pumped from his throat and covered his pajamas. It spurted onto her dramatic blue gown, painting a gruesome design.

Even through her pain, Austin remembered how he'd been run over by a tank during a battle. This time he wasn't so lucky. The bullet must have severed an artery; the old soldier who was not truly so old would soon bleed to death.

Austin fixed her attention on Mrs. Ferguson wailing and rocking her husband in her arms. Austin couldn't help Mr. Ferguson now. The opportunity for undetected flight was too good to pass up. So she fled.

Holding her throbbing left shoulder with her right hand, Austin lurched across to the door, watching Mrs. Ferguson all the while. The woman didn't raise her head, not even when Austin opened the door.

Austin released her shoulder so she could hang on to the banister. The pain intensified and made her woozy. The view of the steep descent frightened her, and she swayed on the top stair.

She knew she didn't have the strength, the wherewithal, to make it down the stairs without falling. But she had no alternative. She started down.

Halfway to the second floor, she stopped to rearrange the blanket and catch her breath. Mrs. Ferguson was still wailing loudly. That was good. If she grew quiet, Austin would have to worry about what she would do next.

Blood was saturating the thick blanket, but it hadn't yet begun to drip. She agonized over slipping on blood but made it to the second story and then started down the second flight of stairs.

Suddenly the blanket slid from her shoulder. Her foot got snared by the cloth, and she fell, bumping down each step until she landed on her bad shoulder.

Austin screamed.

She stuffed part of the blanket in her mouth and bit down hard.

Mrs. Ferguson continued to scream too.

Austin lay on the floor, struggling to regain her wits. She began to crawl, dragging the blanket with her. Every inch forward was torture.

Finally she reached the living room, still able to hear Mrs. Ferguson's cries. But as long as she could hear her in the distance,

Austin felt safe.

The fire in her shoulder was searing. She had to either get out of the house fast or phone for help. Pain made it hard to think straight.

Chto delyat? Chto delyat? The words kept circling in her mind. She wanted to bang her head on the wall to stop the repetition.

She managed to stand, then shrieked, frightened by the stranger she saw in a mirror; the girl who looked back was unrecognizable. Her mouth was slack, eyes wild. Her face was as red as the blood that covered her sweater.

This person had seen terror.

Austin peered deep into the reflection of her eyes. She willed herself to get centered.

The trick worked. Her body sagged, and she took deep breaths. She would find a phone and call for help.

Good God, this was where she'd begun this misadventure, looking for a phone. Events had come full circle.

This time, however, finding the phone in the Ferguson's kitchen was easy. She dialed the operator and was asking for help when she realized how silent the house had become. She could no longer hear Mrs. Ferguson's cries.

"Send someone to Rabbit Street. Hurry"

"What? Are you sure that's the right name?"

"Yes, Rabbit. Rabbit Street." She wanted to scream again. "Wait. No, it's Lappin, Lappin Avenue. The Fergusons live here. Send the police. A woman's trying to kill me. She already shot somebody."

Austin banged down the phone.

Footsteps plodded down the wooden staircase. Austin staggered from the kitchen into the living room, heading for the front door. She hoped to grab her coat and purse but would leave them if necessary.

Then Mrs. Ferguson ran into the room. The demented woman still held the gun.

Her face and hands were covered with blood. Her blue gown looked like Jackson Pollock had experimented on it.

"My husband is dead," Mrs. Ferguson shouted, "and you killed him."

"I did not!" Austin yelled back, unable to control herself any longer. "The gun was in your hands, lady."

"You'll pay for my husband's death. You pushed to discover who murdered Reginald Simpson, just couldn't let it alone. I warned you. My notes told you not to. If you'd followed orders, then Gordon would be alive. Here, take this." She thrust the gun at Austin. "With your fingerprints on the murder weapon, it'll be my word against yours."

Austin backed away, still clutching the blanket to her throbbing shoulder. She refused to take the gun, knowing this woman laid traps. Why else would a crazy person offer her the gun?

"Your husband is in jail for killing Reg. You'll go to jail for killing my husband. How fitting." Mrs. Ferguson laughed and laughed until tears rolled down her furious face.

Austin reconsidered taking the gun. But if she tried to take it, would Mrs. Ferguson "accidentally" shoot her too? Even if she got the weapon, would she have the nerve to fire it at her attacker, even in self-defense?

The faceoff continued. The women began a macabre dance, feinting and scuffling around each other. The gun flopped so wildly that Austin feared it would go off and shoot her a second time.

In the distance a siren wailed. As the sound grew closer, Mrs. Ferguson halted in the middle of the floor. She seemed immobilized.

Austin saw her chance. She grabbed the army blanket, flung it over the woman's head, and tackled her. Both of them fell to the floor, shouting, and Austin landed on top. The gun bumped and slid a few feet away.

Austin sat on the lump that was Mrs. Ferguson and let the blood from her shoulder pour all over the army blanket and blue gown. She watched her blood mingle with the blood of poor Mr. Ferguson.

Footsteps pounded up the porch stairs. Someone hammered at the door.

"I can't move, I'm busy," Austin yelled as loudly as she could. "You'll have to get in by yourselves."

Minutes later, three policemen burst in. One of them was DS McKinnon.

From her spot atop Mrs. Ferguson, Austin stared up at him, overpowered by a mix of exhaustion and triumph. "I'm glad my hunch was right. See, it turns out you really are my policeman."

CHAPTER THIRTY-ONE

David and Austin lay in each other's arms. He was snoring softly. She was watching the snow fall silently on the fir trees beyond their bedroom window. In the late afternoon dusk, white flakes coated everything, imparting a dreamlike quality to the world. Awe filled Austin's heart at the perfection and purity of the scene. She hadn't known that snow could be so exquisite or life so sweet.

She turned her gaze to the desk calendar that stood on the table beside their futon. Almost two weeks ago she'd discovered the corpse of Reg Simpson lying on the kitchen floor of the United Church. She marveled at how she and David had survived the storm that threatened to dash their lives and young marriage against the rocks of catastrophe.

With David's snores tickling her ear, she recalled the awful howls Mrs. Ferguson made when policemen took her away for booking. At the same time, DS McKinnon had hustled Austin into his car and then raced to the emergency room at Toronto General. A doctor treated her gunshot wound and admitted her to the hospital for observation over the weekend. The Klimenkos had rushed to her bedside after McKinnon called to tell them what had happened at the Ferguson home.

Larissa ran into Austin's hospital room with uncombed hair and wild eyes. "Why didn't you call me?" she wailed.

"You know I have trouble finding phones. Don't you remember?" Austin said.

"You goof, if you weren't all bandaged up, I'd punch you in

the shoulder." Larissa rolled up a visitor's chair and sat beside the bed. "Next time you're off chasing killers, you'd better take me with you."

"That's not a good idea," her father said. "Neither of you should get involved in something like this ever again; you both were very foolish. Things could have ended badly."

"But they didn't, sir, and everything is okay now. I can't tell you how much your support helped me through this ordeal."

She stretched out her good hand to the Klimenkos. When her professor took it into his damaged one, she wondered if she would ever have the nerve to ask what had happened to him. Or if he would ever tell her.

On Saturday in the hospital—nope, she wouldn't be saying *in hospital*, like the Canadians—Austin spent most of the day sleeping. Larissa was her only visitor, and she stayed just thirty minutes, not wanting to wear Austin out. On Sunday Larissa came in the afternoon and to Austin's surprise, Pete turned up too.

He stood beside her bed and shuffled his feet, looking awkward and out of place in the antiseptic medical setting. "I've come to say goodbye," he said.

"Where are you going?" Austin asked.

"My brother left for Calgary, and I'm joining him. Also, I'm still worried about the senator and Darrel. I don't want them to be able to find me."

"Oh, Pete, I'm so sorry. Do you really need to do something so extreme?"

"Nothing left in Toronto to hold me. Besides, my brother says he wants company."

"Phil?"

"Yeah, him. How'd you know?"

"I heard some things." Austin hesitated, wondering whether to ask about the rumor.

Pete raised the issue himself. "What everyone's saying is true, you know. Phil was a snitch for the Mounties, but he says it was nothing much, just enough low-level junk info to keep them off his back. He came up from the States and got into trouble over drugs right away. The RCMP did a deal with him in return for stuff about our anti-war group."

Austin whistled. "Sounds like big-time trouble to me. How do you feel about this?"

"What can I do? He's my brother. If I'm in Calgary with him, maybe I can get him back on track and keep him there." He pulled his cigarettes out. "Can I smoke in here?"

"I don't know. Maybe you'd better not."

Pete pocketed the cigarettes. "Hey, Austin, speaking of drugs, I ran into Reg's pusher yesterday. Do you know Don Snyder?"

"Never heard of him."

"He just got back from Montreal. He'd left town the morning after Reg's murder and didn't hear about it until yesterday. Said it explains why Reg was a no-show for the drug buy he was going to make on Halloween night."

"Don Snyder?"

"Yeah."

"Initials DS, same as my husband's. Good, that ties up one loose end, but I've got one more."

"Don't know what you're talking about, this DS stuff, but I'm happy to help."

"I hate to ask, but did you ever see any evidence of Reg stealing money from the group? You knew him better than anyone else did."

Pete looked out the window and scratched his head. He finally sighed, then turned his gaze back to Austin. "Reg didn't exactly steal money. He was just borrowing it for a while. Told me he'd put it back after he got paid in a couple of weeks for a little job he did for a prof. He was desperate to buy supplies to have flyers and posters made, for the good of the cause, you know. He'd blown through all his money and wasn't used to being short. I warned him he'd get into trouble, but as usual, he didn't listen. Why is that important now?"

"You're right, it's not—just one last little niggle to check off so I can put this case behind me." She tilted her head and smiled up at him from the hospital bed. "You could say I have a bad case of Nancy Drew-itis."

He chuckled. "Gotta admit you're nicer than I thought. Good luck to you and your husband, and I hope you stay out of trouble now, at least for a while. Speaking of trouble, will you let me know if Darrel Smith or Senator Simpson does anything funny?"

"I will, I promise. I'm not especially worried about the senator; I expect he'll have his hands full with the congressional investigation. But Darrel bothers me, I admit. Your warning's good for me to keep in mind."

"When I get settled in Calgary, I'll let you know my whereabouts."

"I'm really glad you stopped to say goodbye, Pete."

Austin left the hospital the morning of November 11, Remembrance Day. All around her, people wore red poppies. There'd been so much death in all the wars—and recently more deaths related to those wars, even after they'd ended: Reg, the angry son; dear Mrs. Duncan; and pitiful Mr. Ferguson, who survived years of military combat only to die at the hands of his own wife.

Austin returned to the Klimenko house and from there called her parents to share the good news that David would soon be released from jail. "I realize I sounded confident earlier. Well, I wasn't, Daddy. But all's well that ends well." She'd learned that saying from him, even before she'd taken a course on Shakespeare in college.

She talked with her father a long time, glad that her mother was out playing bridge. Austin asked questions about his service in World War II that she'd never thought to ask. Her father's answers helped her understand the pressures soldiers faced, day and night, sometimes for months on end.

"I doubt if I'd make a good soldier. Couldn't bear all that without cracking," she said. "I'd snap during the first battle."

"It's not the intensity of warfare that's the worst thing," her father said. "It's the duration. From what you tell me, Gordon Ferguson saw continuous fighting during the Italian campaign and then was sent straight to Belgium, where everyone knows how difficult the Battle of the Bulge was. I was lucky. My military service wasn't nearly as hard as his."

"And I'm so thankful."

"Also, he lost his only son in battle. We mustn't forget that."

"I will never forget." Austin felt sorrow at the memory of Charles Ferguson, whom she never met, and his father Gordon, whom she knew and liked. "Remembrance Day poppies will never be the same."

After Austin hung up the phone, it rang almost immediately. Earleen was calling again from Texas with the latest on Senator Simpson's political troubles.

"A congressional investigation will look into how his war medals were awarded. Looks like his hassles are just revving up."

"Thanks for keeping me posted," Austin said. "Did you manage to uncover anything about Darrel too? The night of my run-in with Mrs. Ferguson, he was supposed to meet Larissa at a restaurant, but he stood her up. Darrel's bad news, and Larissa's meeting with him might've gone wrong anyway."

"I tried really hard but couldn't find out anything about him."

"Never mind. The case is solved, David is exonerated, and Darrel can disappear forever for all I care."

"So congratulations on bustin' David out of the pokey."

"Aw, shucks. It was nothing."

Austin and Earleen laughed, vowing to meet in Texas whenever Austin could get away. Austin dodged the question of whether she'd ever be able to live in America again.

The following day Austin had another doctor's appointment.

After that, Larissa helped her prepare the apartment for David's homecoming. They brought in his favorite foods and added flowers for decoration. They cleaned so thoroughly that even Austin's mother would have applauded.

And finally, David had walked out of the Don Jail a free man. The Klimenkos and DS McKinnon were there with Austin. David strode toward them through the halls of the old prison with confidence. His short hair and clean-shaven face made him look crisp and efficient.

"Look at him," Larissa had whispered to Austin. "He's like a conquering hero."

Austin flung herself into David's arms. After a few minutes, she composed herself and introduced David to Larissa and her father.

DS McKinnon held himself back from the happy group. When David became aware of the policeman, he walked to him and offered his hand. "Thank you for your help and support, sir."

The two men shook hands. Austin looked on and beamed.

As their party of five exited through the main door, Austin gazed up at the forbidding gargoyle guarding the portal, and feelings of triumph and hope flooded through her. The Don Jail was losing an inmate—her husband—but Austin had ensured that the right person would replace him, albeit in the Ontario prison for women. She hoped never again to see the carving and waved it goodbye in a parting gesture of defiance.

Everyone agreed to regroup for a proper celebration the following weekend. McKinnon and the Klimenkos moved away to their separate cars, leaving David and Austin alone in the parking lot. He helped her into the Beetle, careful not to touch her wounded shoulder, and drove slowly out onto the street. "It's glorious to be outside," he said. "The air smells so good and fresh."

"Hmm, yes," she murmured, luxuriating in his presence, bursting with joy and warmth.

He drove west across the Don River Valley. "The trees are all bare now. When I was arrested, there were still leaves on them. The two weeks I passed inside were like an eternity. I feel it should be Christmas already."

"Being together again is even better than Christmas."

"I have to warn you about something, Austin." He looked at her sideways. "I'm going to continue with my anti-war work. I know you're not crazy about it."

"You'll get no objections from me, honey. While you were in jail, I got a crash education about the damage that war does, even to people who never fight a battle. I'm so proud of you."

Within twenty minutes they had reached their apartment. They got out of the car, and David stared at their building with a big grin on his face. "Home. It's good to be here." He started up the sidewalk.

"Wait a minute," Austin said. "I've got to do something."

David watched as she walked to the corner mailbox, gave it a loving pat, and circled back to his side.

"What was that about?" he asked.

"Just my way of thanking Canada for having the grace to correct an error. This is a pretty nice country, you know."

His answering smile was so wide that it threatened to break his face in two. "That's what I've been saying."

Then together, hand in hand, David and Austin entered their building, and soon they were ensconced in their apartment. While he showered, she made his lunch—a little slowly because of her wounded shoulder.

Beside her David woke up from his afternoon nap and stretched. He put his head on her good shoulder. "My angel. The thought of you kept my heart ticking while I was in jail."

She kissed him as eagerly as her shoulder would allow. "You'll never know how much I missed you."

"You're amazing. I'm going to have to get you a white horse."

"Why?"

"Don't rescuers always ride them?"

Austin giggled and ducked her head in an attempt to look bashful. "Hey, we're a team. You'd have done the same for me."

"Things will go right from now on." David sat up and leaned back against a pillow. "Now then, let's plan what we should do next."

"*Chto delyat?*" She sat up also, careful not to lean on her bad shoulder, and scooched up to lean against him.

"You said that before. What does it mean?"

"Just a phrase I picked up from Russian history. *What's to be done?* It helped me direct my efforts when I was trying to spring you from the hoosegow."

"Okay, I get it. Sounds to me like that expression means we should take our future into our own hands, not be complacent, and seize the initiative."

"Hadn't thought of it quite like that, but you're right."

"So, how about now? What's to be done now?" He caressed her cheek softly with his fingertips. "Seems to me we should take stock of what we're doing, see if we're on the right track."

"Sounds good." She pulled back, restless all of a sudden, and moved to the foot of the futon where she sat cross-legged, facing him. "First, though, I need to fill you in on a few things that happened while you were away."

"Anything important?"

"You could say that—pretty important." She picked up a pillow and held it against her stomach.

David tickled her foot. "So, quit teasing and tell me."

"I went to the doctor a few days ago and—"

"Will your shoulder be okay? You look like the war wounded."

"Don't say that. I never want to think about war again."

"Okay, sorry. Go on, tell me."

"I haven't been feeling well lately. I figured it was just the stress of your being in jail and my being up here in Canada and so far from family and Earleen. I wasn't sure though, so that's why I scheduled a checkup."

Austin turned the pillow over and gave it a punch. "Turns out my queasy stomach had nothing to do with stress." She paused, took a deep breath. "David, we're going to have a baby."

His eyes widened, and his mouth formed a large *O*. "A baby? That's wonderful." He joined her at the foot of the futon and took her in his arms, covering her with kisses.

"Ouch," she yelped. "You're hurting my shoulder."

"I forgot. I'm just so excited at the news. Does anyone else know?"

"Just us, so far. Let's call our parents tonight and share the great news." Austin felt so happy that she expected to see joy bubble out of her and cover the bedspread.

David looked thoughtful. "You know what this means, don't you?"

"Big changes."

"It means we can raise our own little Canadian. That way, if it's a boy, he'll never have to worry about the draft."

Austin looked deep into David's eyes and then kissed him on the nose. "I'm glad you're pleased about the baby." And to herself she added, "We'll just see if we raise this child in Canada or not. Time will tell."

David wiped off the wetness left on his nose by her kiss. "Your smile just went into Mona Lisa territory. What're you thinking?"

"Oh, just that life really is a mystery."

Smiling more broadly now, she nestled against his chest.

If Austin had learned anything from her study of history, it was that while the past was set in stone, the future was framed by hope and possibility. And she couldn't wait to turn to the next page.

Kay Kendall is an international award-winning public relations executive who lives in Texas with her husband Bruce, their five house rabbits, and spaniel Wills. She's now working on the next Austin Starr mystery, *Rainy Day Women*.

CPSIA information can be obtained at www.ICGtesting.com
Printed in the USA
LVOW11s1756310816

502664LV00009B/914/P